The Drop Edge of Yonder

Also by Donis Casey
The Old Buzzard Had It Coming
Hornswoggled

The Drop Edge of Yonder

An Alafair Tucker Mystery

Donis Casey

Poisoned Pen Press

Copyright © 2007 by Donis A. Casey

First Edition 2007

10 9 8 7 6 5 4 3 2 1

Library of Congress Catalog Card Number: 2007924785

ISBN: 978-1-59058-446-0   Hardcover

Poisoned Pen Press
6962 E. First Ave., Ste. 103
Scottsdale, AZ 85251
www.poisonedpenpress.com
info@poisonedpenpress.com

Printed in the United States of America

Acknowledgments

Love and thanks to my siblings: Chris, brother and web master; the "real" Martha, and Carol, who helped me reconstruct our mother's recipe for okra pie. I especially want to express my gratitude to my cousins the Morgans, Charles Lee and his wife, Jean, for inviting me to visit the farm outside of Boynton for the first time in almost thirty years. If I hadn't spent so much magical time on that farm when I was a child, these books would not exist. Thanks also to June Smith and Ardith McKeaigg for hosting me so graciously when I spoke at the Boynton Historical Society.

As always, to Butch.

The Family Tree
August 1914

(1) Jim Tucker — Sally — (2) Peter McBride

Josie m. Jack Cecil
- Maxine
- Reginia

Charles m. Lavinia

Shaw m. Alafair Gunn
- Martha age 22
- Mary 21
- Alice m. Walter Kelley 20
- Phoebe m. John Lee Day 20
  - Zeltha

Hannah

James m. Irene
- Jimmy
- Jerry
- Katie

Sarah m. W.J. Lancaster
- Gee Dub 17
- James (d.)
- Ruth 15
- Charlie 13
- Bobby (d.)
- Blanche 9
- Sophronia 8
- Grace 21 mo.

Howard m. Vera
- Bill
- dau. (d.)

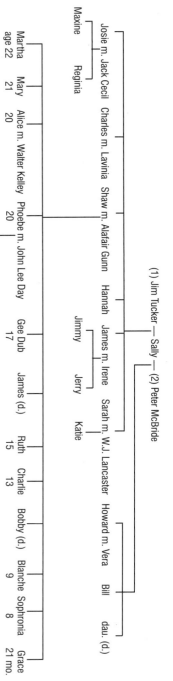

Chapter One

When I think about that day, Mama, here's what sticks in my mind. I remember waking up on my back in the middle of the field. All I could see was the sky through the leaves of the oak tree, and grass all around me. At first, I didn't know where I was, or what had happened to me. But I had a thought. I don't remember what it was. It was gone just about the minute I woke up.

Yet it was a mighty important thought, and if I could just call it to memory, I'd know who did this awful thing. All I know about this thought is that it had something to do with the Fourth of July.

It had been a hard couple of years for Calvin Ross, what with his wife dying, his girls growing up before his eyes, and his sister coming to live with them. The town of Boynton was growing so fast that his dairy business could hardly keep up with the demand, and the work was brutal. Calvin was glad of that, though, since it kept his mind off of what the future held for himself and his three pretty daughters. Since their mother died, Calvin was generally chary of any fellow who came around his daughters. But when Laura, his eldest, had told him that she was in love with the McBride boy, he had been pleased.

For red-haired, dark-eyed Bill McBride was not just a respectful and promising young man who had asked for Laura's hand in the proper fashion, he was the youngest son of that worthy gentleman, Peter McBride, patriarch of one of the more influential clans in Muskogee County, Oklahoma. Bill's substantial family loved Laura, as well, and it did Calvin's heart good to see his daughter happy again after the long, sad year that followed her mother's death.

Therefore, Calvin was not worried when Bill showed up at his farm that hot, windy August evening in 1914, on a fine-looking little roan mare, and asked if Laura could come out for a ride. Bill was accompanied by his twenty-one-year-old niece, Mary Tucker, and Mary's fifteen-year-old sister Ruth, since it would never do for the betrothed couple to ride out alone. Both of the Tucker girls were on their own horses. The plump and good-natured Mary seemed amused at acting the chaperone for her young uncle, who was only three years her elder. Ruth, looking fresh-faced, her wild auburn curls tucked up under a big straw hat, was as champing-at-the-bit to be off as her steed.

Calvin was glad to give his permission for Laura to go. Her chores were done and Iva, Calvin's widowed sister and house-keeper, wouldn't be making supper for at least an hour. Laura would be well chaperoned and well protected, and she was a good rider. The usual riding paths around the area were well used and safe. There was no reason for Calvin Ross to feel the slightest trepidation when his daughter rode off into the evening with her beloved and his nieces. She turned in the saddle as they rode away and waved a cheery good-bye to her father.

Ruth and Mary Tucker rode ahead of the affianced pair most of the way, though Ruth often headed her blaze-faced gelding off into the woods or trotted up the road and back if it struck her fancy. Mary was content to trot along ten yards or so in front of the couple and think her own happy thoughts, her full calico skirt hitched up over her stockinged knees, her younger brother Gee Dub's outgrown boots on her feet and his beat-up cowboy hat on her head, admiring the dusky evening and contemplating supper. Time to oneself was rare for the second of ten children. Bill and Laura contentedly rode along behind, knee to knee, and made their plans for the future, only vaguely aware of what the Tucker girls were up to, until Ruth slowed her pace enough to drop back alongside her uncle.

Bill and Laura fell silent and looked over at the girl, curious.

"I see a lot of bees, Uncle Bill," Ruth observed.

"It's getting evening, Ruthie. They're heading home."

"I know it. I see a lot of bees heading home to that particular big old oak up ahead to the right."

Laura sat up straight in the saddle. "Ruth has sharp eyes, Bill! I see them, too, swarming yonder. I expect there's a hive in that tree."

Mary cantered back toward them just in time to hear Laura's comment. The prospect of an adventure elicited her ready grin. "Want to rob a beehive, Uncle Bill?"

Bill laughed. "Well, let's see what's what, first. Maybe there's a hive worth bothering with up there, and maybe there ain't."

The four young people rode up to the big oak, which was situated just off the side of the road in an open area. The dense shade of the old tree discouraged growth under its canopy, so there was plenty of room for all of them to mill around on horseback underneath and peer up into the branches, looking for a beehive.

"I saw several bees going off up into this area." Laura pointed to a large branch that joined the trunk fairly high up on the tree. "I don't think we're going to see anything for sure from down here. Somebody's going to have to climb up there."

"Reckon that's me." Bill sidled his horse up next to the trunk and reached up to grasp a limb with both hands. He released his booted feet from the stirrups and nimbly pulled himself up into the foliage. In the effort, his hat was scraped off his head by an errant branch, and Ruth stepped down out of her saddle to retrieve it. Mary reached over her horse's neck and took his mare's reins.

Laura lost sight of him for a minute, but could follow his progress by the rustling as he climbed higher into the leaves. Finally, she caught sight of a flash of red hair halfway out a major limb.

"There's a hive up here, all right," Bill called. "A big one, too! Do you think your daddy would like some honey, Laura?"

"Hey, we want some honey, too," Ruth protested.

"Don't worry, Ruthie-girl," Bill's voice soothed. "This looks like it's got enough honey for everybody. You think you can make me a smudge and get it up here?"

"You think you can rob that hive without burning the tree down?" Mary countered.

Bill's head popped into view as he pushed branches aside with his hand. "Why, I'm wounded by your lack of faith in my abilities, Mary. I've smoked out many a beehive in my time and never started a conflagration once."

Mary was already on the ground with Ruth, hunting for materials of the proper length, texture, and moisture content to make a smoky smudge for calming the bees before stealing their honey. "This tall grass here isn't green enough…" Mary called out, but before she could finish her thought, a loud crack and a zing cut her off. The horses started.

There was an instant's silence before Laura said, "What was that?" But all knew very well that it was rifle fire.

"That was close!" Mary exclaimed. "Where did it come from?"

No one had time to speculate before a second shot rang out and hit high up in the oak tree.

Bill yelped in surprise, and Laura called his name, alarmed, while trying to calm her skittish horse. Bill dropped to the ground, tried to stand, but stumbled and went to his knees.

"That coyote is shooting at us." He sounded calm and deliberate. "Y'all girls get on your horses and ride like the devil. Laura, you too."

"You're hit!" Laura wailed, and started to dismount.

"Laura!" Bill's tone was severe enough to startle her. "Do as I say. I ain't hit bad, just grazed the calf…"

The third shot hit Laura's horse in the withers. He bucked and reared, and Laura, unprepared, went flying and hit the ground hard. A fourth shot pinged into the ground close to Bill's feet.

"Ride, you girls, ride!" Bill yelled. "Get help!"

Ruth was in the saddle and racing back up the road as Bill's last word hung in the air. Mary ran toward her uncle, but he waved her off. "No, Mary, get to Laura. Get her out of here. I'm okay, I can stand."

Mary paused and took in the situation in a flash. Bill was hit in the leg and struggling to get up. Laura was down in the grass, conscious or not, Mary couldn't tell, and her horse was skipping and bucking across the meadow with a gunshot wound in its withers. Mary looked off toward the woods, from where she thought the shots had come.

"Can you get to your horse, Bill?" Mary called, as she moved toward Laura.

She never heard the answer. She heard a crack and a hot pain exploded over her left ear, and everything went dark.

Mary's mother, Alafair Tucker, stepped out onto the back porch from her kitchen, fanning herself with a dishtowel. The August evening was sweltering, and Alafair had suddenly found herself so uncomfortable in the hot kitchen that she had had to come outside to try and catch a breeze. The sun was just westering, and the family would be clamoring for supper before long.

Her two-year-old, Grace, had followed her into the yard, and was making a beeline for the path to the barn. The children's house pet, an elderly yellow shepherd named Charlie-dog, was close on her heels. Alafair puffed, distracted by the child's break for freedom. Ever since one of the barn cats had had kittens, it was nearly impossible to keep Grace away from them.

"Grace…" she called, but just as the child stepped out of the gate, the big red rooster, master of the family flock, rose up from nowhere, a miniature demon out of the ground, squawking, spurs at the ready and wings ablur, and jumped at Grace. The dog yipped and beat a hasty retreat.

Alafair started as Grace shrieked and made an about-face back toward the house, narrowly escaping a flogging. Alafair lengthened her stride and scooped the child up into her arms and banged the back gate shut in the rooster's face. She hadn't seen him among the other chickens scratching in the dirt close to the yard.

Grace let out a wail, but Alafair could tell she was startled rather than injured, and she patted the toddler's leg. "It's all right," she soothed. "That old rooster didn't hurt you. He was just trying to protect his family."

Grace sniffled, her eyes round as dollars, but she was comforted by her mother's assurance that she wasn't hurt. "Bad rooster," she pronounced.

Or at least that was what her mother understood, given that she was as yet unable to articulate the letter "r."

"Yes, that woostoo is bad." Alafair glanced down at the dog, who was cowering at her feet. "You're a fine protector." Her voice was heavy with irony, and the dog slunk off to nurse his shame in solitude. She wondered absently why the usually placid old rooster had suddenly taken to flogging anyone who crossed his path, but the thought didn't engage her for long. She adjusted Grace on her hip and let her gaze wander into the distance.

She had no reason to think so, but Alafair knew something was wrong. She had been stirring the soup pot when she felt it, the disturbance in the rightness of things. She was anxious now, for no good reason, she knew. Even so, she began to tick off her family members in her mind, placing the whereabouts of each child, and her children's father. She knew exactly where each was supposed to be, and what he or she was supposed to be doing. She didn't worry about Mary and Ruth any more than the others. They were with their Uncle Bill, who knew how to take care of anything that might arise.

She was just turning to go back into the kitchen when she heard a sound on the wind that caused her to pause. It sounded like a woman moaning. She blinked and listened for a minute, not sure of what she was hearing. It was the wind sighing through the elms around the house, but it was something else, as well. A woman crying, she was sure. Her heart leaped. She turned to go back into the house to send her youngest son, Charlie-boy, to fetch his father, when she heard the horse galloping up the drive from the road.

My head was aching something powerful, and though I didn't have any idea about what had happened to me, I knew I was hurt. I wondered if maybe my horse had thrown me on my head. It came to me that I had been out riding with somebody. I was getting little pictures in my mind that didn't line up. I saw Ruth tearing out at a gallop like Beelzebub himself was after her. That's what came to me, Mama, that the Devil was loose. Laura was there. I got a flash of her dun gelding rearing up and her going a-flying. I remembered Bill, then, up in the tree. Something about craving honey. Robbing a beehive.

Mary swam up from unconsciousness with an effort. The first thing she was clearly aware of was the loud whir of cicadas, and at first she was comforted by the familiar sound. The burning feeling over her ear sharpened her senses, and she raised her hand to her head and opened her eyes at the same time. She found herself lying on her back in a cradle of grass, staring at the darkening sky through a fan of oak leaves. Her honey blond hair had mostly escaped from its long braid, and her head was spinning, and ached like blazes. The fingers that had touched the sore spot on her temple were bloody. She peered at them, perplexed, unable to remember for a moment where she was or what had happened.

She raised her head just enough to peer over the grass. Bill's filly and Laura's gelding were grazing quietly under the oak tree. Mary could see a trickle of blood running down the gelding's withers. He was favoring that rear leg, but from what Mary could tell, the horse was only creased. Everything else in the small meadow was quiet. Neither Laura nor Bill was anywhere to be seen.

Mary stretched up on her knees, then slowly got to her feet. The late summer grass rustled in the desultory breeze. The cicadas were deafening, which made her head ache more than it already did. She took a tentative step, then another. The mare lifted her head to look at the young woman, then resumed grazing.

Mary didn't walk very far before she saw the red hair in the grass, under the oak tree on the opposite side of the trunk. She forgot caution and her pounding head and ran to the prone form under the branches. She fell to her knees beside her uncle and put her hand on his back. He was lying with his face turned toward the tree and both arms flung out over his head, very close to where she had seen him last. It was late in the evening, now, and the light was fading fast, but Mary could see well enough to know that he was dead. The dark, matted, sticky place in his coppery hair showed plain enough that the bullet had caught him in the back of the head and laid him out instantly.

Mary was so dumbfounded that it took her a few minutes to realize that the whimpering, sobbing noises she was hearing were coming from her. She sat back on her heels and looked around. The sun was down and the light was nearly gone. The heavy August air had stilled and the dry grass and leaves had quieted. The only sounds were the relentless cicadas and the intermittent movement of the horses. She stood up and dried her eyes on her skirt tail before she began a methodical examination of the meadow. She fully expected to find Laura lying dead in the tall grass, but she did not. She could tell by the way the grass and undergrowth was crushed and broken that there had been a lot of activity in the clearing since the four of them had ridden up to rob a beehive. There was a wide trail going off into the woods to the west that had not been there when Ruth had ridden off.

Mary considered following the path of disturbed grass into the woods to look for Laura, but hesitated when she heard the scuffle of some small animal off to her right. She stood still for several minutes, listening to the night critters come alive. She turned around and caught sight of Bill, just a dark shape on the ground now, and choked back a fresh spate of tears.

She couldn't leave him, now, not with the scavengers coming out and him lying there all dead and stretched out under the oak. She settled herself on the ground next to her uncle's body, to keep him safe until help came.

◇◇◇

Mary sat by herself in the dark for what seemed to her a long time before she heard a horse galloping up the road toward the clearing. The moon had not yet risen, so she could not tell whether the man who guided his horse off the road toward her was coming to help her or not. She hunkered down in the tall grass a yard or two from Bill's cold form, unwilling to reveal herself, until the rider halted in the middle of the clearing and called, "Laura!"

Mary stood up. "Mr. Ross. Over here."

"Laura?" Calvin Ross repeated. Mary could just see his head turn toward the sound of her voice.

"It's Mary Tucker, Mr. Ross, just under the oak tree, here. Can you see me?"

Calvin swung down out of the saddle and took a few steps toward her. "Mary?" he ventured. "Where is Laura? Where are Laura and Bill? Your sister came riding up to the house like old Nick hisself was after her and said somebody was shooting at you here at the big oak. I come as fast as I could. Where is Laura? Are y'all all right?"

Mary started to cry again. "Laura's gone, Mr. Ross. I don't know where Laura is, but Uncle Bill is shot dead."

Calvin stiffened. "Shot."

"Ruth rode to get help but I must have got grazed. By the time I came to, Uncle Bill was dead and Laura was gone. I think whoever did it took her, Mr. Ross. There's a trail through the grass there that leads off into the woods. I think she must have fought him."

Calvin said nothing. He asked her no questions, offered no speculation or comfort. He mounted his horse, pulled his shotgun from its holster on his saddle, and headed off into the woods, leaving the weeping young woman standing alone in the dark.

Chances may have been slim that Calvin would find Laura by plunging into the dark woods by himself, but Mary was not surprised that he did it. There was nothing he could do to help

Bill, now, and every minute that passed, the trail to his daughter grew colder. Mary settled back down on the ground, waiting for Ruth to come with the sheriff.

Calvin's hoofbeats faded into silence, and the crickets joined the chorus of cicadas as the night deepened. Mary wished she had some light, and she felt some anxiety that a big cat might catch the smell of blood, but she wasn't particularly afraid to sit there on the ground in the dark next to a dead body. Even if the spirits of the dead wandered the earth, like her half-Cherokee grandmother believed, Uncle Bill would never hurt her. He had been her favorite uncle, after all. He was by far the youngest of her aunts and uncles, only a couple of years older than Mary herself. He had always been patient with all his many young nieces and nephews, and the best fun to be around. She had often played duets with him, he on the mandolin, she on the fiddle. She reached out and put her hand on his back. She could feel through his shirt that he was cold, and lifeless as a stone. Once, she remembered, he had held still for a quarter of an hour while she and her sisters had counted his freckles…

"Miss Mary!"

A man's voice saying her name caused Mary to start and jump to her feet. The sudden movement caused her aching head to spin and her vision to blur, and she reeled, clutching at the trunk of the oak tree to keep from falling. Someone grasped her arm, and she shrieked and tried to jerk away.

"Miss Mary, Miss Mary," the man said again. His voice was familiar. He seemed familiar altogether, hovering over her, holding her arm gently. She stopped struggling, suddenly aware that he was trying to help her. She blinked and her vision cleared enough to recognize her would-be rescuer.

"Kurt," she managed.

Kurt Lukenbach was one of her father's hired men, a German immigrant and an expert horse trainer and smith. He was an enormously tall young man with clear blue eyes and light brown hair. A scar, white against the tan of his face, ran down his left cheek from the corner of his eye to his jaw, but rather than mar his looks, it was rather rakish. As long as Mary had known him, Kurt had been exceptionally quiet and reticent, but Mary was quite fond of him even so. When Mary's father Shaw Tucker had hired him more than a year earlier, his English was barely understandable, and she had enjoyed helping him firm up his grip on the language.

"I meet Mr. Ross on the road," Kurt was saying to her. "I just was walking home from town when I hear that something has happened here in the clearing. *Lieber Gott*, Miss Mary, you are hurt! Sit down here…" He paused, and Mary felt his body stiffen as she leaned against him for support. He had seen Bill.

He didn't ask her anything. He urged her around to the other side of the tree trunk and sat her down on the ground. Then he pulled a bandanna from his back pocket and pressed it against her wound.

She became aware that she could hear the sounds of several men on horseback riding toward them from the road. She could hear them talking as they grew near, and she could identify the voices of her father's cousin, Sheriff Scott Tucker, and his deputy Trent Calder. Her vision was too blurry and the dusk too deep for her to identify the first horseman to crash through the brush, but Kurt murmured, "Micah." Another of Shaw Tucker's horse trainers, another friend of Mary's. By ones and twos, half a dozen or so other men followed him in quick succession. Ruth was not with the group, as far as Mary could see, but she was surprised to hear the voice of her grandfather, Bill's father, Peter McBride.

The sheriff must have stopped by Grandpapa Peter's farm for reinforcements. Mary recognized two of the men who were carrying torches as Grandpapa's hired hands. Her heart curdled. Cousin Scott had no idea what he was leading Grandpapa into.

The horsemen rode into the clearing and spread out, calling for Bill, and Laura, and for Mary, but there was such a lump in her throat that Mary couldn't reply, try as she might. It was Kurt who stood up and called to the sheriff.

Sheriff Scott Tucker drew a breath to call out to the others, but hesitated when he realized what he was seeing by the light of the torch that his deputy was holding. The look that crossed his face caused Mary to sob, and Scott dismounted quickly and knelt down beside her. Kurt deferentially moved away.

Scott felt Mary's face and head. He pulled the bandanna away from her temple so he could inspect the oozing wound. "Who shot you, Mary?"

Still unable to speak, she shook her head, and Scott enfolded her in an embrace. While she cried, the sheriff reached out one hand and tentatively examined the hideous wound at the back of Bill's head. He looked up at Trent, who wordlessly remounted his horse and rode across the meadow to inform Peter McBride.

"Mary, honey," Scott said, "listen to me, now. I sent Ruth on home to get your daddy. Your daddy will be here directly, honey, and then you can go home. Can you stop crying and tell me what happened? Who shot Bill, baby girl? Where is Laura? Do you know who done this?"

With a giant effort of will, Mary swallowed the lump in her throat. She pushed away from Scott and wiped her eyes with the back of her hand. "I don't know, Cousin Scott. I tried to see who was shooting but a bullet knocked me cold before I could see anything. All I know is that it came from over there. Then when I came around I found Uncle Bill shot. I don't know where Laura is. Her daddy rode through here a while ago. I don't know how long. I've lost track of time. But he tore off looking for her. Then Kurt showed up and helped me." To her own surprise, she began to weep yet again. She would have thought that she had shed every tear she possibly could.

Scott hugged her and patted her back soothingly. "All right, sugar, all right. We'll talk later. Listen, I think I hear your daddy coming right now."

But all Mary heard was her grandfather, across the meadow, make a sound so full of grief that it sent chills up her spine.

Chapter Two

Do you remember the Fourth of July, Mama, when we all went to the party in town and had ice cream and watermelon, hot dogs and pie, and watched the parade? The Veterans band played on the bandstand and we all sat around on folding chairs and listened to them. Remember how happy everybody was, how Daddy and his brothers and the boys all set off firecrackers and laughed and teased? Bill and Laura were there, too, and the Turner boys, Art and Johnny. And Trent Calder, Kurt and Micah, Aunt Josie's girls Maxine and Reginia, and all of Cousin Scott's boys. Everybody for miles around was in town. It was a happy day!

I wonder if that memory came to me in the field just because it was so nice? Even though I hadn't yet realized what had happened to Bill, maybe I knew in my soul that I was about to be grieved something awful.

Alafair Tucker banished her husband, Shaw, to sleep in the parlor with the boys, and spent the night sitting next to their big double bed, where she had secured Mary. She watched all through the night, keeping the nightmares away from her daughter through sheer will. She leaned across the bed and stroked Mary's forehead at any sign of distress, and sang to her softly, the same song she had sung to all her children when they were little and in need of comfort.

"Oh, where is my kitty, my little gray kitty?
Oh, where, oh, where has she gone?
I've looked in the cellar, I've looked in the attic,
And nowhere can kitty be found.

Kitty, Kitty. Oh, where are you hiding today?
Kitty, Kitty. Oh, come forth and join in our play."

Mary slept the sleep of exhaustion, never moving, even when the rooster crowed in anticipation of dawn. Alafair didn't stir either, but sat there in her rocker next to the bed instead of generaling her family through the start of the day, as she usually did. Every one of her large brood knew the situation, and Alafair was content that they could competently take up the slack.

She heard her oldest girl, Martha, slide out of bed before the cockcrow had faded away, and the soft metallic sounds of the kitchen stove being fired told her that Shaw was up and about as well.

Martha's nightgowned form appeared in the bedroom door, her dark hair hanging loose about her shoulders. "Mama?" she whispered. "How's Mary?"

Alafair turned in her rocker to look at Martha through the dawn gloom. "All right, I think. She's quiet now. The kids still asleep?"

Martha nodded. "Ruth's up, and Daddy and Gee Dub and Charlie. Took Ruth a long time to go to sleep last night, judging by how she tossed and turned. She's rattled, I expect."

"How did Grace do?" The two-year-old usually slept on a cot in her parents' room.

"Good. She liked being in there with us. Me and Ruth will get the kids up and dressed and take care of breakfast."

"Thank you, honey. I'll be in directly."

Martha had no more turned around to go than Shaw tiptoed into the room. He was still in his nightshirt, his dark hair uncombed and his face unshaven. His hazel eyes looked very dark this morning, uncharacteristically sunken and haunted. He smoothed his droopy black mustache with the back of his fingers and managed a smile for her sake. Alafair rose from her rocking chair and crossed the room to meet him. They reached out and took one another's hands.

"How's she doing?" Shaw kept his voice low.

"She seemed to get through the night well enough. That graze on her temple ain't much more than a scratch. She cried a little in her sleep early on, but settled pretty well as the night went on. I'm going to let her sleep."

Shaw looked over Alafair's head at his slumbering daughter. "She had a rough day yesterday."

Alafair peered up at him. "How are you?" Shaw had been very fond of his young half-brother, and was shaken by his mother's and stepfather's grief, as well.

Shaw didn't reply immediately, and Alafair put her hand on his chest to soothe his heart.

"I'll do, I guess," he finally said.

"It was a terrible thing, Shaw. I feel scared, knowing that some lunatic is abroad. All night, I kept thinking I could see somebody lurking in the shadows just outside the bedroom window, but every time I got up to look closer, all I could see was just the shadow of that lightning-blasted hackberry in the moonlight."

Shaw nodded. "This would spook anybody. I just came in here to tell you that I'm heading over to Ma and Papa's directly. I'm taking Gee Dub with me, but the two hired men will stay close. Already sent Micah over for John Lee," he said, referring to his son-in-law, who resided on the adjoining farm. "I reckon they can all help with the search for Laura." He leaned in close to whisper in her ear. "As for the rest of y'all, stay close to the house, now. I took the Remington out of the cabinet and loaded it. I put it up on the rack over the front door, along with a box of shells, in case you need it quick."

Alafair nodded. "Martha will have to go to work, but I'll put the rest of the kids to getting the chores done. Ruth's here to run the house and Mary can watch Grace. I need to be getting over to your mama's before noon."

Shaw glanced at Mary. "You putting her to work, as well?"

"Best thing for her. The baby always makes her laugh."

"Why, honey, everything makes Mary laugh. She's always been our laughing girl. How's she going to laugh again after this?"

Tears started to Alafair's eyes when she saw the unshed tears in Shaw's, and she couldn't help but embrace him. "Don't you worry, darlin'. There will be reason to laugh again, if I have to bust down the Pearly Gates to find it."

The children were dressed and breakfast was well underway when Alafair finally made her way into the kitchen. Ecstatic to see her mother, Grace clambered down from her chair at the table and ran to Alafair with a piece of bacon clutched in her fist. She was followed closely by Charlie-dog, who had always had an affinity for whoever was the youngest in the family, especially if the child was eating bacon. Alafair picked Grace up and automatically wiped the toddler's face with the tail of her apron. From the stove, Martha cast her mother a glance over her shoulder.

"Charlie and Blanche are milking," Martha informed her, before Alafair had completed the morning inventory of her offspring, "and Ruth is in the hen house."

Alafair nodded. Ruth was in the hen house, Martha at the stove. The twenty-year-old twins, Alice and Phoebe, both married, were currently fixing breakfast for their own husbands. Seventeen-year-old Gee Dub was in the parlor with his father, cleaning the rifles they had just taken from the locked gun cabinet. Mary was sleeping still. Charlie, age thirteen, and nine-year-old Blanche were milking. Sophronia, eight years old, was setting the table and trying to run herd on Grace, the child who had usurped Sophronia's position as the youngest of the family.

Everyone in her family accounted for, Alafair sat down at the table with Grace in her lap and spooned oatmeal into the child's mouth.

Shaw appeared at the kitchen door with his hat and coat on, and tall, lanky Gee Dub following on his heels. "Reckon we're off, darlin'."

Alafair looked up at him, surprised. "Aren't y'all going to eat?"

"No time, honey. I want to round everybody up and get over to Papa's before the sun is well up."

Alafair leaped to her feet and plopped Grace down in the chair, where the child serenely went on feeding herself oatmeal. "Martha, let's fix your daddy and the boys some bacon sandwiches they can take with them."

"Now, Alafair," Shaw protested, "we got to get going."

"Hush, now." Alafair flew into action, grabbing a paper-wrapped loaf of bread from the cabinet. "We'll have you a passel of food before you get the horses saddled."

Shaw gave her an amused smile, but didn't dawdle. "Come on, son," he said to Gee Dub, and the two of them headed for the front door.

"You be careful, son," Alafair called to their backs, and the ever quiet Gee Dub gave her a wave of acknowledgment before they disappeared. Alafair shook her head to herself as she began slicing bread for the bacon Martha was frying. "I declare, Martha. Sometimes men don't think at all. Your grandma surely isn't going to be in any mood to feed them."

"How is Grandma?"

Alafair shrugged as she buttered the thick slices of bread. "Daddy said she was holding up when he was over there last night. I think she's trying to be strong for Grandpapa. All your daddy's brothers and sisters were there, except for Uncle Charles, of course, but him and Lavinia should be here this morning, I expect. Aunt Josie and Aunt Sarah spent the night over there." She paused. "Did you hear that noise last night? Like somebody howling?"

Martha didn't look up from her cooking. "I heard the wind blowing off and on. I was hoping it might bring a rain, cool things off." She forked out the cooked bacon and added more slices to the hot grease. "I'll send Charlie into town to tell Mr. Bushyhead I won't be in to work at the bank today. I'm sure it's all over town by now, what happened to Uncle Bill."

"You sure it would be all right?"

"I think Mr. Bushyhead would be surprised if I showed up, considering."

"Good, then. I'll feel better with you here to run herd."

The conversation was interrupted by the creak of the screen door as it opened to admit Phoebe, whose husband, John Lee, had been recruited by Shaw to join the search party. Alafair put down her bread and went to usher the heavily pregnant young woman to a chair.

"Beebee!" Grace squealed, always overjoyed to see a new face. She launched herself at her sister's knees as oatmeal splattered and her spoon clattered to the floor.

"Did you walk all the way over here?" Alafair was not ordinarily one to cosset a healthy expectant mother, but Phoebe's face was drawn and her eyes red.

"Don't fuss, Mama. The walk is good for me," Phoebe protested, but she allowed her mother to push a comfy pillow behind her back as she sat down in the kitchen chair. "Oh, Mama, ain't it awful about Uncle Bill? How's Grandma and Grandpapa? Have they found poor Laura? How is Mary? Why didn't somebody come over and tell us last night?"

"Now, honey, don't fret yourself." Alafair resumed her place at the cabinet to help Martha assemble sandwiches. "It ain't good for the baby. There's plenty of people to help, and the best thing you can do is stay as calm as you can so nobody has to worry about you. Grace, what are you doing?" She pulled the toddler out from under the table where she and the dog were stretched out, eating bits of spilled oatmeal off the floor with her dropped spoon. Alafair plopped the unperturbed child back into her chair, retrieved a clean flour sack from a drawer, and she and Martha began to pack up bacon sandwiches.

"But who would do such a thing to Uncle Bill?" Phoebe insisted. "I don't think Bill had an enemy in the world. Not one!"

Alafair cast her a dark glance. "Oh, there's a hidden viper somewhere."

Chapter Three

The parade was the best one yet, Mama, all us kids agreed. When the Grange went by, Grandpapa and Daddy and the uncles all looked so fine on the beautiful red Tennessee Walkers that Grandpapa raised. And Daddy was carrying that big flag! Blanche and Fronie were on their Sunday School float. Blanche got to be Betsy Ross, but Fronie was all dressed up like a Revolutionary War soldier. We laughed at that, but Fronie thought she looked mighty fine in her short britches. Charlie walked by with the Boys' Ag chapter, herding that curly black calf he won a ribbon for later at the County Fair in Muskogee. That saucy Art Turner tried to throw a pebble at the calf so he'd shy, but Uncle Bill poked Art in the ribs and made him miss. Art couldn't hit the side of a barn with a handful of beans, anyway.

I had to explain everything to Kurt. I thought that was kind of funny, since he's been in America for years. He cheered 'til he was hoarse. I never saw him so lively, not before or since.

The first day after Bill died was long, hot, and disturbing. Mary slept all morning and most of the afternoon. Shaw and Gee Dub were away all day with the sheriff's posse, looking for Bill's killer and any sign of Laura Ross.

Shaw had ordered Kurt and Micah to remain on the premises to care for the animals and, incidentally, watch the house.

In the afternoon, Doctor Addison dropped in to check on his patient, and told Alafair not to worry overmuch that Mary was so lethargic. Her wound was superficial, and he expected that her lack of energy was mostly shock and grief.

"Let her sleep, Alafair," he advised.

And so Mary slept all day, while Martha and Alafair took turns sitting beside the bed for no good reason, really.

Ruth was jumpy as a cat, starting at every noise and shadow, and Alafair had some trouble keeping her distracted. Finally she sent Ruth to the barn with Grace to play with the kittens, and Charlie, who seemed to have aged from thirteen to thirty overnight, went along to keep an eye on them.

It didn't help matters that the rooster attacked the three youngsters the instant they set foot out the gate. Alafair stood looking out the screen, shaking her head, as Ruth shrieked, grabbed up the baby and ran for the barn. Charlie was having none of it. He seized the bird by the neck and marched it, flapping and squawking, to the chicken coop, where he threw it inside and unceremoniously slammed the door on it.

Phoebe stayed with them all day, ostensibly to help. But instead of the sweet and gentle girl that Alafair knew, this hot, pregnant, and upset Phoebe prowled the house, fanning herself and snapping at Blanche and Sophronia. The usually noisy little girls skulked around in the shadows, wide eyed, and tried their best to be invisible.

Alafair pushed her damp hair out of her face and tried to comfort her children in the way each needed most at the moment, trying to be patient, praying that God would bring the world around right sooner rather than later.

Later in the day, Alafair let the girls clear away dinner and entertain Grace while she seized rags, a mop, a pail of water, and a gallon jug of vinegar from her pantry. She rolled up her sleeves and tied on her apron and kerchief, preparing to get as much housecleaning done as possible before she had to cook and pack food for Bill's visitation at her mother-in-law's house the next day. Not that cleaning did much good, she thought, as she poured vinegar into the bucket of water. This time of year, every door and window was open at all times, and dirty-footed people were tramping in and out of the house all day long. It seemed like a continual haze of reddish dust hung in the air and filtered in through the screens and settled on the floor and furniture. She dusted and mopped every morning, and by afternoon, a new film of dust covered everything in the house.

Well, she comforted herself, if I didn't make an effort we'd be buried up to our necks in a week. She hefted her supplies and headed into the parlor, but stopped in her tracks at the door. Charlie, who she had thought was off in the paddock with the hands, was sitting in one of the armchairs by the settee. This was such an unexpected sight that, for an instant, it didn't register on her who she was looking at. Charlie was a fun, energetic, mischievous boy, who was normally either gone off on some adventure or buzzing around noisy and bothersome as a fly. The fly had most unusually alit in the parlor.

"What's wrong, Charlie-boy. You ailing?"

His dark blue eyes, normally so distracted, gazed at her steadily. He was slouched in his seat, clad only in a faded shirt and overalls, his bare feet stretched out in front of him and his forearms relaxed along the arms of the chair. "Naw, I ain't ailing, Ma. I wanted to talk with you a minute."

This was unexpected indeed. At thirteen, Charlie was of an age when the desire to hold thoughtful conversations with his mother was as rare as snow in August. Alafair set her bucket on the floor, bemused. But she assessed the situation quickly enough. She crossed the room and sat down in the second armchair across from the boy. "Are you feeling bad about Uncle Bill?"

He didn't answer her question, but a sad smile flitted across his face, and he wiped his blond forelock out of his face with the flat of his hand—a move that reminded her startlingly of Shaw. Charlie sat up straight and pulled his legs back toward the chair. Alafair noticed that his overalls were too short. He had always been a leggy boy, all bones and knobby joints, but lately he'd started fleshing out, as well as spurting up. He was usually such a dickens, though, that Alafair hadn't realized 'til this minute that she could begin to see traces of the man to come in her youngest boy.

"I've been talking with Daddy and Gee Dub," he was saying, "about how somebody could just come up and bushwhack Uncle Bill and them like that. I've been mighty worried because that dog is still on the loose."

Alafair nodded. Charlie had been only three when his younger brother died, too small to remember. The first time a young person realizes that death is something that really does happen to people he loves, the world shifts in a profound way.

Charlie continued. "Daddy and Gee, they can go out with the posse and hunt for him, but then you and the girls get left here all alone. Why, that bushwhacker, he could pick y'all off like birds on a branch. So I asked Daddy if I could stay around the house and watch out after y'all, at least until they catch the skunk."

"What did Daddy say?"

"Well, he said he'd already worked out a watch detail with Micah and Kurt, but he expected that three pairs of eyes was better than two, so he'd work me into the roster."

"So is this your first watch?"

"I'm going out to spell Micah right now. But I figured to tell you about it first, so you'd know what's going on."

"All right, Charlie. That's good to know."

She had thought that now he'd conveyed his message, he would jump up and disappear out the front door in a blur, but he leaned forward and clasped his hands between his knees. "I know I ain't exactly Bill Tilghman, Ma, but I'll do the best I can. Sometimes a yappy little dog keeps the critters away as good as a big old mastiff."

"As far as I'm concerned, you've got a heart like a mastiff, son."

He gave her a skeptical smile as he stood. "At least I'm doing something besides jumping out of my skin."

◇◇◇

Early the next morning, dressed in her good blue cotton dress and her second-best hat, Alafair arrived at the McBrides' sprawling two-story farmhouse on the outskirts of Boynton. She found dozens of buggies, wagons, and the odd automobile parked in front of the house in haphazard array. Death had struck the family, and the entire community had gathered to lend support. As her horse trotted up the long access road pulling her buggy, Alafair waved at Shaw's brother-in-law, Jack Cecil, driving past her in the opposite direction. Sitting next to him in the buggy was Doctor Jasper Addison, whose long white beard streamed in the breeze as they shot by.

She pulled up into the yard and climbed down to retrieve her food baskets. The long front porch was overflowing with grim-visaged older men, standing around in groups or seated in cane-bottomed chairs, discussing the tragedy in low tones. Alafair recognized them all—Shaw's uncles, by blood and marriage, neighbors, Mr. Bushyhead the banker, Mr. Lang the grain merchant, Mr. Turner the stable master. Alafair's son-in-law, the town barber Walter Kelley, strode down the porch steps to relieve her of her basket of food as she approached.

Walter was married to Alafair's daughter Alice, Phoebe's most unidentical twin. Alafair had been unhappy in the extreme when Alice chose the much older barber as her mate. He was glib, handsome, and, to Alafair's mind, shifty, but Alice had been so happy during the last year that Alafair had softened toward him.

"Miz Tucker," he greeted.

"Looks like everybody in town is here," Alafair observed.

"Anybody who's not here now has been or will be. Fortunately there's enough food to feed the whole town."

Alafair nodded. "Good thing. Shaw's mama won't have to worry about cooking for a while. How're they holding up?"

Walter shrugged. "They're pretty shook, I can tell, but you know how it is. This thing happened so sudden-like, that I don't reckon it's hit them yet. The uncles practically had to tie Mr. McBride up to keep him from joining the posse. Finally told him that Grandma would be needing him, but the truth is that the sheriff don't need to keep track of wild old fellows like Peter McBride while he's trying to catch a murderer."

"And Grandma Sally?"

"You know Miz McBride. She loved that boy like glory, but you couldn't crush her with a rock."

"Is there any news?"

Walter nodded. "Why, yes there is. We just heard a few minutes ago that somebody found Laura…"

Alafair's heart leaped into her throat. She stopped walking. "Lord have mercy! Is she killed?"

"No, no, she's alive. But I don't know nothing more than that. Don't know who found her or where or what happened to her. Jack Cecil rode in with the news just before you came."

So that was why Doctor Addison was with Jack. Alafair sagged. "Praise Jesus!"

Walter ushered her into the house. "One blessing, at least."

They passed into the foyer, from where Alafair could see through the open French doors to her left into the enormous parlor.

The room was packed with women. Sally and Peter McBride, Bill's parents, were seated on parlor chairs off to the side, surrounded by daughters, daughters-in-law, and granddaughters. Most of the furniture had been moved aside and two sawhorses were set up in the middle of the room. The new Christian Church preacher, Mr. Lacy, was hovering solicitously around the bereaved parents.

Alafair caught her mother-in-law's eye, and Sally gave her a wan smile. She looked much as usual, except for the swollen eyes. "They haven't brought Bill home yet?" Alafair asked Walter, under her breath.

"He's still with Mr. Moore, the undertaker," Walter murmured. "I expect they'll be bringing him home any time, now."

Alafair's daughter Alice and Shaw's eldest sister, Josie Cecil, rose from their chairs and crossed the room into the foyer to help Walter and Alafair with their baskets. "We're putting the food in the kitchen, Mama," Alice said, by way of greeting. "How's Mary?"

"She's up and about. The wound on her head is just a graze. She's awful quiet though. Don't have much to say."

"Still in shock, I'm guessing," Josie offered.

"That's what I think," Alafair agreed. "How are y'all doing, Josie?"

Alafair's concern weakened Josie for an instant. She turned her head to look out the window just long enough to gather her reserves before answering. "Holding up."

Since Alafair was properly handed off, Walter returned to the porch and Alafair and Alice followed Josie's substantial form straight through to the back of the house and into the big kitchen. The giant kitchen table was completely covered with food, so Josie and Alice began unloading Alafair's baskets onto an available countertop.

"I just heard that they found Laura," Alafair opened. "Walter says Jack just came in with the news. What do you hear? Do you know how she is? I passed Jack and the Doc on the road as I came in."

Josie nodded. "Jack just came by to give us the news and fetch Doc Addison. He didn't give us too many details, but I gather that it was her daddy that found her early this morning. She was sprawled out unconscious in the middle of the road, right between the meadow and her daddy's house."

"I declare!" Alafair breathed. "She couldn't have been there last night. Shaw said that they searched all around that area before the moon went down and it got too dark to see. Has Laura told them anything?"

"I don't think so. She's still unconscious or somehow unable to speak. Jack says she looks pretty tore up."

"Did he think…could they tell if she was…" Alafair was unable to finish the thought aloud, but Josie understood her perfectly well and shot her a rueful glance.

"Don't know. Jack told me privately that he wouldn't be surprised, but even if the Doc finds it to be so, I imagine Calvin won't want it getting around."

"Poor child," Alafair said.

"At least she's alive, though."

"She may not feel so glad to be alive herself," Alice interjected. "She sure did love Bill. I know I'd want to die if anything happened to Walter."

Alafair and Josie both smiled. Spoken like a proper newlywed. "I imagine you're right," Alafair agreed.

"Especially if she's ruined…" Alice added, but Alafair cut her off.

"Hush, now, sugar. Let's not get such a rumor started, especially since we don't know any such thing."

Alice's fair eyebrows lifted. "Well, it wouldn't hardly be her fault."

"Even so," Josie said.

Alice puffed, full of disdain for such an old-fashioned attitude, but said, "I expect you're right."

A commotion at the front of the house interrupted the conversation and pulled the three women back into the parlor in time to see everyone moving into the foyer and toward the front door. Josie put her hand on her sister Hannah's arm. "What's happening?"

Hannah looked back at them, her hazel eyes refilling with tears. "Mr. Moore's hearse just pulled up."

Bill's parents had stood, but neither of them made a move. They just stood there in front of their chairs, their faces blank, staring through the doors that led into the front entryway. Sally clutched a handkerchief, her knuckles white. Peter put his hand on Sally's shoulder.

Alafair looked away from them, her eyes pricking. She tried not to think of the times that she had stood in their place, attempting to hold it together for the sake of all the dozens of people who had come to comfort her, when the last thing she wanted in the world was to be comforted.

Hannah and Josie moved to their mother's side, and Alafair felt Alice's hand slip into hers. They walked together to the window. The back of the hearse was open, and the fine ashwood coffin with brass handles was already being slid out into the waiting hands of the volunteer pallbearers. Alafair was gratified to see that Walter Kelley was among them. The three men on one side of the coffin were Shaw's Tucker uncles, the brothers of his late father Jim, Sally's first husband. When Sally had married Peter McBride after Jim's death, Peter had been as inexorably and thoroughly absorbed into the Tucker clan as if he had been born to it. Technically, Bill McBride had not been at all related by blood to these three old gentlemen, but Alafair doubted if that fact had ever occurred to any of them. Bill had called them all "Uncle," after all.

The six men hoisted the coffin to their shoulders and paced up the porch steps and into the house, where they lowered it reverently onto the sawhorses in the middle of the room. Mr. Moore unclamped the lid and he and his assistant lifted it off and set it against the wall. A low noise, almost like a sigh, rippled through the room. All Alafair could see from where she stood was the tip of a freckled nose, a smooth pale forehead, and a shock of coppery red hair, and then not even that as her eyes flooded. She heard Alice stifle a sob.

The crowd rustled like wind through a wheat field and parted to give Sally and Peter access to their son. The three daughters, Josie, Hannah, and Sarah, followed close. The family stood with their backs to Alafair, so she was spared the sight of their faces. She knew how they looked, though. She pulled a handkerchief from her sleeve and wiped her eyes.

More noise and voices outside caused her to turn and look out the window behind her. The men in the family who had ridden with the posse had arrived and were dismounting and handing their horses off to the boys. Alafair was interested to see that Micah had shown up, and was discussing something with one of the posse members. She caught sight of Gee Dub's dark, curly hair before he disappeared around the house, leading three horses by the reins.

Shaw and his brother Charles walked into the house together, and hesitated when they saw the tableau of their sisters and parents standing before the coffin. Only Josie turned to look at them. Shaw's eyes swept the crowd and alit on Alafair and Alice. Some of the stiffness went out of his stance when he saw his wife and daughter standing by the window, and they smiled at one another. He looked dusty and red-faced with the heat, his shirt sleeves rolled up above his elbows. The other two brothers, James and Howard, came into the house, followed close by several cousins, sons and nephews, including Sheriff Scott Tucker, who moved to the side to stand by his father, Uncle Paul. Phoebe's husband, John Lee Day, came in and gave Alafair a discreet wave. The four Tucker brothers joined the immediate family by Bill's side.

They all put their arms around one another and stood in a knot, this family all together for the last time. The only sound was occasional soft weeping, and through the open windows, the shifting of horses in the yard. The few young children in the room clung to their mothers' skirts in silent awe. Alafair stood holding Alice's hand, studying her husband's family as they clung to one another. Four dark-haired men, all six feet tall or close to it; three tall, dark-haired women, surrounding two little parents. Howard was the only blood child of Peter McBride, now. She wondered if it had dawned on him. Howard was the only one of the entire brood with blue eyes, like his father. Even poor dead Bill, who had inherited Peter's red hair, had had dark hazel eyes like his Tucker siblings.

Well, people died. Even young, healthy, promising people like Bill McBride. But this…this murder. Absolutely senseless, as far as Alafair could see. Bill had loved her family, and had hung around the farm a lot. He was not much older than her older girls, after all. He and Shaw and the boys had planned a dove hunting trip for the fall.

This would not do. Someone evil was abroad, someone who had no compunction about killing an innocent young man and savaging a seventeen-year-old girl, and almost as bad in Alafair's eyes, shooting at her daughter. Mary had been lucky. Why hadn't the killer kidnapped Mary instead of Laura? Maybe he thought he had killed Mary. Apparently he had tried to do just that. Was his plan to steal Laura all along, and Bill and Mary were just in the way?

Alafair stiffened and her grip tightened on Alice's hand. Did the killer realize that Mary had not seen him? Would he try to finish the job? As much as she wanted to talk to Shaw about what the posse had found, she was suddenly desperate to get home. She pulled Alice toward her and whispered in her ear.

"I don't think they need me here, right now," she murmured. "Tell your daddy that I had to go home and check on Mary. I'll be back later. Be sure and find out everything you can."

Alice's blue eyes widened, but before she could comment, her mother was gone.

Chapter Four

After the parade, all of us young folks had pulled the chairs around the bandstand into a big circle, and we were sitting there eating hot dogs and ice cream, drinking Co'Colas and telling stories. All the fellows were telling about lawbreaking that they'd seen with their own eyes. You know fellows. They were all trying to outdo each other, and impress us girls, I think. Whereas we were trying not to get mustard on our summer dresses. Laura was in a fine mood that day. She was going on to Bill about his freckles, accusing Art Turner of having a secret sweetheart, and teasing Kurt about the way he talks. How they both blushed!

Art was giving as good as he got. He's the teasingest fellow that ever was, especially with the girls. He never met a girl that he wouldn't try to tease until she cried. I've never figured out why he's that way. Martha says he thinks it's funny, but I always thought he's just mean. If he thinks that's the way to impress a girl, he's entirely misguided. After a while, I noticed that Bill looked a little put out with Art, but his sass was just rolling off Laura like water off a duck's back. Bill and her had just agreed to marry, and she was mighty happy. We all were. Johnny Turner broke right down and cried. Nobody is more sentimental than Johnny.

Mary was sitting on the porch with Grace in her lap and Charlie-dog the shepherd at her feet when Alafair drove up to the house. In the distance, past the vegetable garden and next to the barn,

Alafair could see Charlie and Kurt in the corral, doing something with a couple of mules. Charlie waved at her, and she waved back. She noticed that Kurt was wearing a gun belt.

Phoebe was on the porch swing, fanning herself with a paper fan and looking sweaty and uncomfortable, her auburn curls frizzling out like a halo from the twist on top of her head and sticking to her neck. Mary and Grace had apparently been napping in the heavy heat, but they perked up when Alafair's buggy appeared. Grace scrambled out of Mary's lap, and was crawling up the front gate in excitement by the time Alafair had dismounted the buggy. Alafair swung the gate open, giving the little girl a ride that made her squeal with happiness.

Alafair picked her up. "You been behaving yourself for Mary and Phoebe?"

Grace patted her mother's face with one hand and wrapped her dusty bare legs around her mother's waist. "I helped Mary."

"Did you?" Alafair walked up onto the porch and sat down with the toddler in a slat-back chair.

"She was a big help." Mary gave her mother a look that said she could have done without that kind of help. "She and Phoebe dusted the piano while Ruth and I did up the dishes."

"It was very musical," Phoebe added.

"I'm sure it was." Alafair reached across and plucked Grace's rag doll from Mary's lap and handed it to Grace. "Here's your baby, honey bit. I see her bed over yonder at the end of the porch. You go on and lay her down for her nap."

Grace was amenable. She jumped down and ran on tiptoes to the makeshift doll bedroom she and her sisters had constructed from rags, buckets, baskets and boxes, accompanied by the dog, leaving the women to talk.

"How're you feeling, darlin'?" Alafair asked Mary.

Mary touched the bandage at her temple. "Not too bad. Still got a headache, and it stings off and on. Sometimes I get blurry in this eye, but it clears up directly. Main thing is I just want to sleep. I can't get woke up." She hesitated. "I don't want to get woke up," she admitted.

Alafair nodded, unsurprised. That had always been her own reaction to trauma. She just wanted to go to sleep and not have to think about it any more. She gazed at Mary a minute, stifling a desire to take her into her arms. Mary looked sad. It was not at all a normal look for Mary, who had always been Alafair's happiest child. Nothing had ever perturbed Mary, until now. In fact, Mary was the one who had always taken it upon herself to cheer the unhappy with a joke and a smile. She had the easiest, sweetest laugh Alafair had ever heard. Alafair caught her bottom lip between her teeth to keep from crying. Yes, if someone had held a gun to Alafair's head and forced her to say, she might have said that laughing Mary was her favorite. Alafair swallowed the lump in her throat.

Lord, I would do anything, she prayed, to get that smile back, to hear that laugh again.

"Doc Addison said he'd be back sometime today to have another look at you," Alafair said. "Don't know when, though. I just saw him leaving when I got to Grandma's. Seems Laura got found by her daddy, and the doc was on his way to see her."

Both girls sat up straight at this news, but Alafair forged ahead before they could ask questions.

"All I know is that she's alive. Jack Cecil told Josie that her daddy found her in the road, unconscious, and they don't know if she saw anything or not."

"Well, is she all right?" Mary asked.

"I don't know. They told me that she was beat up, but that's all. I expect your daddy will have more news when he gets in later."

Mary and Phoebe glanced at one another, distressed, before Phoebe asked, "How's Grandma and Grandpapa?"

Alafair shrugged. "I didn't get to talk to them, there was too much commotion, too many folks. Oh, but they looked to be feeling bad when I left. Mr. Moore brought Bill home. They set him in the parlor. Daddy's whole family was there, all your aunts and uncles, so that's good for Grandma. Alice and Walter were there, too. I couldn't stay, though. I just felt like I'd be more use at home. What have y'all been doing since I left?"

"Phoebe and me haven't been doing much of anything," Mary told her, "except for watching Grace. Seems we're invalids, to hear Martha tell it. I saw that you have a peck of okra in the kitchen. We were talking about chopping okra directly."

"I hate cutting up okra," Phoebe fretted. "I hate the way it makes your hands smell. You can't get that smell off your hands for nothing." She shifted in her seat and eyed Alafair ruefully.

Alafair smiled. She knew this was Phoebe's mood talking. Phoebe loved fried okra, and was always ecstatic when the first tended pods were ready in the summer. "Honey, I've got okra up to my chin. I've pickled enough okra to last ten years, and it's still coming on like wildfire. Maybe I'll make it into a fried okra pie tonight. You always like that."

Phoebe's eyebrows peaked with interest, but Alafair turned back to Mary, intent on her original topic. "Everything been quiet? Where is everybody?"

"Charlie is back in the paddock with Kurt, helping him with the mules. Martha and Blanche are out on the back porch sorting clothes for mending or the rag bag. It's too hot to do it in the house, but if they sat out here with us, we might try to help, don't you know. I think Martha sent Ruth and Fronie to rake the chicken yard and feed the chickens. Neither one of them wanted to do it, but Martha figured Ruth needed a task. Fronie's got scared of that old rooster since he's taken to trying to spur everybody. She whined about it so much that Martha stalked out there and ran that bird off with a broom." She chuckled, momentarily raised from the doldrums by the memory of Martha's pique. "I think in the end Fronie and Ruth were more scared of Martha than the rooster."

"Bad rooster!" Grace interjected. Everyone laughed, and Alafair was suddenly grateful that the rooster had gone bad and was providing the kids with a distraction.

She stood up. "I think I'll go around and check on the girls."

Mary nodded, listless again, but Phoebe gave her mother a narrow look. "Is something on your mind that we ought to know about?"

Alafair almost smiled at being so transparent. "No, of course not," she lied. She passed through the parlor on her way to the back porch, shedding her hat and rolling up her sleeves. Every window in the house was wide open, but the sultry air was still and offered no breeze to relieve the heat. She glanced up at the loaded rifle in the gun rack over the door. The sight comforted her.

She checked the drip pan under the ice box and was dismayed to see that it was full. She had just emptied it that morning. The block of ice that Shaw had fetched from town on Saturday hardly lasted half a week in this heat. Never one to waste water, she pulled the pan from under the ice box and carefully emptied it into a bucket to use for mopping or for watering the suffering garden.

This small activity in the stifling kitchen made her thirsty, so she poured herself a glass of cool water from the crockery jug on the windowsill in the kitchen and drank it down before going out onto the screened-in back porch.

Martha and Blanche were sitting next to one another in two wooden chairs with a pile of clothing between them. Several smaller piles lay in front of them and to the sides as they sorted the clothing by color and state of repair. Through the screen, Alafair could see Sophronia and Ruth, both topped with big shady straw hats, raking the chicken yard.

Alafair kissed the top of Blanche's dark hair before she pulled up a chair of her own. Martha's eyes widened. "You're home sooner than I expected, Ma."

"There were so many people there that I figured I was more in the way than a help. I imagine I'll be over there plenty in the next few weeks. You wouldn't believe how much food folks took over. Your daddy and Gee Dub and John Lee won't be very hungry when they get in this evening." She sat back in her chair and folded her hands in her lap. "Looks like y'all are about done. Blanche, honey, go on into the kitchen and wash some rice for me. I'm thinking a pot of rice and a fried okra pie will be just about right for supper tonight."

"But I ain't quite done here, Mama," Blanche pointed out.

"I'll help Martha finish up."

"I'm not sure how much rice to wash."

Alafair calculated in her head for a second. "Use about three of those scoops. Use the big sieve."

"But it's hot in there, Mama," Blanche protested. "I'd rather sit here on the porch and help Martha."

Alafair was unmoved. "I swear, you're lazy as Uncle Ed, girl. Why, one time he hid under the porch with the dogs all day so his Pa wouldn't find him and make him split kindling. Ended up nearly eat up with flea bites. Now, just get in there and don't dawdle, and you'll be done before you know it."

Blanche rose and reluctantly opened the screen to go into the stuffy kitchen.

"And don't forget to pick through the rice for rocks before you wash it," Alafair said to the girl's back.

Blanche didn't exactly roll her eyes, but the set of her mouth conveyed her exasperation as she disappeared into the house. Alafair tried not to laugh.

She picked up a shirt and turned her attention to Martha. "Everything been all right here? Have you seen anybody around?"

Martha looked at her oddly. "Nobody that shouldn't be around. Why? Has somebody seen that killer around here?"

"No, no. Not that I heard. It's just that until they catch the miscreant I'd just as soon keep a close eye on everybody. Oh, I forgot to tell you that Calvin Ross found Laura beat up but alive this morning."

"I declare! I was just about sure they'd find her dead. Did she tell them who did it?"

"The story I heard was that she ain't in a condition to talk, but your daddy will know more about it than I do. How has Mary been?"

"Well, now. She's not herself, that's for sure. She seems like to cry at any minute. It makes me sad just to look at her. She's always been the happiest person in any room. I hope they find the killer soon, so maybe she can start to get over this. I miss her laughing."

Alafair sighed. "I sure wish I could have spared her this. Ever since your daddy brought her home I've been trying to figure a way to ease her heart."

A smile bent the corners of Martha's mouth. Her mother would never change. "Some things even you can't do, Mama. Everybody's got to bear their own burdens."

"Maybe," Alafair begrudged, unconvinced. "The thing that confounds me is that as far as I know, there ain't no one on earth who had bad feelings toward Bill McBride. Do you know anything that might be useful, sugar? You and Bill were pretty close to the same age, after all."

Martha looked down at the pile of baby smocks in her lap. She didn't want to think about Uncle Bill. She had been fairly successful, thus far, in keeping her grief at bay. She knew how she would feel when she finally had to visit Grandma and Grandpapa, and see Bill's earthly remains for the first and last time. She knew how she was going to feel at the funeral, when they would all walk to the cemetery behind the hearse, and she would have to watch her grandparents struggle to contain themselves, and maybe her father, too. Her father seemed to be holding up well, but she could tell that this was harder on him than he was letting on. And Mary, who had been Martha's closest companion all her life, who had had to see poor Bill all shot up and dead…

No, Martha could handle her own grief. It was the broken hearts of those she loved that she couldn't bear. She took a deep breath and looked up at her mother. "I don't know much more than you do, Ma. Since we grew up, I've mostly seen Bill at family get-togethers, or when he would come over here to work with Daddy and the boys, or play with the kids. He liked Micah and Kurt, too." She sighed. "Just last Sunday, when him and Grandma and Grandpapa were over here for dinner, Bill was telling Mary and me about the house and land he has his eye on to buy, before him and Laura marry. And about making another trip to Waco in the fall to look at some mares for Grandpapa." She was unaware that she was referring to Bill in the present tense.

"Piece of land?" Alafair interrupted.

"Orlen Kelso's old place, out south of town. Bill said he gave Orlen one hundred dollars earnest on it." Martha hesitated, thinking. "Wonder what Orlen will do with it now?"

"What did Bill say about his trip to Waco?" Alafair urged.

Martha looked back at her mother and shrugged. "Bill goes down to Waco about every year now, to buy or sell horses. Used to be he'd go down there with Grandpapa, but for the past five years or so, he's been making the trip on his own, or sometimes with Uncle Howard, I think, or sometimes with some of his friends. I expect Grandpapa trusts Bill's business sense, by now. He always did have a feel for the horses." She paused. "I don't expect any of this has anything to do with why Bill got killed."

Alafair nodded. "I know, honey. I'm just casting my net wide. What else is there to know about Bill?"

Martha's gaze shifted back to her mother's face. Is this helpful, her expression said, this dredging up happy times, gone forever?

Alafair read her expression, and smiled. "Tell me, honey. If I knew more about the youngster, I might get an idea what happened to him."

Martha didn't argue. "Bill came into the bank a time or two, whenever he was in town, just to say "hey." He was good friends with Trent Calder, and them and the two oldest Turner boys, Art and Johnny, used to go hunting and fishing. I think the four of them would go to the picture show together every Saturday night, at least until Bill got engaged to Laura. Bill was sweet on the Kellerman girl, Shirley, for a while, but once he met Laura, that was the end of that. At least for Bill. I don't think Shirley was happy about it. He liked to visit with Alice and Walter since they got married. He liked to ride in Walter's motor car."

"You never knew him to get in a fight, or have words with some other young fellow?"

"Oh, no. Bill never was one to spoil for a fight. But you know how hot-headed Art Turner is, what a wild and untamed mouth he's got, not like his brother Johnny at all. Bill and Trent were always pulling him off somebody and soothing any feathers that got ruffled. Funny how Bill and Trent are so calm, them both being redheads."

Alafair leaned back in her chair and folded her arms across her chest, abandoning any pretense of sorting clothes. "Hmm," was all she said.

"Not much help," Martha admitted.

"I wouldn't say that. I wonder if Scott knows to talk to the Turner boys?"

"I imagine Trent would put him on to them. Besides, maybe it wasn't Bill at all that was the target. Maybe it was Laura, or even Mary. Maybe the killer didn't have any target at all. Maybe he was just in the mood to shoot somebody, and the four of them wandered by at the wrong time."

"I'd almost rather that," Alafair told her, "than think he targeted them."

Blanche appeared at the screen. "Ma, I got the rice all washed and in the pot. How much water do I put in?"

Alafair stood up. "I'll be right in." She followed Blanche, but paused before she went into the kitchen and looked back at Martha. "Keep thinking, sugar. Somehow we have to figure out how to get Mary to laughing again, and a little justice might go a long way to do just that."

Chapter Five

Trent Calder had a bunch of tales about lawbreakers, due to his being the Sheriff's deputy and all. He told the funniest story about his own uncle Roy Calder—remember him, Mama? He wasn't exactly a genius in the criminal department. Trent related as how Roy and his son Doug broke into the lumber yard after a snow storm and stole a bunch of boards. The next morning Trent just followed their footprints from the lumber yard right to their house. Can you imagine? Trent near to fell off his chair laughing. Said that while he was arresting them, he couldn't help but point out that they'd have done better to wait until after the melt, either that or do their burgling during *the snow storm.*

While Trent was telling his story, I noticed Shirley Kellerman standing over by the bandstand. She was trying to make like she was listening to the band, but I could tell she was trying to hear what we were laughing about. I felt sorry for her. She could have joined us, if she'd a mind to. It was her own idea to keep apart from us. Art Turner saw her, too. He nudged Johnny and nodded over that way. They whispered together a bit, and Johnny looked annoyed, I thought. I'd bet money Art wanted to engage in some mischief at Shirley's expense, but Johnny must have talked him out of it, because they joined back in the storytelling directly.

The long, sweltering day had just about come to an end by the time Shaw and Gee Dub and Micah, the hired man, finally made their way home. The last fading light was lingering on the horizon when Alafair heard them ride past the house toward the stable, and it was entirely dark by the time they trudged up to the house and filed into the kitchen through the back porch. The younger children were in bed. Only Martha and Mary were with Alafair in the kitchen when the men came in, trailing Kurt Lukenbach and Charlie, who had come up from the stables to meet them when they arrived.

Gee Dub had two shotguns under his arm, both unloaded with the breeches broken, and he slipped past his mother and sisters into the parlor to lock the guns in the cabinet. Kurt and Micah both stood by the door with their hats in their hands and greeted Alafair and the girls solemnly, asking after Mary's health. Shaw hung his hat on the hook by the back door and lowered himself tiredly into a chair at the table beside Charlie.

Two weeks earlier, Alafair would have objected to Charlie's being out so late, but under the circumstances, his thirteen years made him old enough to pull a man's duty when he was needed.

He had stepped up without complaint. His blue eyes gazed at Alafair steadily, his sandy blond hair suffering serious hat distortion—sweaty, spiky at the crown and plastered down in a ring around his head. Alafair opened her mouth to admonish him to wash before bed, but decided to wait until later when the men were out of earshot and the boy's dignity wouldn't be compromised.

"Ma, I'm mighty hungry," he said.

Alafair smiled. "Then you fellows better get some grub into you before you get to bed. Busy day tomorrow."

"Alafair, John Lee has gone home to his wife, but I told these boys you'd feed them." Shaw nodded at the two young men still standing deferentially beside the back door.

Alafair waved them toward the table. "Come on, then, boys. Have a seat. There's a pot of rice on the stove, and I can have you some ham and gravy in a jiffy. Martha, fix these fellows up with some sweet tea."

Kurt and Micah mumbled their thanks and seated themselves at the table as Alafair began melting lard in her big iron skillet.

"I'll just have a bowl of rice, darlin'," Shaw told her.

"Me, too, Ma," Gee Dub said as he sat down. "Too tired to do much in the way of digesting."

"How's it going over at Grandma's?" Alafair asked, as she arranged slabs of ham in the hot grease.

"Most everybody's gone home, now, except for Charles and Lavinia. They'll be staying the night."

"What time is the funeral tomorrow?" Mary wondered.

"Ten o'clock. The preacher was there most of the day." Shaw nodded at Micah and Gee Dub. "These two young'uns and Charles' boys got the grave dug in the family cemetery this evening. They're putting him next to Aunt Olive."

"He always liked Aunt Olive," Martha observed.

Alafair removed the slabs of ham and scraped the bottom of the skillet to loosen the luscious brown bits into the grease before she made the gravy. She measured the flour into the grease and stirred the roux until it browned, then added enough milk to fill the skillet. After she had thoroughly mixed the ingredients and moved the iron skillet a little way off the fire, she placed the platter of ham on the table before the two hired men.

Kurt thanked her solemnly, but Micah started a little when she placed the platter before him and looked up at her, bemused. He had been staring at Mary.

Alafair blinked at him thoughtfully before she turned back to her gravy. Micah Stark. What did she know about him? He was something of a jokester, is what she knew. He was a good-looking youngster, in his mid-twenties, with dark hair and merry gray eyes. Average height, funny as could be, he'd take any opportunity to play with the kids. But maybe a little vain, a little enamored of the sound of his own voice. Shaw liked him. He was a good worker, a good carpenter and an efficient horseman.

He had a fun-loving personality, much like Mary's. Did Mary like him? She was friendly with both Micah and Kurt, Alafair knew. She had seen Mary and Micah team up to tease the stolid Kurt, but otherwise, it didn't seem to her that Mary had ever shown a particular preference for one boy over the other.

However…

Alafair absently stirred the gravy until it thickened, then poured it into a bowl, all the while thinking of ways to get Mary's smile back.

Shaw had managed to delay the five ravenous males long enough to say grace, and they were already eating by the time Alafair put the gravy bowl on the table. Shaw and Gee Dub had turned their bowls of rice into a comforting hot cereal with the addition of several teaspoons of sugar, a dollop of butter, and cream. Charlie, Micah, and Kurt had made some headway with the ham and buttered rice. Micah took the bowl from his hostess and began to ladle gravy over everything in his plate while Kurt waited his turn.

Alafair sat down with Martha and Mary on the opposite side of the table from the men. "You boys did a day's work. Grave digging ain't an easy occupation."

"Yes, ma'am," Micah answered, after a hasty swallow, "my arms is about wore off. Can't hardly lift my fork."

"You seem to be doing all right," Mary observed drily, as he shoveled another spoonful of rice and gravy into his mouth.

He chuckled. "It would be a sin to waste cooking like this, ma'am."

Alafair propped her chin on her hand and leaned her elbow on the table. "Where you from, Micah?" Out of the corner of her eye, she saw Shaw look up at her from over his bowl.

Micah grinned and sat back in his chair, clearly relishing the prospect of being the center of attention. Kurt remained engrossed in his food. "Well, ma'am, I'm from Texas, down around Abilene."

"How did you end up here?"

"My daddy moved to Texas from Ohio when I was a tyke and started a business there, Miz Tucker. A cattle company. I expect I'll go into it with him one of these days. But I reckoned I'd better see the country a bit before I settled down to it. Didn't want to live my life never having been anywhere but Abilene. I worked in the oil fields around Houston for a while, then a cattle ranch outside of New Braunfels. That's where I met Kurt, here, too, amongst all them Germans. I told him he wasn't never going to learn the English language proper if he didn't get out with the English speaking people, so me and him come up here together and did some roustabout work in the big oil fields up in Tulsa County, then on down here to the field north of Boynton. We started looking to work with horses after a few months, though. That's what we both like. We was lucky to hear that Mr. Tucker was looking for some help."

"I thought you were from Germany, Kurt," Mary interjected.

Kurt's mild blue eyes widened as he looked up from his ham, vaguely surprised to be included in the conversation. He smiled, and unconsciously fingered the scar on his cheek. The move was not lost on Alafair. "I am."

"What do you think about all this war business?" Gee Dub asked him.

Alafair shifted in her chair, impatient. Talk of the war that had just broken out in Europe annoyed her. People wasted too much time gabbing about something that had nothing to do with them, in her opinion. She had been infinitely more moved by the death of President Wilson's wife just the week before. Those poor daughters…She opened her mouth to steer the conversation back on track, but Kurt saved her the effort.

"Don't mean anything to me. I have been away a long time from Germany." He returned his attention to his supper, content to let Micah continue the story for both of them.

"Yes, indeed," Micah said, "old Kurt here come over from Germany almost seven years ago, but he proceeded to head right to New Braunfels, which if you don't know is nothing but a town full of as square-headed a bunch of Germans as can be found on this side of the Atlantic."

Kurt shot Micah a glance at the remark, but seemed otherwise unoffended.

"It was in about nineteen and eleven, as I remember it. I was running cattle for a Mr. Schwartzenfeld down there when I met this fellow here…" He nodded at Kurt. "…and I told him, 'Kurt,' I says, 'come on with me up to Oklahoma, boy, and we'll get rich working in the oil fields, and you can learn to be a regular American.' As you can see, ma'am, we didn't hardly get rich, nor did poor old Kurt get to be a regular American. But working with the horses and mules is sure less of a backbreaking proposition than being a roustabout, and not half as dangerous, I guarantee."

"Now, that's quite a story," Gee Dub commented, as he spooned more sugar onto his rice.

"It sure is, Gee Dub," Micah agreed. "And you can bet it ain't over yet."

"Got big plans, do you?" Shaw asked, amused.

"Well, yes sir. I expect I do."

Mary, who had been leaning with her elbows on the table, listening intently to Micah's tale, straightened. "Y'all want some pie?"

Alafair was sure the young men would have accepted the offer, but Shaw pushed his bowl away and shook his head. "Thank you, hon, but it's been a long day, and it's going to be a long day tomorrow. I reckon these boys need to get to bed. Take one of the lanterns on the back porch, Micah. It's plumb dark."

Obediently, Kurt and Micah stuffed the last few bites into their mouths and stood to leave. Mumbling their thanks to Alafair and the girls, they headed out the kitchen door to their shared room at the back of the work shed, between the barn and the stable.

Mary and Gee Dub, one injured and one bone tired, also took their leave to clean up and seek their beds. Charlie, saved from exhaustion by his youth, was sent under protest to wash before retiring, leaving Shaw, Alafair, and Martha sitting silently at the table. Shaw drank the last of the sweetened cream from the bottom of his bowl, then looked up to see two pairs of dark brown eyes gazing at him speculatively.

"Did you talk to Scott today?" Alafair asked him. "Have they made any progress in finding out who shot Bill?"

"I didn't get much chance to talk to Scott, but I did get a few words with Trent Calder. He told me that they had trackers out in the woods all day who have come up with a few things. The dogs found a hollow in the woods where they figure the kidnapper had stashed Laura for a bit after he grabbed her. It was all covered with branches and leaves as neat as you please. They found an empty feed sack in it. He expects that the bushwhacker throwed it over her head when he snatched her. Didn't find any ropes or anything to restrain her, though, so she must have been unconscious when he put her in the hole. Scott has been over to the Rosses' trying to get some information out of Laura. Her eyes are open, but she's in some kind of stupor and don't hardly seem to know he's there. Doc Addison says the kidnapper nearly stove her head in, maybe with the butt of a pistol. He thinks whoever done it probably expected Laura was dead or dying when he stashed her in the woods. She was alive enough to crawl up to the road, though, before she passed out again. Calvin thought she was dead when he found her, but when he picked her up he saw she was breathing."

"Did the doc think she'll get better, Daddy?" Martha asked.

Shaw shrugged. "He said she might come around and be just fine. Or maybe she won't."

"That poor girl," Alafair muttered.

"Did the doc get the bullet that killed Uncle Bill?"

"He did, Martha. Said it's a 7 by 57 millimeter rifle bullet. Hattie at the general store would sure know if anybody had ordered 7x57 clips recently, since she don't sell that many seven millimeters before hunting season."

"Poor Laura," Alafair reiterated. "Poor unfortunate girl, and her mother dead and all. I think I'll go on over there tomorrow morning early and see if I can do anything for them."

"I hear Calvin wants to keep the girl secluded for a while," Shaw told her.

"Still, it can't hurt to offer."

Shaw said nothing, but his eyes crinkled and his black mustache twitched. Alafair would never stay out of it if she thought she could be of some help to a young person. Besides, if anyone could help, she would be the one.

Alafair patted the table with her hand. "Now, I'm wondering if one of those hired boys of yours might be able to help cheer up Mary."

Shaw hadn't expected this comment at all. His eyebrows shot up. "Micah and Kurt? What makes you say that?"

"Well, it's plain she likes them."

"All the kids like them," Shaw pointed out. "Don't mean anything."

Alafair eyed him for a moment, deciding to use some care with this subject. Shaw was easily spooked when it came to talk of his daughters and men. "It's just that Micah is a lively youngster, and it looked to me like Mary was enjoying his palaver."

Shaw looked at Martha, who was sitting with her arms crossed over her chest, observing her parents and keeping her own counsel. "Have you heard your sister say anything about liking Micah Stark?"

"Mary likes everybody," Martha told him. "She's as friendly as an old dog. She thinks Micah is funny but too cocky for his own good. I thought for a while that she had eyes for Kurt, but she mentioned the other day that Kurt hasn't got two words to say for himself. She hasn't said anything about either of them lately, at least not to me."

"Where did Kurt get that scar?" Alafair wondered.

"I never asked," Shaw said, "but he once mentioned a run-in with some barb-wire."

"Doesn't seem to bother him," Martha told her. "Though when we were in Boynton a couple of Sundays ago, Laura and Mary were saying they were going to paint a scar on Micah so the two boys would match up. Micah was laughing like the rest of us, but Kurt acted like he'd rather be somewhere else."

"Kurt seems like a gentle soul, though," Alafair opined.

"Seems like," Martha agreed. "Mary said he was a comfort to her when he came across her in the field the other night. She always speaks warmly of him, when she speaks of him at all."

"Just what is it you intend to do, Alafair?" Shaw challenged, half joking. "How do you intend to get these young folks together? The cotton is going to be coming in for the first picking within the next few days and the head feed will need to come in not long after. I've been making arrangements for extra hands with my brothers for most of the last month. Those are going to be two busy fellows directly. I don't see how I can spare either of them for spooning at least until winter sets in."

"I'd have never pegged you for a matchmaker, Ma," Martha teased. "You could have picked somebody for Mary with more wherewithal than those two hired men."

"Matchmaking!" Alafair exclaimed, affronted. "I never said any such thing. I was just trying to come up with some way to distract Mary from her troubles for a while."

"Some things only time will heal, darlin'," Shaw told her, serious again.

◇◇◇

After everyone in the family was finally abed, Alafair made the rounds of the house to check on the children before she lay down herself. The night was sticky. Gee Dub and Charlie, Blanche and Sophronia had dragged cots and pallets out onto the big front porch to sleep, and Grace had thought that such a capital idea that she had insisted on sleeping between the girls. All the doors and windows of the house were wide open, and an occasional sultry breeze billowed the curtains in the girls' bedroom, where Martha and Ruth lay asprawl on one of the double beds and Mary lay in a little ball on the other.

As she bent over Mary to brush a wisp of damp hair out of the young woman's face with her fingers, Alafair noticed that Mary was clutching something to her chest. The room was dark enough that she had to lean close to see that it was a book.

She gently eased it from Mary's hand and started to lay it on the side table, then hesitated. Not a book. She could tell by the size of it that it was the journal that Mary had kept since she was about ten. Alafair had seen it before, tucked into a box of personal treasures that Mary kept in a drawer in the chiffarobe, along with ribbons and an odd piece of jewelry or two.

Having always lived in such close quarters that the idea of privacy was unknown to her, Alafair had idly thumbed through it once or twice, when she was putting away the girls' clothes. It was filled with Mary's impressions of the latest book or poem she had read, recipes for her favorite dishes, a joke or witticism she had heard. Alafair had found it sweet and amusing, but not particularly revealing.

But that was before. Alafair gazed at the dark shape in her hand. What had Mary been writing lately? Was there something in here that Alafair could use to help Mary in any way?

Well, it was far too late and too dark right now. Reluctantly, she placed the journal on the table. "Sleep tight, darlin'," she whispered.

Through the bedroom window, she could see the tree branches moving in the moonlight, and for a second, thought she saw a human form in the shadows. She moved closer to the open window, but could see nothing. She shook her head. Since it had been struck by lightning the year before, the big hackberry tree had taken on a weird, angular shape, with a multitude of odd protuberances, like waving arms and peeking heads. Surely that's what had fooled her. It had fooled her before.

She made her way to the front screen and stood looking out for a minute, enjoying the rustling, chirruping peace of the night. She had just turned to go to the bedroom when she heard the moaning sound. She stopped in her tracks and listened intently for just a few seconds before she heard it again, distinctly. It was a woman, that was for sure, moaning, so sad, like her heart would break. Alafair eased open the screen and stepped out onto the porch. There was little breeze, now. The trees were still, and all she could hear were the myriad singing insects. She tiptoed from child to child and bent over each cot and pallet, but all were sleeping the peaceful sleep of the innocent.

Alafair walked down the porch steps in her bare feet, and a little way into the yard, where she stopped and listened again. Who are you? she thought.

"Speak to me," she whispered. "Tell me what you want."

But nobody answered.

Chapter Six

*After Trent's story, Walter told about how he got jumped by a robber
in his own back yard a few years back, who stole all the money that
he was taking home with him for the night from his cash register
in the barber shop. Walter said the thief was hiding in some bushes
and waiting for him in the dark. He jumped out and grabbed the
money pouch right out of Walter's hand and ran like a turkey before
Walter even knew what happened. Turned out to be that Williams
boy. Remember how his ma nearly sank through the floor when the
judge sent him to jail for six months for strong-arm robbery? People
just don't think about how what they do affects the folks that love
them. And then, sometimes you just don't know that what you've
done has caused someone pain. Anyway, thinking about poor Miz
Williams made us sad for a minute, and after that, the stories took
a turn down a darker road...*

Very early the next morning, just as the sun was rising, Alafair
allowed her girls to get breakfast, filled a basket with food, and
went to the barn to hitch her little gray filly, Missy, to the buggy.
One of Shaw's hunting hounds, the aptly named Crook for his
broken tail, jumped into the back seat and squirmed with joy
when Alafair didn't order him out. He never missed an opportunity for a buggy ride when he was allowed. She pulled out of
the barn and was just passing the house on the way to the road
when Mary met her at the front gate and waved her to a halt.

"What's on your mind, punkin'?" Alafair asked.

"Daddy says you're going over to the Rosses'."

"I am. Going to take them some food and find out if Calvin will let me see Laura for a minute."

"You going to try to get her to tell you who hurt her?" Alafair blinked at her before she answered. "I expect not. I hear that Laura is in a state and not talking to anyone. Beside, I reckon Calvin wouldn't allow me to be pestering the child. I'd just like to take her a bit of comfort, if I can."

"I want to come with you."

"Are you sure?" Alafair was surprised. "We've got Bill's funeral later. It's like to be an upsetting day as it is."

Mary climbed up next to her mother in the buggy and Crook tried to nuzzle her ear. She pushed him away absently, then arranged her skirt over her knees before she answered. "Ma, I'd feel better if I did something useful about this situation. Anything. I can't stop thinking about what happened. There was nothing I could do. There was nothing anyone could do. My mind is a-roil, all the time. I can't sleep but I have bad dreams. My heart is sore. I feel so sad. I haven't felt so sad and scared since Bobby died and I feared you and Daddy would lose your minds. I thought that there wasn't enough sad left in all the world to feel that way again, that we had used it all up. But now I've gone to that well again, and I'm sorry to find that it's as deep as the ocean."

Alafair's heart shrank at the mention of her little son who had died of poisoning years before, but it was Mary's distress that caused the lump in her throat. She put her hand on Mary's knee. "Honey, when a body grows up, you find that life is just like that. There is an endless supply of sad. But there's an endless supply of joy, too. It comes and it goes, just like winter turns into spring, just like night turns into day. Everything passes, even the worst of your grief. The way to live a happy life is to trust that everything is as it should be, even if you can't see it at the time. You'll do better if you can endure the bad and rejoice in the good."

Mary smiled at her mother's platitudes. "I know grief passes, Mama, or at least grows less. But I feel like it might pass quicker if I could just do something."

Alafair patted her knee. "All right, then. We'll see what we can do." She picked up the reins and clucked at the horse, and they trotted out onto the road.

Calvin Ross' beautiful little dairy farm abutted Shaw's parents' land on the west, within walking distance of the town of Boynton. The property was fronted by a rail fence. A stone gate was topped by a huge sign announcing "Ross Dairy Farm" in festive blue and yellow lettering. The long, low barn stretched off to the left, behind the neat little dairy and office building. Straight ahead, at the end of the drive through the gate, sat the two-story, rail-porched Ross home. Appropriately, the house and all the outbuildings were painted butter yellow. By the time Alafair and Mary arrived, Calvin's farm hands had finished the milking, and as they drove past the dairy, they found Calvin and the man he employed to make his deliveries loading the dairy wagon with canisters of fresh milk, tubs of butter, and cheeses.

The driver had climbed into his seat and Calvin was just closing the doors on the milk wagon when Alafair pulled to a stop. As his delivery man drove away, Calvin eyed them warily, trying to decide whether he was up to accepting any more condolences at the moment, but he walked over to the buggy and smiled at them, friendly enough.

"Calvin," Alafair said, "we brought you some vittles."

"Thank you, Alafair, but I expect we've got enough vittles to last a spell."

"Well, we brought 'em," Alafair countered, undeterred. "Might as well leave 'em. If you and the girls don't need them, the hands might enjoy a meal."

"That's neighborly of you." Calvin gave in to the inevitable. "Just take them on up to the house and leave them with Iva.

She'll see that they get put to good use." He paused and studied Mary. "How you doing, Mary, honey?"

"I'm all right. How is Laura, Mr. Ross?"

Calvin's lips thinned and he shook his head. "No change, as far as I can see. The head wound looks bad to me, but the doc says he don't think her skull is busted so bad it won't mend. She ain't uttered a word since it happened. Sometimes she just sleeps, or stares off into space. That's bad enough, but ever once in a while she takes a notion to wander, like she's looking for something. Won't say nothing to us, but she's like to crawl out her bedroom window and hie off into the night, if we don't keep a sharp eye on her. The sheriff keeps wanting to talk to her, but it don't do no good. I'm bound to tear my hair out with worry. Doc Addison says to let her rest, don't let nothing fret her, so that's what I'm doing."

"How're the other girls?"

Calvin shrugged. "They're young, Alafair. They're helping out as best they can, trying to get her to eat, helping Iva with the chores, and all."

"Well, it's a nasty business, Calvin. I won't be easy 'til they catch the skunk who did it."

"He better not rest easy, either." Calvin's face hardened. "If he crosses my path, I'll save the county the cost of a trial."

"I understand, Calvin. Just be careful. Don't leave the girls without a mother nor daddy either."

Calvin looked down at the ground and shook his head, smiling at his own folly. "I hear what you're saying, Alafair." He looked up at her. "But I've never been so riled."

Alafair had nothing to say to this. She wasn't inclined to try and talk him out of it when she rather agreed with him. She picked up the reins. "We'll take this food up to Iva. No need to disturb yourself. I can see that you're busy. We've been praying for y'all, Calvin."

"Thank you, Alafair," he called as she pulled away from him. "We could use it. Take care, Mary."

Calvin walked back toward the dairy barn and Alafair drove the buggy around to the back of the house, so they could unload the food into the kitchen.

"You never asked Mr. Ross if we could see Laura," Mary pointed out.

"Don't see why we need to bother the poor man with it," Alafair told her as they climbed down. "We'll see what Iva has to say. Crook, stay put." The dog settled down in the back of the buggy, where he would stay, since he had been ordered, until they came back.

Iva herself came out onto the back porch to greet them. She was Calvin's sister, a childless widow, who had been living with the family since the mother had died. She resembled Calvin quite a bit, Alafair thought, tall and rangy, hair gone prematurely gray, but a pleasant face. A pleasant manner, too. She had only been in town for a little more than a year, and was still learning the particulars of her new neighbors.

"Why, it's Alafair Tucker, isn't it?" she greeted, relieving Alafair of her basket as she walked back up the steps. "And Mary! I'm glad to see you looking as well as you do, honey."

"Thank you, Miz Grady," Mary said.

"I swear, everyone has been mighty generous," Iva told them, as she ushered them into the kitchen. "We've been eating as much as we can, and I've been feeding Calvin's workers like kings for the last couple of days, but in this heat, I'm afraid food is going to go to waste."

"I thought of that," Alafair assured her. "That's why I've brought you some of my canned goods, and Mary here made up a package of her own dried noodles."

"Why, that will come in handy! Calvin and the girls do love their chicken noodle soup. Now, sit down and have some cake. Miz Kellerman from the church brought it last evening, and it's too good to be let go to waste."

"Miz Kellerman. Isn't her girl Shirley a friend of Laura's?"

"They know one another, but Shirley was more a friend of Bill's. She cooled toward Laura when Laura and Bill started stepping out together. I know Miz Kellerman really admires the McBrides. Now, eat some of this cake."

"Thank you, Iva, but we can't stay too long. Bill's funeral is later today, you know."

The pleasant look melted off Iva's face and she sat down heavily in a kitchen chair. "I know."

"Are y'all going?" Mary asked her.

"I am, and maybe Laura's sister Betty. Calvin hasn't got the heart, he says. The youngest girl, Joan, will be staying here to look after Laura."

"You don't think it would help Laura if she went?" Alafair asked. "Bill was her intended, after all. I'd think she'd want to take her leave of him."

Iva shook her head. "Laura doesn't know if it's day or night. She's been told that Bill is gone, but I don't know if she understood. The wounds on her head don't look quite so bad now that we got them cleaned up, but I'm afraid her mind is just a mess. Sometimes she acts like she understands you, and sometimes she doesn't. When we get her up to change her clothes or make the bed, she's as limp as a sack of cobs. But if you take your eye off her for a minute, she's liable to walk right out of the house!"

"Calvin said she's taken to wandering."

Iva sagged at the sheer pathos of it all. "I wonder sometimes if she isn't looking for something, but who knows what's going on in that poor muddled brain of hers? Her right hand doesn't grip well, and her right eye wanders now and then. I don't think she's aware of anything, but Calvin is convinced that she knows more than we think. Why, he's afraid that if we took her over there and she saw poor Bill in his coffin, she'd just fall right down dead."

"So it's bad as that."

"It is. This very minute, the child is in her room yonder, lying in a pile on her bed. Maybe she's sleeping, maybe she's just a-staring at the wall. She's said nary a word, nor even cried. I know she understands us sometimes, if we tell her to roll over or something like that, but sometimes she just doesn't seem to understand at all."

Mary caught her lip between her teeth and looked at her mother expectantly. Alafair leaned back in her chair with a thoughtful expression on her face, and briefly drummed the kitchen table with her fingertips. "Iva," she said at last, "would you let us look in on Laura for a minute?"

Iva's forehead crinkled. "Oh, I don't know, Alafair. Calvin doesn't even want the sheriff talking to her any more. He says she's been through enough right now."

"I don't intend to interrogate the girl, Iva. I'd just like for Mary and me to sit with her for a little bit, let her know that she has plenty of people who love her and are thinking of her and praying for her. Calvin don't have to know. We wouldn't stay more than a minute."

Iva pondered, clearly torn. "I doubt if Laura will even know you're there," she warned. "But still, I can't see as how it would hurt." When she stood, Alafair and Mary stood as well, and followed her through the kitchen and the parlor, into the tiny back bedroom on the first floor where Laura was ensconced.

It was a bright, pleasant little room. The one large window, shaded on the outside by a big leafy locust tree, was propped open with a length of broom stick to admit the breeze. The head of the narrow bed was centered against one wall, and a small chest with a mirror on top was centered against the wall opposite. Two kitchen chairs sat on either side of the bed, and a third was pushed into a corner. Too many chairs for the little room bespoke of recent visitors.

Laura herself lay on her side, facing the door, her blue eyes wide open, but vacant. Her head was swathed in bandages stained pink in several places where her wounds had seeped blood, but her face appeared untouched. Her mouth drooped slightly at the right corner and her right eye appeared to be looking somewhere slightly different than the left. Her fine, pale blond hair had been pulled back and tied at the nape of her neck in an attempt to keep it neat. Her white cotton gown was clean, but damp with sweat. She didn't acknowledge her aunt when

Iva bent over the bed and spoke her name. In fact, she gave no sign that she was aware of their presence at all.

But Iva talked to her just the same. "Laura, Mary Tucker is here to see you, darlin' girl, and her mother, too. You remember how you always said you loved Miz Tucker, don't you, honey, and how Mary and her sisters were like your own sisters? Well, they've come to see you now. Don't you want to sit up and make them feel welcome?"

Laura didn't speak, nor take her eyes off the open door. Her only response was to move her hands from where they lay cradling her cheek and clasp them together at her breast. Iva straightened and gave Alafair and Mary a helpless shrug.

Alafair nodded at Iva, acknowledging that she knew what she was up against, and removed her hat, all business, now. "It's all right, Iva. Just leave Mary and me alone with her for a minute. Maybe we'll just sit with her and be quiet. You can come roust us out when you think it's been long enough."

Iva ceded the bedroom to them and withdrew. Alafair sat down in one of the bedside chairs and motioned for Mary to do the same.

"Poor Laura," Mary murmured. "Oh, Mama, I feel so helpless. What can we do?"

Alafair reached out and put her hand on Laura's hands. "Just touch her, honey." She leaned forward, her face inches from Laura's. "Laura, darlin', it's Miz Tucker, and your friend Mary. Everything's all right, now, sweetheart. Ain't nothing going to happen to you now. There's nobody here going to hurt you. You're in the circle of your family."

Mary, who had placed both hands on Laura's side, wasn't weeping, exactly, but her eyes were spilling over with tears that ran down her cheeks unnoticed. "Laura," she said, taking her mother's lead, "why don't you come back to us? We sure miss you."

Laura closed her eyes.

Alafair leaned in even closer and put her hand on Laura's cheek. "Sugar, Bill wouldn't like to see you like this. Bill is in heaven, now. He's looking down on you, he's going to watch over you for as long as you live. Bill loved you more than anybody, still does; and you know he wants you to be happy."

Mary's eyes widened. She was surprised that Alafair was taking such a straightforward tack. She sniffled, trying not to break down.

Laura made a little mewling sound.

"You got to live, honey," Alafair said to her. "For Bill's sake, and for all the folks that love you. You've got to come back."

Laura's shoulders began to shake. Alafair rose from her chair, sat herself down on the side of the bed, gathered the girl up in her arms like she was cradling a baby, and began to sing to her.

"I went to the stable and best as I was able
I looked down the old wooden spout.
I went to the wood pile and stayed there a good while
But never would kitty come out.

Oh, kitty, kitty, oh where are you hiding today?
Oh, kitty, kitty, come forth and join in our play…"

Laura moaned, then started to sob like her heart would break. Alafair rocked her back and forth, and Mary, crying herself now, patted her leg.

Iva rushed back into the room at the sound of the sobbing, and stood amazed in the bedroom door. "I'll declare," she managed.

Alafair crooned to Laura wordlessly, rocking her and comforting her as best she could. She had to consciously keep from squeezing the breath out of the girl. Her arms were covered with goose flesh and her hair was practically standing on end; for when Laura began moaning and crying, Alafair recognized the voice she had been hearing on the wind.

Chapter Seven

At first, the stories the boys told were all about folks who were too stupid to make a success of being criminals, very funny and all. But then all of a sudden, we were talking about murders. John Lee told about when his little sister found their dad shot to death in a snow bank, and him and Phoebe just gave everybody goose bumps telling how they both reckoned John Lee himself came close to hanging for it. Gee Dub made us all both laugh and shudder with the tale of how Charlie found the dead woman in Cane Creek—running his fingers through her hair in the water. Gee Dub didn't say it, but everybody was thinking about how that woman was Walter's first wife. Alice didn't particularly like that story, as you can guess, Mama. She doesn't like to think that Walter had a life before she came along and married him.

Alafair and Mary were driving up onto the road from the Ross farm, when Mary nudged her mother's shoulder and nodded at a horseman riding toward them from the west.

"I believe that's Micah," Mary said.

"I believe you're right," Alafair agreed. She clucked and snapped the reins, and they pulled out onto the road just as Micah reached them. He fell in companionably beside them as the buggy slowed its pace. Crook apparently caught the scent of something interesting, for he jumped out and disappeared into the long grass.

Micah touched his hat brim with his fingers. "Howdy, ladies."

"Hello, Micah," Mary responded. "What are you doing out this way?"

"Well, Miss Mary, your daddy sent me to talk to his brother Mr. James Tucker about the cotton harvest. Seems Mr. James' crop is about ready to drop off of its own accord, and he has contracted with the pickers to work his place this coming Tuesday. He was wondering if Mr. Tucker would be willing to come by and help out, and Mr. Tucker wanted me to tell his brother that he'd be delighted."

It was the usual arrangement. Every year at the end of August or early September all the relatives and neighbors worked their way around each other's farms helping the migrant pickers bring in the cotton crop. The harvest usually began with the farms farthest to the south of town and worked north. James Tucker, whose farm was located about three miles south of Boynton, usually put in one of the larger cotton crops in the vicinity, and was part owner of the local gin.

"Why, Daddy will be seeing Uncle James in an hour or so," Mary said.

"Yes, ma'am, but I expect he thought it would be unseemly to discuss business at their brother's funeral."

"You're coming the long way around if you've just been to James'," Alafair noted.

Micah's excitable horse, annoyed at having to adjust his pace to the buggy's, skipped a bit, and Micah pulled the roan's head up and patted his neck before answering. "I am, Miz Tucker. Corky here is feeling frisky this morning, so I took a long circle around on my way back, letting him run it out. Lucky I run into you."

"Don't let us hold you," Alafair said.

"Why, I'd much rather keep you lovely ladies company."

Mary laughed, and Alafair's mouth quirked. The boy was full of bull, but Alafair was glad that he had amused Mary.

"Y'all been visiting with Mr. Ross?" Micah asked. "Did you see Miz Laura?"

"We took some food by," Mary told him. "Miz Grady let us have a look in on Laura."

"How is she feeling? Does she remember anything, yet?"

Mary shook her head. "I wish I could say she does. I thought for a while that Mama had got her back with us, but she just cried for a bit, then went to sleep without saying a word. Miz Grady did say she seemed eased some. She asked us to come back any time."

"I'm mighty sorry Miz Laura ain't doing well. Why, everybody in town is asking about her. Just this morning Mr. Turner at the livery stable wondered if I'd heard anything new. Seems his boys were particular friends of Bill McBride, and Laura, too. Poor old Kurt is awful upset about the whole business. Can't stop talking about it."

Alafair perked up. This was not the first time she had heard the Turner boys mentioned in the last few days. She tried to remember who else Martha had mentioned as a friend of Bill's. The Turner boys, and Trent Calder, the deputy. Martha had said that Bill liked to visit Alice in town and ride in Walter Kelley's automobile. Shirley Kellerman, Alafair remembered, had been sweet on Bill once, and Laura's aunt Iva had mentioned Shirley's displeasure at Bill's engagement. She would try to talk to some of the young people at the funeral later to see if she could glean a hint of something that would help the sheriff catch Bill's murderer.

"Are you going to the funeral?" Mary asked Micah, and Alafair started as though Mary had read her mind.

"Afraid not. Mr. Tucker has me and Kurt busier than a couple of beavers at a wood-gnawing contest. Seems we'll be taking care of all the stock by ourselves while Mr. Tucker is busy with the cotton harvest. Got to get them all in so we can keep an eye on them. I paid my respects to Mr. and Miz McBride yesterday."

They reached the entrance to the farm, and Mary made to get out of the buggy to open the gate, but Micah stopped her.

"Allow me." He leaned over and unhooked the chain without dismounting, then grabbed the postern and trotted the big gate open in a wide arc. Alafair drove through and down the drive toward the house, and did not stop as Micah closed and refastened the gate. Micah loped past them and doffed his hat grandly in the way of a good-bye.

Mary puffed a laugh as he receded toward the stable. "He's a big old bag of wind, but he's funny."

"Would you call him a friend?" Alafair asked.

"Well, I like him all right," she admitted.

"How much do you like him?"

Mary shot Alafair a look. "I don't like him *that* much. What are you thinking, Ma? You trying to get me married off?"

"I'm trying to get you to feeling better." Might as well be straight. "Seems like the young'un amuses you."

The comment brought the last few days crashing back down on Mary, and she sagged. "Wish I didn't have this funeral to go to."

Alafair drove the buggy into the barn, but made no move to get out right away. Mary looked over at her, curious. Alafair turned on the seat and draped her arm over the back. "I was thinking. After the funeral is over, while everybody is still around, I figured I might talk to some of Bill's friends, see if I can get a handle on who wanted to do Bill harm, or get hold of Laura. You said you wished you could do something helpful. You want to help me try and figure this thing out? I expect friends of Bill and Laura may be more willing to talk to you than to me, anyway."

Mary sat up. "I'd like to do that more than anything, Ma. Surely we can find out something to help Cousin Scott."

Alafair smiled at Mary's enthusiasm, at once touched to see the spark that lit her blue eyes, and alarmed that perhaps she had a bit too much faith in her mother's problem-solving ability. "Now, honey, we may not come up with anything useful."

"I bet we do, Mama. But even if we don't, at least I'll feel like I'm not just sitting around all pathetic while Bill's killer frolics around uncaught."

Alafair eyed her skeptically, but nodded. "All right, then. While we're taking care of the horse and buggy here, let's decide who's going to talk to who and what we're going to say. And by the way, honey, don't tell Daddy what we plan to do."

"You think he'd try to stop us?"

"Well…no. Probably not. Him and Scott never take my snooping very serious. But there's no reason to get him all stirred up."

When they finally got into the house, they found Ruth at the stove, red-faced, a smock over her dress, standing over a pot of boiling water with a long-handled wooden spoon in her hand. A dishtowel was spread on the cabinet, upon which stood two glass lamp chimneys. Ruth greeted her mother and sister absently before she retrieved a third chimney from the water by inserting the spoon through its open top and gingerly lifting it out, letting the water drain out the bottom. She arranged the bulbous glass cylinder next to the others to dry on the towel. Alafair had purchased three new kerosene lamps, and the glass chimneys had to be boiled before the first use, to keep them from cracking.

Alafair stopped in her tracks when she saw what Ruth was doing, and Mary, unprepared, ran into her mother's back.

Alafair clapped her hands onto her hips. "Ruth, are you boiling those new chimneys right now? It's almost nine o'clock! Y'all should be getting ready for the funeral. And besides, I told Blanche to do that hours ago, after breakfast. Now you've got to take time to douse the stove, and the kitchen will be hot all day."

Ruth, spoon poised in the air, stood dumbfounded for a moment at her mother's unexpected rant. Mary smothered a laugh, and slipped past Alafair and out of the kitchen, leaving Ruth to her fate.

"Everybody is getting ready right now, Ma," Ruth said, when she finally found her voice. "I'm just finishing this up for Blanche because Grace got scratched by the rooster while her and Charlie were picking beetles off the potatoes, and she wouldn't let anybody but Blanche doctor her."

"Is the little gal all right?"

"Oh, it was nothing, just a scratch, but you know how she is. When she gets it in her head that one of us is her favorite person of the day, there's no use anybody else trying to do anything with her."

Alafair shook her head, but couldn't help a chuckle. Grace was a smart and good-natured little girl, but she did have her willful ways. "I declare, I don't know what's got into that bird. He's going to find himself in a pot along with some noodles if he don't mend his ways."

Ruth relaxed when her mother softened, and allowed herself a smile. "Blanche did get the wicks soaked in vinegar so they won't smoke, and they're dried and back in the lamps. Fronie's already over to Phoebe's, and Daddy said he'd take Blanche and Grace over there directly."

"Are my greens and dumplings boxed up?"

"Right over there, Ma."

"Okay, honey, you go on along and get ready. I'll finish up here."

After Ruth left, Alafair cleaned up the kitchen, then inspected the mess of turnip greens and fatback she had made. The big pot was packed in a wooden crate with straw all around to keep it hot. After the funeral, she would bring it back to the boil on her mother-in-law's stove, and make cornmeal dumplings in the pot liquor.

Everything seemed to be in order, and she turned to go kiss Grace's scratch and pass judgment on her children's funeral attire before changing into her own. It was a comfort to her to turn her mind to the needs of the living.

The funeral was just as hard as Alafair had feared. Neither Sally nor Peter wept, but throughout the service Sally's little body trembled like a leaf. Whether it was from the effort it was costing her not to cry, or from rage, Alafair couldn't tell. Sally McBride was tenderhearted and tough as nails at once, so it could very well have been either. Peter McBride was silent and shrunken

into himself, the strain of his loss making a shadow of a man whose personality had always filled any room he entered.

Shaw and Josie stayed close to their mother, Howard and Hannah close to Peter, and Charles and James hovered near their brother's casket. The youngest sister, Sarah, acted as the family's ambassador-at-large, taking care of business with the undertaker or the minister, relaying the order of the day to anyone who expressed an interest. Their spouses, grown sons and daughters, aunts, uncles, and cousins gathered around and followed along, trailing the younger children and grandchildren. Alafair had Ruth by one hand and Charlie by the other, both youngsters solemn and uncharacteristically quiet. Her older children, Martha, Mary, and Alice, sat together at the service and walked together to the cemetery, along with the sons-in-law, Walter Kelley and John Lee Day. Phoebe, almost too pregnant to walk, had stayed home with Grace. Blanche and Sophronia had been given the option of going to the funeral or staying with Phoebe, and Alafair had been relieved when both chose to help Phoebe.

Alafair had expected Gee Dub to attach himself to his brothers-in-law or his age-mate cousins, but he hovered about in her vicinity so pointedly that she figured Shaw had told him to keep an eye on his mother.

Bill was buried in the family cemetery in the grove behind the McBride house, between his favorite Aunt Olive and patriarch Great-Grandpa Tucker. When the last words were said over the grave and the mourners turned to go back to the house for a funeral dinner, Alafair and her children made a brief stop at the nearby graves of her two boys who had died in infancy. When they left the grounds, three of Bill's nephews were filling in his grave.

After dinner, Mary and Alafair drew aside into a corner of Grandma's house long enough to review their strategy. Alafair would talk to Mrs. Kellerman, though Mary would not be able to talk to Shirley. She had not come, and Alafair resolved to find out why. Bill's friend Johnny Turner was there, but not his brother Art, which seemed to be a fruitful line of questioning for Mary to pursue. Trent Calder was spotted filling a plate in the kitchen. He was potentially a rich souce of information, but trying to get anything out of Trent was like pulling teeth. The women determined that he would be less suspicious of Mary's questions than Alafair's, and they briefly plotted a plan of attack before separating to take the field.

Mary repaired to the kitchen to find Trent, and Alafair went into the parlor, where the first people she laid eyes on were Scott and his wife, Hattie, sitting next to one another on the love seat in the corner. Their twenty-five-year-old son Stretch was sitting beside his mother in a kitchen chair, with his arm draped over her shoulders. Hattie's thin, freckled face was mottled from weeping, and she looked up, dabbing her eyes with a handkerchief, as Alafair walked over. Scott and Stretch both gave her a pale smile. She expected they were relieved to see someone approaching who was more skilled at offering comfort than they. She smiled back.

"Oh, Alafair!" Hattie emitted a shuddering sigh. "What an awful thing for poor Aunt Sally and Uncle Peter. Why, if it was one of my boys, I just don't think I could stand it." She shot her son an accusing look. "They none of them better get hisself into a situation, is all I got to say."

Stretch Tucker, who, true to his nickname, was easily a head taller than either of his parents, gave Alafair a long-suffering glance before he answered his mother. "We aim to stay out of trouble as best we can, Ma."

"The sad thing about this, Hattie," Alafair observed, "is that Bill and the kids didn't get themselves in a situation."

"No, indeed," Scott concurred. "Can't blame anybody for this but whoever did the shooting."

Hattie sniffed. "Scott sees some ugly things about folks in his work, Alafair, but this just don't make no sense at all."

Alafair folded her arms across her chest and shifted her weight to one foot. "Are you making any progress in finding out who did it, Scott?"

He shook his head, more in exasperation than in denial. "This killer is a slippery one. He knows how to cover his tracks, that's for sure. I even called in old Joe Dan Skimmingmoon, the tracker for the Muskogee Police Department. If he can't follow a trail, it can't be followed, I reckon. He'd see signs, but then lose the trail directly. Haven't found anything for the dogs to get a scent from. Best thing I can think to do right now is to investigate Bill himself, see if I can't figure out who might have taken against him for any reason, unlikely or not."

"Knowing Bill, that's a hard way to go."

"That's the truth, Alafair. I've been talking to every friend Bill ever had, and most of his kin, too. Of course, I get the same story from everybody. If there ever was a ruckus, Bill was the first one to make the peace. The only *compadre* of his I haven't spoke to yet is Art Turner. He's down in Tishomingo at his grandma's and couldn't make it back in time for the funeral, according to his dad. I had Mr. Turner over to the office and together we telephoned the post office down there, to see if we could get the boy back up here straight away, but I ain't heard anything back as of yet. The Tishomingo postmaster told me he had seen Art a day or so ago, and the boy had said he planned to stay on with his grandfolks for a week or so. So we know he was there, at least."

"Did you talk to Bill's friend Shirley Kellerman? I see her mama over yonder, but I never did see Shirley at the church or the grave site either one. That surprises me some. Him and Shirley had known each other since they were kids. Used to play together and all."

Stretch removed his arm from Hattie's shoulder and leaned forward, interested. "I wondered about that myself." He ran his hand across the light russet-brown frizz he had inherited from his mother and looked up at her through the sharp blue eyes he had gotten from his father. "I heard she was awful broke up when she found out Bill was dead."

"The Kellermans are on my list," Scott said, "but I haven't talked to them yet. Trent seems to think Shirley was mighty fond of Bill. It's a long shot that she'd know something helpful."

Alafair turned to gaze thoughtfully at Shirley's pretty, dark-haired mother, who was standing with a couple of other women in the corner next to the fireplace. "Still, maybe I'll ask her why Shirley didn't make it today…"

Scott nodded. "Let me know if you find out anything interesting," he said, and she nodded absently. She was barely aware of Scott's ironic smile as she began to move away.

Hattie eyed her husband suspiciously. "You're mighty easy going about her asking questions of folks that might know something of killing," she said, after Alafair was out of earshot.

"I noticed that myself," Stretch added.

Scott gave a rueful shrug. "I don't know if it's just an accident or luck or what, but in the last couple of years, she's managed to find out things I couldn't that helped bring a couple of murderers to justice. I expect folks will tell her things they won't tell me, since she can't throw them in jail. But however she does it, I'm not too proud to stand back and see what she comes up with."

Mrs. Kellerman was a member of Alafair's church, and therefore Alafair knew her and her family rather well. Mrs. Kellerman was a short, curvaceous woman with a very pretty face set off by large black, doe-like eyes. Her daughter Shirley bore a strong resemblence to her. But personality-wise, mother and daughter couldn't have been more different. Mrs. Kellerman was sweet, pleasant and ever helpful, whereas Shirley was…well, to Alafair's way of thinking, Shirley was spoiled rotten. She was her parents' only daughter, and the youngest child to boot, and her mother had made very sure that Shirley had never had to ask for anything twice in her entire life. Or even once, if her mother could manage to guess her wishes.

"Them kids were more than just friends," Mrs. Kellerman assured Alafair, between bites. The two women were seated at one end of the long dining room table, nibbling on chocolate cake and managing to have a fairly private conversation in spite of the dozens of people milling around the food-laden table.

"Or at least they used to be. Shirley had it in her head that she loved Bill, and was hurt bad when he fell for Laura. In fact, I was afraid that girl would go completely around the bend when she heard they were going to get married. She was not more than twelve years old when she decided that Bill McBride was the one for her." Mrs. Kellerman paused to study her forkful of cake. "I wouldn't have been unhappy if that match had worked out, to tell you the truth," she admitted.

"But didn't Shirley wish Bill and Laura well, under the circumstances?"

"She was hurt and angry at first, don't you know, and thought Bill was mistaken. She thought he should reconsider, but she's too good a girl to really wish unhappiness on anybody. Anyway, I was actually afraid that Shirley might do herself an injury when Bill died. She's such a sensitive girl. I'm sure she was feeling guilty for having uncharitable thoughts about Bill and Laura earlier. I expected the funeral would be too upsetting for her, so I sent her on the train to stay with my sister in Oklahoma City for a spell. That's why she isn't here."

"There was never any understanding between Bill and Shirley, was there?" Alafair asked. "If there was, I never heard about it."

"No, at least not as far as Bill was concerned. You know how young girls are, though, once they get something into their heads. I told her, though, that if he couldn't see that she was twice as…" She hesitated, apparently thinking better of passing on that particular mother-daughter exchange, and ate her bite of cake.

By the time Shaw and Alafair were ready to leave for home, it was evening. The children, all but Gee Dub, had been sent home with Martha and Mary earlier to take care of milking and feeding the animals, and to take their Saturday baths.

Shaw was particularly subdued, unutterably depressed, Alafair knew, by his brother's funeral and the grief of his mother and stepfather, though he was making an heroic effort not to show it. When the three of them finally walked out of the house, into the dusk and toward their buggy, Alafair gave her son a wordless glance. Gee Dub didn't acknowledge by word or look that he had gotten her message, but he climbed up into the driver's seat ahead of his father and took the reins. Alafair and Shaw sat next to Gee Dub in the buggy seat as he drove his parents home. Shaw had removed his tie and collar and sat in silence, with his best suit coat draped over his knees.

Gee Dub, too, had peeled down to his shirtsleeves. He concentrated on the road as he drove, comfortable to be quiet, as always. They were passing the Ross farm, just before the turn to the road out of town, when Gee Dub jerked the buggy to a halt. The horse snorted in protest, and Alafair and Shaw looked over at their son, surprised.

"Look yonder," Gee Dub said, before they could ask him what was the matter.

Alafair turned her head to look in the direction he had indicated. The Ross house sat at the end of the shaded drive a few yards off the road, looking completely devoid of interest, to Alafair's eyes. Gee Dub tossed the reins to Alafair, jumped from the buggy, and ran toward the house.

"Lord a'mighty!" Shaw exclaimed, and lit down after the boy, leaving Alafair sitting on the seat in a state of complete confusion.

Gee Dub began yelling, "Mr. Ross! Mr. Ross!" as he neared the house. Calvin flung open the front door, roused by the commotion, but Gee Dub and Shaw veered off toward the side of the house and an open bedroom window.

A pale yellow tongue of flame extruded briefly from the window, then disappeared, and Alafair was out of the buggy and on the front porch before her brain had consciously registered what she had seen. By the time she and Iva Grady and the two younger Ross girls rushed through the house to Laura's bedroom, Gee Dub had already hoisted himself through the window and ripped the flaming curtains from the rods.

Laura Ross was lying on her bed, her ankle tied to the bedpost by a strip of cotton sheet, staring into some world known only to herself, unconcerned about the little fiery fingers that were beginning to consume the bedclothes. Her aunt tore loose the tether as her sisters grabbed her up out of the bed, and Laura allowed herself to be hustled from the room amidst shrieks of alarm and rough treatment that made no inroads into her private darkness. Alafair dashed the white coverlet to the floor and stamped the flames to oblivion.

Sheriff Scott Tucker, still dressed in his funeral attire, stood next to the locust tree by the bedroom window with Calvin Ross, Shaw, and Gee Dub, and examined the burned and muddy curtains. Alafair was in the bedroom, standing next to the open window, ostensibly examining the scorched wall and ceiling. She could hear the outside conversation perfectly.

Scott extended the evidence toward Calvin. "Like y'all thought, somebody set these curtains afire on purpose. See, here's where the fire started, on the end here. Then when it was good and burning, it sparked the bedcovers. I'll tell you, Mr. Ross, it's a mighty lucky thing—a miracle, I'd say—that Gee Dub here has such sharp eyes and was passing by just when he did. If that fire had burned one minute more, it would have flashed up the wall and ceiling and you'd have lost your house and your daughter, at least."

"Jesus Lord!" Calvin breathed. It was a sincere prayer. "What am I going to do with the poor addled child? I didn't think she was of a mind to take her life. I already have her tied to the bed like a wandering calf. Am I going to have to keep her trussed up head to toe?"

Scott blinked at him. "It wasn't Laura did it, Mr. Ross." He was matter-of-fact about it.

"It wasn't Laura?"

"No, I don't think so. Looks to me like it was done from the outside. Somebody stood right here, bold as brass, pulled the end of the curtain out the window and dabbed it with kerosene. Then he fired it with a match and flung the curtain tail back inside.

Whether he knew Laura was in the room I don't know, but it's common knowledge around here that she's in a bad state."

"It wasn't Laura?" Calvin repeated stupidly.

"Couldn't have been," Scott explained patiently. "Smell the kerosene on these curtains. There's no jar or bottle of kerosene to be found. Besides, I looked at Laura's hands pretty close. As short a time as the curtains were burning, she would have had to have a kerosene smell about her, and she did not. Nor did she have the smell of sulfur on her fingers, or a smudge, like she had just lit a match."

Calvin had gone beet red, like the top of a thermometer that is about to explode. "Someone tried to kill her? Someone tried to kill her and all of us in our home?"

Shaw, standing a pace behind Calvin, reached out and put his hand on the man's shoulder to calm him. "You thinking it's the same person murdered Bill and kidnapped Laura?" Shaw asked Scott.

"Well, it don't look good. If you don't mind, Mr. Ross, I'm going to post a guard out here until we catch this dog."

"But if he didn't kill Laura in the first place, why would he be trying to kill her now?" Gee Dub interjected.

Scott eyed Gee Dub with interest, then shrugged. "I expect he thought he did kill Laura in the first place, and now he's returned to try again. Maybe he's afraid she'll come around and remember, and then he'll get caught. Tell me, Gee Dub, what made you look over here from the road when you did?"

Gee Dub considered, then answered, "I don't rightly know. Something caught my eye. A movement. I thought I saw something move over to the side of the house, just under this tree. Maybe it was the fire."

"You didn't see a person?"

"Nossir. Something moving, is all. I don't know what."

"I'll tell you what, Gee Dub. I want you to ponder on it for a while, see if something floats up that you can get a hold on." Scott squatted down close to the ground to examine the dust beneath the window. He picked up a half-burned matchstick and examined it thoughtfully.

"Whoever done this is either stupider than a bucket of oats," Scott said to nobody in particular, "or he has more nerve than he has any right to. Look here. He laid his rifle down on the ground, a bad mistake on his part. He must have seen y'all and had to run before he could cover his trail, which he has done a masterful job of up until now. Look at these butt plate marks—it looks to me like two X's, then a space, and two more X's. Mighty slim stock on this gun. Here's a gouge in the ground—a bolt, I think. A bolt action rifle. I can't get a handle on the shape well enough to recognize the make. Now, this is quite a break for us. He carries an uncommon firearm."

He paused and gazed at the ground. "Lots of prints here. I see Shaw's and Gee Dub's coming up from the road. It's a mess. Somebody don't belong here, though." He pointed to a heel print to the right of the window that didn't look any different from the other scuffs, as far as Calvin was concerned.

Scott stood up and meandered down the side of the house and toward the back. He caught a glimpse of Alafair before she took a step back from the window as he passed, and smiled, but made no other indication that he'd seen her. He paused before disappearing around the corner and looked back at Calvin. "I see a partial trail here, Mr. Ross. I'm going to follow it and see where it gets me. Stand guard on those marks under the window. I want to make some drawings. Keep everybody inside till I get back."

Chapter Eight

Trent had a bunch of stories that were just too grisly for words. Cousin Reginia and Alice finally couldn't take any more and stood up to leave, so Trent apologized and said he'd stick to funny stories. We talked for a bit about Bill and Laura's wedding plans. Their engagement was pretty sudden, and we were all surprised. Laura was the most popular girl in town, and there were plenty of broken hearts among the fellows when Laura finally made her choice from all her suitors. I was sure glad, though. She couldn't have chosen a better man than Bill.

Then Bill jumped in and said that before we quit the scary tales, he had one that would stand our hair on end. So Alice and Reginia got curious and sat down again.

By the time they got home, it was long after dark. The children were asleep, some on the porch, some on cots they had dragged out under the trees by the side of the house. Except for Martha, who met them in the drive with a drowsing Grace in her arms.

"Where have y'all been?" she demanded, her anxiety making her short.

"Now, now, don't worry, honey," Shaw soothed. "We're sorry to be so late, but on our way home, we run into some excitement as we were passing Calvin Ross' place."

Gee Dub took the mules and wagon to the barn after Shaw and Alafair climbed down. After her parents had filled her in on the story of the Rosses' narrow escape and Gee Dub's heroics, Martha brought them bowls of cold canned tomatoes with chopped onion and fresh warm cornbread with butter. They sat themselves down on the porch, exhausted. Both of Shaw's hunting hounds, Crook and Buttercup, trotted up the steps and lady themselves at his feet, and Grace hoisted herself into Alafair's lap, complicating the logistics of her supper.

"Come on, Grace-pie," Martha urged, "let Mama eat." She tried to lift the toddler out of Alafair's lap, but Grace shrieked in protest and clung leech-like to her mother's neck.

"She's been missing me, I reckon," Alafair said. "It's all right, Martha. Just move up that little table from the corner of the porch for me and Daddy to put our bowls on, and I can manage."

Martha obliged, and Alafair ate her tomatoes with one hand and cuddled drowsy, thumb-sucking Grace with the other. "Thank the Lord for all these grown-up kids," she noted to Shaw.

"They do make life easier, waiting on us and all."

"As well they should, after what they put us through when they were little."

Martha chuckled, but to Alafair's surprise, offered no riposte. "So did Cousin Scott come up with anything by following that trail from the Rosses' house, Daddy?"

"Scott tracked him all the way to the back of Calvin's dairy barns, where the varmint had stashed a horse. After he mounted up, he took off toward the creek, where Scott lost him in the water. When we left, Scott was riding in one direction up the creek bank, and one of Mr. Ross' hired men was riding in the other, looking for where the horse came out. I expect they didn't get far before it got too dark to see. Scott will be on it tomorrow first light, I reckon."

All the children were sleeping, or at least abed, on the porch and in the yard, where it was cooler, occasionally mumbling or tossing uncomfortably in the heat. Alafair inventoried the children and noted two missing. Gee Dub, she knew, was in the barn taking care of the mules and wagon. Her heart skipped a beat. "Where is Mary?" she asked Martha.

"She went over to Phoebe and John Lee's after the funeral. John Lee just brought her back not five minutes before y'all came in, and they took her horse to the barn." Alafair nodded, relieved. Mary was with her brother and her brother-in-law, then, and safe. Alafair and Shaw finished their supper in silence, and Alafair sat back in her chair, watching the stars sparkle in the night sky.

Snuffling noises from her lap brought her attention back to Grace. "This child is asleep," she announced.

"I'm thinking it's getting about bedtime for all of us," Shaw said.

"I'll just put Grace down and clean up the dishes." Alafair moved to get up, but Martha stood and held out her arms.

"I'll take her."

"Why don't you do the dishes for Mama, and I'll hold the baby for a spell," Shaw interjected.

Alafair transferred Grace's limp little form to Shaw and rose from her chair. "I see Gee Dub coming up to the house from the barn. I'm going to go check up on Mary."

She met Gee Dub half way on the path between the house and the barn. He was carrying a lantern, and he lifted it when Alafair approached, illuminating his own face as well as hers. His dark eyes glinted at her from under his hat brim. His cheek was still smudged with soot. He pushed the old slouch hat back on his head with his fingertips when he recognized his mother. She had to look up at him.

"Mary and John Lee still in the barn?" Alafair asked him.

"She is. John Lee just rode off. After we got our stock took care of, she sat down on a feed sack with a lamp and her little journal. Said she wanted to write down some thoughts before she forgot them." His eyebrows rose as he described this odd behavior.

"I'd just as soon she not be off by herself since this murderer is still around for sure."

"She was keen to get rid of me, Ma. Besides, Charlie-dog is in there with her. But I'll go on back if you want."

"Well, that's all right, son. I'm going to get her. Did you tell her what all transpired at Mr. Ross' place?"

"I did. She didn't have much to say about it."

"You go on back up to the house. It's sure enough past everybody's bedtime."

"Take this here lantern, Ma," he insisted. "I reckon I can find my way back from here without falling on my face."

Alafair continued on her way, holding the lamp down at her side and watching where she put her feet on the uneven ground. The moon had not risen, and the night was very dark, but noisy with insects. The air had that dry, dusty, ripe smell of late August to it. The lamp blinded her to the rest of the night, and she moved through a world that only existed in a pale yellow circle of light around her. She had almost reached the barn door when a movement caused her to stop in her tracks and peer intently into the shadowy darkness outside her light bubble. She put the lantern down on the dirt path and stepped outside its glow. If she had indeed seen a person, he could certainly see her by the lamplight. She stood in the dark and blinked for a moment, allowing her eyes to adjust. Whatever it had been, a darker shape against the darkness, by the corner of the barn, she couldn't see it now. She walked an arc around the side of the building, making sure that nothing was there to threaten Mary inside, oblivious to any danger to herself.

There was no one. She heard nothing, saw nothing. Satisfied that no one lurked in the shadows, she retrieved her lantern and pushed open the barn door enough to let herself inside. Mary was sitting on a feed sack, just as Gee Dub had indicated, next to a lantern of her own which was hanging from a nail in a post. Charlie-dog was stretched out comfortably on the floor next to her, and his tail thumped out a languid welcome when Alafair entered. Mary was writing in her journal, which was perched on her knees, her free hand cuddling a gray barn kitten in her lap.

Alafair could hear her singing softly to herself.

"I took my dog Rover and looked the fields over
to see if my kitty was there.
No dog could be kinder but he couldn't find her.
Oh, where can my poor kitty be?

Kitty, kitty, oh where are you hiding today?
Kitty, kitty, come forth and join in our play…"

She stopped singing and looked up when she heard her mother. "I hear y'all had an adventure."

Alafair nodded. "It's an alarming thing. This fellow seems determined to do away with someone else. Did Gee Dub tell you that he probably saved Laura's life, and maybe the entire Ross family?"

Mary's eyebrows elevated. "He told me that y'all saw the fire and that him and Daddy pulled the burning curtains down."

"Well, it was Gee Dub that did both them things."

Mary smiled a quirky Tucker smile. "He didn't go into detail. Just like Gee Dub." The kitten was in the mood to play, and Mary was having some trouble keeping it from pouncing onto her journal pages. She set the kitten on the floor. It took a couple of playful swipes at the patient dog before it bounced away to join its mother and litter mates behind a hay bale in the corner.

"Gray kitty, just like the song." She nodded at the kitten. "Comforts me." She looked up at Alafair. "I'm glad you're here, Ma. I was hoping you'd get the idea and come to find me. I want to talk to you about what we found out at the funeral; compare, see if we come up with something useful." She hesitated at the look on Alafair's face. "What's wrong?"

"Have you heard anybody knocking around here since Gee Dub left?"

"No. He just left a minute ago. What do you mean?"

Alafair shook her head and sat down next to Mary on her own feed sack. "Oh, nothing. I declare, I'm so chary with all this business that I think I'm seeing things that aren't there. I wish you wouldn't wander off on your own, though, especially after what happened tonight. Not until this prowling murderer is caught."

Mary was unmoved. She could see the concern on her mother's face, and understood it well enough, especially considering the fire, but since Bill's death she hadn't been able to roust up any emotion stronger than a dull sadness. "I like it in here, Mama. It's nice and quiet, and I can think. Nobody hovers around me asking me how I feel all the time." It dawned on her how that might sound to Alafair, and she smiled sheepishly.

Alafair smiled back. "I can understand that. But you've got to be careful for awhile. At least keep one of the dogs with you."

Mary laughed and looked down at the drowsing shepherd at her feet. "Charlie-dog would just lick the miscreant to death."

"I doubt it. But keep one of Daddy's hounds, Buttercup, or Crook, if you'd rather. I'm serious, now."

"I know you are, Mama, but don't worry. I'll keep a better watch on myself from now on. I don't want you fretting."

"Thank you, sugar. Now let's see if we come up with anything." Alafair hung her lantern on a hook and leaned over to see what Mary was writing. Mary casually put her hand over the page.

"Of all the folks my age that we mentioned, I did talk with everybody but Art Turner and Shirley Kellerman, who didn't come to the funeral. Art's brother Johnny was there, though. I asked him why Art didn't come, if they were such good friends of Bill's, and he said that Art was down in Tishomingo with their grandma and couldn't get back in time. He told me that Art left for Tishomingo the day Bill was shot, and they didn't even think to let him know about it until yesterday, when Scott came to talk to them. Mr. Turner made a telephone call from the sheriff's office in Boynton to the post office in Tishomingo and left Art a message."

"That's interesting. I spoke with Scott, and he mentioned that telephone call his own self. The postmaster said he did see Art on the day after Bill was shot, though. Art said he figured he'd stay on with his grandfolks a day or two more. So, if he was out of town…"

"Trent Calder told me the same tale," Mary interrupted her, "and he said that Cousin Scott was sending him down to Tishomingo on the train this very afternoon after the funeral, to talk to Art and check his story."

"So Scott has some reason to suspect Art ain't telling the whole truth?"

Mary shrugged. "He must, or he wouldn't send his deputy all the way down to the Texas border. Trent didn't tell me straight out what's making Scott suspicious, but from things he said, as well as something Johnny said, I'm guessing that Art and Bill had some kind of disagreement the morning of the day Bill died."

"A fight?"

"Something near enough to it to get Scott sniffing around."

"Scott didn't mention anything about it. What did Johnny say?"

"Well, he said he expected Art probably felt mighty bad about Bill getting shot, since the last words they had were bitter ones. I tried to get him to tell me what they fought about, but he didn't want to rake it over."

Alafair crossed her arms over her chest and pondered this. "I'd love to know," she mused, then snapped to attention. "What else did you find out?"

Mary studied her journal for a moment, then dropped it flat in her lap and lifted her gaze to middle space. "Shirley Kellerman's friend Annie Dunn told me Shirley was awful upset. I think she loved Uncle Bill, and was hurt bad when he fell for Laura."

"Shirley's mama said there was never any formal understanding between them."

"No, I'm sure there wasn't," Mary agreed. "Bill and Shirley had known each other since they were kids, used to play together and all. But since they grew up, I don't think they ever did more than talk sweet to one another at church, or maybe banter a little if they met in town. But that doesn't keep a girl from giving her heart unasked. Even so, Ma, I can't imagine that she could have done anything to hurt Bill. And if she has bad feelings toward Laura, she's kept them to herself."

"She didn't keep them from her ma, though. Miz Kellerman and I talked for quite awhile at your grandma's house after the service. Miz Kellerman is right worried about Shirley. She said she had been afraid that the girl would go completely around the bend when she heard that Bill McBride was going to marry Laura Ross. When Bill got killed, Miz Kellerman worried that Shirley might 'do herself an injury,' is exactly what she said to me. I figured she was afraid that Shirley would make a scene at the funeral, so she sent her on the train to stay with her aunt in Oklahoma City for a spell. That's why she wasn't there today."

"My goodness!" Mary exclaimed. "Could it be that some plot of hers, maybe to get Laura out of the way, didn't go exactly as planned, and Bill got killed by accident? But Shirley is such a silly creature. Does she have enough wit to plan and carry out a devious plot?"

Alafair laughed a humorless laugh. "Nothing would surprise me about anybody, honey. Maybe it wasn't her planned it. Maybe she asked someone else to do it, or mentioned it to somebody who took it upon himself."

"Well, what do we do now, Ma?"

"I think we made some progress. Last week, I couldn't think of one person in the world who might have a reason, however weak, to kill Bill. Now there are two. Seems Scott is trailing Art Turner, so I don't think there's any need for us to do anything there. But Shirley Kellerman…Let's think on it tonight, and try to come up with someone else we can talk to about her, someone who might know something helpful." She took Mary's journal from her and closed it, then gently smoothed a stray tress from Mary's forehead. "Now, let's go back up to the house before your daddy sends a posse after us. How are you feeling, sugar pie? You're looking pretty wore out. How's your head?"

"I'm all right, Ma," Mary assured her patiently. "I'm tired and sad, it's true, and I have this dull headache that won't go away. I think it's getting better, though."

Alafair reached for the bandage on Mary's temple, but Mary caught her hand and lowered it into her lap as tactfully as she could. "I forgot to tell you about Phoebe," she said, and was satisfied to see Alafair's face change as she introduced a new subject of concern. "She was restless as a cat in a box tonight. The heat is bothering her something awful. She kept complaining about her back hurting. Poor old John Lee was hopping, bringing her pillows and ice tea and all."

"Oh, my! Sounds like her time is near. I wish I had thought to have one of you kids spend the night over there."

"I'll go back," Mary volunteered.

"No, no, it's too late, now." Alafair shook her head. "I reckon if they need us tonight, John Lee can be here in five minutes. The first one always takes a long time, anyway. You can go over first thing in the morning, if you want. Maybe Daddy will spare one of the hired boys to go with you and stand lookout. I'll send Charlie, too, to fetch and run if need be."

"And miss church?"

"I doubt if Phoebe will feel up to going. And I expect the Lord can find y'all at Phoebe's as well as at church." She and Mary gazed at one another for a second. Alafair knew perfectly well that the idea of facing every solicitous soul at church in the morning didn't fill Mary with joy. Mary, on the other hand, was struggling with her guilt at being so happy to get out of going.

"Of course, I could send one of the other kids," Alafair said, breaking the silence.

"Oh, no, that's all right," Mary answered so quickly that Alafair couldn't help sputtering a laugh.

The two women left the barn, lamps in hand, and, bolting the barn door behind them, made their way back to the house with the dog trailing behind them. A faint glow lit the front windows, and Alafair could see one figure on the porch, rocking back and forth languidly in the swing. The iron bedstead that sat at the corner of the porch in summer was made up, and Alafair knew within reason that the two dark, motionless lumps thereon were Blanche and Sophronia. Mary went up the steps ahead of her, and Alafair heard Mary and a male voice murmur an exchange before the girl went into the house. Charlie-dog padded across the porch and flopped himself down under the little girls' bed. The long-legged form in the porch swing was holding the baby in his arms. Alafair raised her lantern to see the pair better in the dark. She had been so convinced that it was Shaw holding Grace that when the light fell on Gee Dub with his sister in his arms, Alafair could hardly credit her eyes. The lantern light accentuated the planes of Gee Dub's face, making him look more gaunt than he was—making him look startlingly like his father, like a grown man.

"I thought you were Daddy," Alafair managed.

Gee Dub raised his eyebrows. "Daddy's run out to the stable for a bit. You know how he has to make sure us fellows took care of the stock so as to meet his particular requirements."

Alafair hung her lantern on a nail and sat down on the swing next to her son. Suddenly she was feeling old, and melancholy. "From what Mary tells me, Phoebe will be having her baby right soon."

"I guess I'll be an uncle."

"And I guess I'll be a grandma."

"I didn't like to mention it."

"I appreciate it." Alafair leaned back into the swing, picking up Gee Dub's rocking rhythm. "You know what's in just two weeks," she said, after a brief silence.

"I do. That would be my birthday."

"Your eighteenth birthday, if I figure right."

"You do."

"You'd better start thinking about what you want for your birthday dinner."

"I'm pondering on it."

"You weren't even as old as Grace when your daddy finished building this house," Alafair told him. "And now you're practically a man."

For a moment, Alafair thought he had nothing to say about this. He shifted the toddler on his shoulder. "Daddy would more than likely disagree with you," he said finally.

In the darkness, Gee Dub couldn't see the smile that crossed Alafair's face. "You'd be surprised what Daddy thinks." She stood up. "Bring her inside when you get your fill of toting her. I'm going to bed."

As she closed the screen behind her, she slipped her hand into her skirt pocket and fingered Mary's journal. Mary must be distracted indeed, Alafair thought, to allow her closely guarded musings to fall into her mother's hands.

She sat down in a parlor chair and pulled the table lamp a little closer. Alafair hoped Mary was so preoccupied with her own thoughts that when she found the journal in its place tomorrow, she wouldn't remember that she hadn't put it there herself. But even the threat of being caught red-handed didn't deter Alafair from settling in for a long read.

Chapter Nine

That was it, Mama. That's what I was thinking about when I first opened my eyes in the field. Not that somebody had been shooting at us, or that Bill was hit in the leg and Laura was off her horse. Not even that I had no idea what had just happened to me, or why I was lying on my back in the grass staring up at the sky. I was thinking about that time we were all sitting around the bandstand telling stories about crimes we'd seen with our own eyes. At first the tales were funny, then the boys got to trying to scare us all. Then Bill started to tell about the trip he took down to Waco a few years ago, when he'd seen a murder...

It was a miserable night. Every one of the kids except Grace had found him or herself a place to sleep outdoors, leaving the parents practically alone inside. Alafair's bedroom was situated at the corner of the house in such a way that the open windows caught whatever breeze arose and funneled it over the bed. Alafair and Shaw clung to the edges of the bed, as far away from each other's body heat as they could manage, and Grace preferred a quilt on the relatively cool floor under the window to her little cot.

Alafair was drifting in and out of a heat-soaked fog, and at first she wasn't sure whether the activity she was hearing in the yard was real or a dream. But when Shaw sat up and swung his legs over the side of the bed, Alafair dragged herself up into consciousness.

"What is it?" she asked him.

"I hear voices in the front. I think it's John Lee."

Alafair was wide awake instantly. She picked up the sleeping baby and made her way through the parlor, and found herself standing on the porch in her nightshift before she had entirely thought about it.

Charlie met her at the screen door. "John Lee just rode up. Phoebe's asking for you, Ma."

"Is the baby on the way?" She walked past him toward the edge of the porch. She could see John Lee's form on his big gelding, leaning down to speak to a knot of kids over the fence. He straightened when he recognized Alafair.

"It's Phoebe, Ma," he called. "She thinks it's her time." Alafair couldn't see his face in the dark, but his voice sounded just the littlest bit hysterical.

"How far apart are the pains, John Lee?" Alafair asked.

"Every ten minutes or so."

Shaw, standing at Alafair's elbow, put his hand on her shoulder. "You go on home, boy," he called back to his son-in-law. "Gee Dub will go get Doctor Ann. Tell Phoebe her mama and me will be there directly."

John Lee was gone before Shaw finished talking, loping across the barnyard on the most direct route back to his bride.

The children crowded around their parents, excited and all talking at once. The three dogs, Charlie's yellow shepherd and Shaw's two hounds, milled around among the humans, wagging happily. Gee Dub crashed into the house to pull on his pants and boots, and Charlie tugged at his father's nightshirt sleeve. "Can I go with Gee?"

Grace, finally disturbed by the noise, shifted on Alafair's shoulder and lifted her head, curious.

"Calm down, now." Shaw raised his voice to be heard over the din. "We can't all go. Phoebe's house ain't big enough to hold all of us. Charlie, you can go with Gee Dub. Go put your clothes on. Mama, you need any of these girls to go with you?"

"I might could use Mary to fetch and tote. The rest of you girls need to get in bed and try to get back to sleep. Church in the morning. Now, now," she warned, over the chorus of moans, "it's like to be way into tomorrow before this little baby comes on into the world. I doubt if you'll be missing anything. Ruth, take Grace and put her down with you on the back porch. Rest of you, back to bed. And Martha's in charge now, so mind her."

Gee Dub came back out. Alafair noted that he was carrying a rifle, and she wondered what Shaw had been saying to him since the fire. Whatever it was, she knew Gee Dub was a good hand with a gun, and she approved of the precaution, especially under the circumstances. He was followed by Charlie, who was still tucking his shirt into his knickers. "Should we stop by and let Alice know?" Gee Dub asked.

"No," Shaw told him emphatically. "I don't want you traipsing all over creation in the middle of the night. There'll be plenty of time to tell Alice in the morning. Just go directly to the Addisons' and let Doctor Ann know what's happening, then come straight home."

The boys headed for the barn and the girls slouched off back to bed as Alafair and Shaw turned to go back into the house to dress. Alafair noticed as he ran across the yard at his brother's heels that Charlie was barefoot, but it was too late to deal with it now.

"That boy," she muttered to herself, then turned to her husband after they walked back into the bedroom. "Shaw, I don't like the idea of leaving the girls here all alone what with a killer still on the loose."

"I had the same thought. I figured on rousting out Kurt and Micah and having them take turns keeping watch over the house for us while we're gone."

Alafair grunted her approval as she pulled her chemise on over her head.

The two hands lived in a neat little finished room appended on to the tack and tool shed behind the barn. Their accouterments consisted of two iron bedsteads, a shelf and two clothes pegs attached to the wall, a square wooden table and two slat-backed chairs, and a Franklin stove. Shaw expected to have to walk through the tool shed and pound on the wooden door to rouse the boys, but when he pulled out of the barn in the buggy with Mary and Alafair, he was surprised to see Kurt Lukenbach's angular form already standing in the barnyard, apparently waiting for them.

Shaw maneuvered the buggy around and pulled up next to him. In deference to the ladies, Kurt snatched off his hat. The hat was useless in the dark, but no self-respecting horseman would do without one, whatever the circumstances. "What are you doing out and about at this hour, Kurt?" Shaw asked him.

"I heard commotions. Was thinking maybe I could help with something." He pressed the hat to his chest. "Evening, Miz Tucker…Miss Mary."

Mary made a noise as if to respond, but Shaw was in too much of a hurry to allow pleasantries. "We have to get over to our daughter's place, Kurt. I need you and Micah to watch the house for us tonight. Gee Dub will be back directly, but right now, the girls are alone."

"I'd be proud to, Mr. Tucker," Kurt assured him.

"Where is Micah?"

"Asleep, last I saw."

"Well, you take the first watch, then. Wake him up to relieve you when you get tired."

"Yessir. Don't worry about nothing, Mr. Tucker."

They rattled off down the buggy trail between the two farms, tailed by the two hounds, leaving Kurt standing in the yard with his hat in his hand. Mary and Alafair both turned in their seats to watch him until he plopped his hat back on his head and turned to walk up toward the house.

"I believe that's the most words I've ever heard that boy speak all at one time," Alafair observed.

Phoebe and John Lee were pacing the floor of their wee clapboard cottage when her folks arrived. Phoebe had one arm over John Lee's shoulders and one hand cradling her enormous belly, as though the weight of her incipient offspring were too much to bear without a helping hand. John Lee was relieved to let Alafair take his place as prop. Alafair couldn't tell much about his color in the yellow light of the kerosene lanterns, but he seemed pale, the black stubble on his face contrasting strongly with a washed out complexion. His big black eyes looked like a startled doe's as he glanced over at Shaw, helplessly wondering what his place was in this eminently female enterprise.

Shaw took his arm. "Come on outside with me, now, son," he said in the same gentle voice he used the soothe a skittish animal. "Let's take care of the horses. Then we can sit in the yard for a spell and let the women do their work. They'll call us if they need us."

Neither John Lee nor Phoebe said anything, but they locked eyes as Shaw drew his son-in-law outside. Both were patently terrified, and only too willing to abdicate all responsibility to the experts.

Phoebe leaned against her mother like a dead weight. Her face was flushed, and the fine hazel eyes were frightened and determined at once. Her auburn curls had been twisted up onto the top of her head at one time, but had now mostly escaped and hung in frizzed hanks down her neck and around her face. She was dressed only in a shapeless, mid-length cotton shift that was damp with sweat.

Alafair let Phoebe lean on her and began walking her up and down the combination parlor-dining-bedroom, while Mary hovered about anxiously.

"When did the pains start, sugar?" Alafair asked.

"Something in my back was hurting pretty bad off and on all day. I was thinking I was having a contraction or two this evening when Mary was here. But I just been sure for the last couple hours. Woke me up."

"How far apart are they?"

"I don't know. Ten, twelve minutes or so."

"Has your water broke?"

"No, not yet."

"Well, don't you worry about a thing, honey. Mama and Daddy are here, now, and Gee Dub has gone to fetch Doctor Ann Addison. I reckon it's going to be a little while yet, but this baby is sure on the way. Mary, go outside and set John Lee to drawing some water. Ask your daddy if you can borrow his pocket watch. Then come on back inside and pull down the bathtub, fire up the stove and start heating some water for a nice tepid bath."

Mary immediately banged out the screen door to retrieve her father's watch.

"Oh, Mama," Phoebe protested, "it's too hot for a bath! I couldn't stand it."

"You just trust me, darlin'. We won't make it hot, just warm enough not to chill you. Believe me, it'll make you feel a lot better, relax your muscles."

Mary placed the tin bathtub in the middle of the parlor floor, since the fire in Phoebe's little two-burner cook stove made the kitchen intolerable, then she heated the water in a big kettle to warm the cool water she and John Lee had poured into the tub. Mary was glad to be busy, to think of something besides murder. The physical tasks even eased the continual headache she had been living with for the past week. Mary and Alafair helped Phoebe into the tub, where she melted into the water like butter.

Phoebe took her first free breath in hours. "That does feel better, Mama," she admitted.

Alafair pulled a kitchen chair up next to the tub, sat down, and began laving Phoebe's back with a soft cloth. "It'll help for a while, honey. Mary has more water heating if your bath gets too cold for you. Just let me know when you've had enough and Mary and I will hoist you out." She gestured with her free hand. "Mary, unpack those raggedy old quilts and sheets and them herbs that I brought, will you?"

Mary smiled as she moved to do her mother's bidding. Alafair was in her element, now, sitting in her chair in her coverall apron, her dark hair wrapped in a kerchief, in charge of the situation, directing her children in the business of living.

Between contractions, and momentarily comfortable, Phoebe sagged down into the water, hardly able to keep her eyes open. She sighed. "I feel pretty scared, Mama."

"I know you do, honey."

Phoebe managed a wry laugh. "I imagine you do know, as many kids as you've had. I've just barely got started and I'm ready to quit. Is it always this hard?"

"Pretty much."

"Why did you keep doing it, then?" Phoebe asked her, only half joking.

Alafair squeezed cool water from the rag over the back of Phoebe's neck. "I was always so pleased with the results."

"Now I think you're pulling my leg," Phoebe accused. "You expect I'll be a good mother, Ma?"

"I'm sure of it. And I think you've got yourself a fine man in John Lee. He'll be a good daddy."

Mary interjected herself into the conversation. "And you've already had a lot of practice, Phoebe, what with all the little brothers and sisters you have."

"I have a righteous example in Mama."

It was Alafair's turn to laugh. "Honey, I love being a mama, love having kids around, the more the better. But I sure wasn't born knowing how. If it hadn't been for your two grandmas, I'd have been carried off to the insane asylum twenty years ago."

"I don't believe that," Mary said. "You're so easy at it."

"Oh, mercy!" Alafair exclaimed. "Don't ever think it's easy. It's a lot easier now, now that you older ones are grown up and take so much of the burden off me. I've been lucky. Y'all are pretty good kids, willing, never in any serious trouble, at least to now. But it was a different story when I had five little kids under six years old and lived in that old soddy, just me and your daddy. We lived with my folks in that big old rambling house when Martha and Mary were born in Arkansas. After we moved up by Tahlequah, we lived with your Grandma and Grandpapa

McBride. That's where you twins were born. Then Grandpapa bought their place down here. He helped us buy our first forty acres, and Daddy and his brothers built that soddy. That was the first time I ever lived in a house of my own, such as it was. Your daddy worked like a slave every waking minute.

"Then Gee Dub came along. Grandma and your aunts helped me as much as they could, but they all had their own families and farms to work." She shook her head and barked out a laugh at the memory. "It was like living in a crate full of monkeys. Y'all children are lucky I didn't go crazy as a bug and smother you in your sleep. Then I had your brother James that died after a few days, and I was so overwrought and depressed about it that your daddy asked his mother if me and you kids could come back and stay with her for a spell. Your grandma saved my life, that's for sure, and probably you kids' lives, as well. It couldn't have been much fun for her, a weepy crazy woman and a ragtag bunch of kids underfoot, and Bill was just pretty young himself. But she never was anything but wonderful about the whole thing, and Grandpapa, too. Why, I think he took charge of you older ones more than I did.

"By the time we moved back home, Martha and Mary were getting up big enough to help me a bit, eight and seven, thereabouts, and I had regained my wits, enough to do what needed doing, anyway. You remember any of that, Mary?"

"I remember being at Grandma's, and I remember living in the soddy, but I don't know if it was before we went to live with Grandma or after. I do remember all us kids sleeping together in the same bed like a litter of puppies."

"I remember that," Phoebe said. A distracted look crossed her face, and she struggled to sit up. "I think I'm getting another pain." Alafair grabbed her arm and helped her into a more upright position. Phoebe's face reddened and her knuckles whitened as she gripped the edges of the tub. She made a little squeaky sound as the pain intensified, but bit her lip and soldiered on. Alafair leaned over her with her arm draped across Phoebe's shoulder.

"It's okay, honey," she soothed. "It's okay. I think I just heard a buggy drive up. Doctor Ann is here, I'm thinking. Mary, bring me that big towel. Don't worry, puddin'. It won't be much longer now."

Ann Addison was a full-blood Indian, half Cherokee and half Creek, well versed in traditional native medicine and lore. She was equally versed in the most up-to-date and modern scientific techniques, by virtue of having been well educated, as well as married for the last forty years to the first university-trained doctor in the Indian Territory. Doctor Ann had brought into the world a disproportionate share of the people who had been born in Muskogee County, including most of Phoebe's siblings.

She pulled her pony-and-trap to a halt at the front door and leaped to the ground with her bag in her hand. She was wearing a conical maroon straw hat with a tiny brim, straight from the 1880's, set square on top of her head. Though she usually wore her silver-streaked black hair wound around her head in a tight braid, tonight it was hanging loose down her back, which was her normal practice for attending a childbirth. Dr. Ann was a formidable woman in all ways, tall, muscular, and all bony angles, and she looked at Shaw eye to eye as he came forward to greet her, lantern in hand.

"Where's our little mama?" Doctor Ann was nothing if not straight to the point.

"She's inside with Alafair and Mary, ma'am," Shaw said to her back, as she strode away from him and into the house.

Shaw laughed and looked at John Lee, who was standing at the front of the trap, holding the pony's halter and stroking its nose absently. "Cavalry has arrived, John Lee," he observed, and heard John Lee try to muster a laugh at his witticism. Shaw shook his head, full of pity for the scared boy, concerned about his daughter, but infinitely grateful that this time it wasn't him in John Lee's position.

Together, the two men unhitched and watered the doctor's pony and pulled the trap over to the side of the house, glad to have a useful occupation for a few minutes before they had to return to their vigil in the front yard.

John Lee sighed as he sat down, and Shaw patted his knee.

"Nothing harder than waiting," the older man observed.

"I'll be glad when it's over. Phoebe's so small." John Lee hesitated. "Things can happen..."

"Now, boy, don't get to going down that road. Phoebe's a healthy girl, and she's got the best help in the world with her."

"But..."

"Ssst!" Shaw hissed at him, and John Lee clamped his mouth shut so fast that Shaw laughed. "Don't borrow trouble," Shaw said, more gently. "Just think about the new little fellow or gal that's about to come into your life."

John Lee flopped back in his chair. "Well, that don't make me feel much better, Pa. For the last months I've been studying on whether or not I can be a good father."

"Why, I think you're a natural, boy. Just set him the best example you can."

"I never had a good example myself, until I married into Phoebe's family, at least. Can I teach a boy to be a good man? What if he takes after my father?"

Shaw shifted uncomfortably. John Lee's father had been the scum of the earth. How the son had turned out as well as he did was a wonder. "I'll tell you what I was told before my first one come along. Expect them to be good, and they will be." He laughed. "Sometimes, anyway. Just take it one day at a time, son, and do the best you can. Try to have some fun. Kids are a joy, most of the time. It ain't all so burdensome."

"Well, what if it's a girl? I don't know anything about being a daddy to girls."

"If it's a girl, then you're done for, John Lee. Resign yourself to being led around by the nose like a tame old ox, 'cause she'll charm you stupid."

◇◇◇

Alafair wandered outside just before dawn, leaving Mary and Dr. Ann Addison with Phoebe. Phoebe was laboring hard, now, but the baby hadn't quite crowned, and Alafair took advantage of a lull in the action to catch a breath of cooler air and give the men a progress report. She stood at the screen and studied the scene before she went out. John Lee was sleeping restlessly, fully clothed, on a cot in the front yard, and Shaw was dozing in a chair with his hat over his eyes and his arms crossed over his chest. The screen creaked as Alafair stepped out, and Shaw lifted the hat with one hand and peered at her with one bleary eye.

She smiled and shook her head to indicate that the child had not yet deigned to make its entrance into the world.

"How's Phoebe doing?" Shaw asked, his voice low to keep from disturbing John Lee.

"She's doing good, for a first baby. Things seem to be moving along. A little while yet, I think."

"How about Mary?"

"Well, I think she's about to vow to remain an unmarried lady," she admitted with a twinkle. She nodded toward John Lee. "What about him?"

Shaw stood up. "I'm glad he finally dropped off. He's been so nervous all night I figured his arms and legs was about to fly off. Nobody's going to be worth shooting tomorrow. Or today, I ought to be saying." He dug his knuckles into his lower back and stretched until his spine cracked, then sighed with relief. He looked at Alafair askance. "Did you hear Kurt out here a while back?"

The question was unexpected, and she blinked. "Kurt? No, my attention has been elsewhere, don't you know. What was Kurt doing here? He's supposed to be watching the house."

"He said Micah had woke up and taken over. Said he just wanted to let us know that all was well at the house, the boys got back safe and all, and wanted to make sure everything was all right with us here."

"That's good." Alafair was still unsure why Shaw was telling her this.

"I sent him home," Shaw continued. "After he left, John Lee told me that when he rode up to get us last night he thought he saw Kurt skulking around the house."

Alafair was taken aback. "It was like he was waiting for us when we went to wake him and Micah up," she remembered.

Shaw nodded. "It set me to thinking. Mary told us that he was the first person to show up in the meadow after Bill was shot."

Alafair felt her heart thud and her eyes pop. "Kurt! I can't imagine that Kurt would have something to do with this ugly business. I mean, why would he? As far as I know, him and Bill was hardly acquainted, and if he had ever spoken to Laura, I'm not aware of it. No, wait." She hesitated, thinking of all the times lately that she had imagined a figure lurking just out of sight. "Fire him, Shaw," Alafair burst out in a sudden 180-degree turn from her former defense of the young man.

"Now, wait a minute," Shaw cautioned. "I didn't say I think he did it. It just seems that he's turning up in odd places lately. He is a good shot. I've seen that with my own eyes. So it makes me wonder. But that ain't hardly evidence enough to fire the boy. Likely as not he's innocent of anything but being concerned. He's always been friends with Mary."

"I don't care. I don't care if he's as innocent as a suckling calf. I don't want anybody near my children who is under a cloud of suspicion, not until the culprit is good and caught. Why, we don't know but what Mary is still a target."

Shaw's eyes flicked upward off of her face, and Alafair turned to see that Mary had come outside sometime in the course of this conversation and was standing behind her, quietly listening to her parents speculate.

"Y'all are suspecting Kurt of these awful deeds of late?" Her tone was carefully calm and neutral.

"We're suspecting Kurt of acting strange these last few days," Shaw told her.

"I like Kurt a lot." Mary was matter-of-fact about it. "He's sweeter than pie. He wouldn't do anything wrong."

"You just stay away from him 'til this gets sorted out," Alafair insisted.

Mary's mouth took on an ironic twist. "How about Micah? Shall I stay away from him, too? What if you've set the foxes to guarding the hen house?"

Alafair's eyes narrowed just enough to let Mary know that her comment was dangerously close to sass. "You just be careful not to be alone with anybody who's not kin," she said sharply.

Mary eyed her mother and father thoughtfully. There was no reasoning with them right now, not when they were in the full throes of parental protectiveness. "All right." She conceded more to end the conversation than out of any conviction that they had a point. "Ma, Doctor Ann sent me out to get you. The baby's crowning, and Phoebe wants you."

Phoebe's need for her more immediate than Mary's, Alafair's expression changed utterly in the blink of an eye, and she disappeared into the house. Mary hesitated on the landing and crossed her arms over her chest. "Suppose we ought to wake John Lee?"

"Naw, let him alone. He won't be doing much sleeping for the next few months."

After a moment's consideration, Mary crossed the few steps that separated her from her father and laid her head on his chest. He enfolded her in a hug, as natural as could be, as though she were seven again. Mary closed her eyes, enjoying the feel of his cotton shirt against her cheek and breathing in the familiar smell of wood smoke, sorghum feed, and horse that was peculiar to her father. When she was a little girl, she had always felt completely safe from harm in her daddy's arms, and for a few minutes she let herself go back to that safe place where she knew her parents would never let anything bad happen to her or to anyone she loved.

Finally she stood back. Life was a road that could only be traveled in one direction.

"You feeling all right, honey?" Shaw's hands were on her shoulders, unwilling to release her back into adulthood until he was assured she was ready to go.

She smiled at him. "Oh, I'm just tuckered out. It's been a long few days. I feel like I could sleep 'til Christmas."

The spell broken, Shaw dropped his hands and smiled back at her. "You'd better get back in there and help your mother and sister, now. We can think about sleeping after this child joins us."

◇◇◇

The sun was up by the time Shaw began to hear the wild noises coming from the house that had terrified the liver out of him the first couple of times he had heard them, and he drew John Lee away with him to milk the cow and feed the animals. The two men were just walking back toward the house from John Lee's little barn when Alafair stepped out of the house and waved to them. Shaw read the look of joy on her face.

"Looks like you're a daddy, boy," he said, and just managed to grab the half-full milk pail from John Lee's hand before the young man dropped it and ran.

John Lee flew past Alafair into the house, pausing only long enough to get the word on Phoebe's condition and the gender of his offspring. Alafair waited for Shaw by the front door.

They locked eyes. "Phoebe's fine," Alafair said, first thing. "She did real good. I'm proud of her. It's a girl. She's a little thing, maybe six pounds, Ann says, but healthy and pink. Got a head full of black hair." She hesitated in her recitation. "We're grandfolks, Shaw," she managed, awed. "Don't that beat all?"

She was standing on the landing that served as a porch, and he was standing below her, hazel eyes gazing up at her from under his hat brim. Milk from the pail he was holding in one hand had splashed down one side of his trousers. He was bleary eyed and unshaven, and Alafair wondered if she looked as bedraggled as he did.

Shaw, on the other hand, was thinking that Alafair had hardly changed since the day they married twenty-four years earlier. She still kept her dark brown hair caught up in a loose twist from which tantalizing wisps were always escaping. The expression in her dark eyes was still sharp, opinionated, warm and laughing. When she had something important to tell him, she still unconsciously placed the palm of her hand on his chest, over his heart. She was exactly the right size to tuck the top of her head under his chin, as though they were a pair made to fit together. She was not as willow-whip slender as she had been before she had borne him twelve children, but as far as he was concerned, she had plumped up nicely in all the right places, and her arms embraced him just as warmly. Most of all she was still the sword and shield and heart of her family, the pillar of the house.

"You're the finest looking grandma I ever saw," he said at last.

Alafair laughed. No matter how much things changed, one thing in her world could always be counted on.

Chapter Ten

Remember how, every year, early in the fall, Grandpapa used to send Bill down to Waco? He'd go down to Millard Jackson's JJ ranch, to look over his new crop of foals that we about ready to leave their mamas. Grandpapa and Mr. Jackson have been friends since I don't know when...since they were both pony soldiers together out in the Arizona Territory back in the '60's, right after the war. After him and Grandma started that farm outside of Mountain Home soon after they were married. That's when Grandpapa bought some of his first breeding stock from Mr. Jackson.

Calvin Ross sat upon his front porch with a shotgun across his lap. Even though the sheriff had left a deputy on duty outside the front gate, Calvin had been sitting there on the porch from the moment Sheriff Tucker left his farm after the fire until he couldn't stay awake enough to keep from falling out of the chair. Then he had called his most trusted hired man to relieve him just long enough to eat and catch a nap. And now he had resumed his watch on the porch, shotgun on his knees, while his crew cared for his dairy herd, milked, separated, churned, and readied the delivery wagon for the upcoming week.

For Calvin didn't have time to run a business at the moment. He was too busy pondering his future and the future of his family. He rocked his chair back and forth as he thought. Since he was not sitting in a rocking chair, the *thump, thump, thump* of the front legs on the wooden porch echoed hollowly across the yard.

Somewhere out there in the world prowled a vile excuse for a human being, a damned bushwhacker, the lowest scum in all creation, who was bent on killing his Laura, a girl bright and delicate as a daisy, clever, gentle and loving, guide and comforter of her sisters, helper to her aunt and father. Ruined now, he thought. Yes, surely ruined, her mind broken as well as her body, walking somewhere between life and death, between this world and the world over yonder.

Calvin loved Laura dearly. Or, he loved who Laura had once been. He had no idea if she would ever return to him. But the truth was that while her would-be killer was at large, and as long as her empty shell remained in his house, everything that Calvin still held dear was in danger of annihilation.

It seemed obvious to Calvin that he was going to have to send Laura away—where, he didn't know—not just for Laura's safety, but for the sake of her poor terrified little sisters.

But where to send her, and to whom? To keep her safe, Calvin needed to do this thing in secret. Not an easy proposition when one lived in a town the size of Boynton. There was an insane asylum for white folks that had just opened up near Vinita, but the very thought of sending Laura to a place like that horrified him to the core. Yet what alternative did he have? Laura needed constant care and vigilant attention. The strain on Iva and the girls was already telling. Calvin and Iva's parents were dead, and his late wife's mother was far too elderly and frail for such a task. Perhaps he should ask Dr. Addison for his advice.

"Calvin!"

Iva's voice caused him to start out of his reverie, and he looked over to see his sister scowling at him, red-faced, from the half-open screen door.

"Calvin, if you don't stop whomping that chair on the porch, I'm going to dump this soup I'm making right over your wooden head. The whole house is shaking!"

Calvin mumbled something to appease her, and Iva slammed back into the house. He shook his head, and his gaze wandered back over the yard. He was grateful for the interruption, because the problem was eating him up, and no solution was forthcoming.

"I ain't going to stew on it," he said aloud, but before the last word was uttered, his mind had slid back into its well-worn groove.

Calvin closed his eyes and sat back and thought.

Lord, I don't have an idea one what to do about this. Now, you have seen fit to call that fine boy Bill McBride home. I don't understand why, but I expect you got your reasons, and since he's in heaven, I ain't got no quarrel with it. But you visited this evil on my innocent girl, who never has harmed a living creature in her life, and I just don't hold with that at all. So you'd better get this son-of-a-bitch caught, Lord. (Excuse my language, but you know I was thinking it, so what's the point of being a hypocrite about it?) And if your plan is to let us mortals run around with our thumbs up our fundaments for a spell before we nab the dog and hang him, then you better send me a downright resplendent idea for keeping Laura and the girls out of harm's way, and right quick, too, because it's too big a poser for me to figure out...

Sometimes the Lord doesn't answer prayers in the way the supplicant wants, and sometimes he takes his sweet time in answering prayers at all. But the Lord was on the ball and looking sharp that day, and Calvin opened his eyes to see a dark little woman in a black dress and poke bonnet trudge determinedly through his front gate and toward the house.

He blinked twice and stood as she climbed the steps and halted before him. She looked up, black eyes burning from the depths of her bonnet.

"Calvin," she greeted.

"Miz McBride. Allow me to express my condolences. I was right sorry to miss the funeral."

"I understand, Calvin. I'd have done the same if I was you. How's she doing?"

"Not so good, ma'am. In fact, I think she's standing on the drop edge of yonder. I fear that the merest nudge is like to send her plunging over to the other side."

Sally nodded. "I hear you had some trouble the other night."

"Like to got burned out."

"Jesus burn the sniveling yellow coward in hell."

"Amen."

"When my grandson told me what had happened, I got to thinking that if I was in your shoes, I'd be looking to find some safe place to hide the girl 'til this is over."

"You and me are traveling the same path with that thought, Miz McBride."

"I expect. Well, then, Calvin, I aim to present you with an idea."

Calvin and Sally McBride sat down on the porch, and leaned toward one another, head to head. Calvin listened to Sally for a quarter of an hour, and after she left, he had just about decided that God is partial to the direct approach.

◇◇◇

Alafair didn't get home until late Sunday afternoon. Shaw and Mary had left Phoebe and John Lee's little farm shortly after the baby was born, but Alafair stayed to clean the house, feed John Lee and the doctor, and generally provide support to the new mother. In the mid afternoon, Phoebe's twin Alice showed up all in a flutter of excitement, and Alafair finally felt free to go home and see after her own family. Alice would stay the night. In fact, some female relative, mother, sister, aunt, or cousin, would spend some time with the newly minted parents every day for the first couple of months of their newborn's life.

Alafair was exhausted, but there would be no time to rest in the foreseeable future. Shaw had agreed to help his brothers with their cotton harvests, and before dawn on Tuesday morning, they would be on their way to James' farm for three or four very hard days of picking, hauling, ginning, and baling; and for Alafair and her sisters-in-law, cooking for and feeding a score of workers three times a day.

She had one evening to regain her equilibrium, for tomorrow she had to get her own house in order before the cotton harvest took her away. For the second time in recent weeks, she had reason to be thankful for her grown and half-grown children. She sat on the porch and played with Grace while Martha and Ruth fixed supper and the other children did the barnyard chores. Using her childbirthing adventure and her head wound to good advantage, Mary napped. Shaw, tired out from baby sitting John Lee all night, going to church, and then spending the rest of the day catching up on work, Sabbath or not, sat with Alafair on the porch for a long while, but finally dragged himself out to the stables with Gee Dub to check the horses and mules.

Alafair was about to nod off in her chair when Charlie and his namesake dog startled her awake by gallumphing onto the porch. The dog nosed her knee and the boy bent over her, his face inches from hers, and said, "Mama? You awake?"

"Mercy, Charlie, I'd have to be dead to sleep though all that stomping. Where have you been, anyway? Have you seen your new niece, yet?"

"Yeah, me and Blanche and Fronie just got back from over there. We stopped by the barn to play with the kittens for a spell, but we can't find them. I noticed that only the gray one came out to play day before yesterday when I went to do the milking in the afternoon, nor did we spot any of the other of them all day yesterday. I never thought nothing of it—sometimes their mama keeps them hid—but it's been so long now that the kids are getting worried. Where do you think they've got to?"

"Oh, I wouldn't worry about it, Charlie. I imagine their mother has moved them somewhere. They'll turn up directly."

Charlie bit his lip. "Well, that's what I figured at first, but this evening Blanche noticed that mother cat meowing all distressed around the store room door. Daddy padlocked that door a couple of days ago, after we were in there for some lumber. We left the door standing open all afternoon while we moved some stuff around. I'm thinking the mama cat moved her kittens in there while we was busy, and we locked her away from them. I told the girls I'd get the key from Daddy, but I don't know where he is. They're fretting about them kittens something awful."

Alafair smiled. She could tell by the look on his face that Charlie was doing some fretting of his own over the fate of the missing kittens. Grace, who was standing with her elbow on Alafair's thigh, listening intently, puckered her mouth anxiously. "Kitty?" she said.

Alafair stood up. "Daddy's gone out to the stable with Gee Dub, but I'll fetch the spare key and we'll have a look in the store room. Are the girls out there now?"

"They're waiting for me."

Alafair went into the house and retrieved the iron key ring from its peg by the back door, and walked out to the store room shed behind the barn. Charlie, Grace in his arms, trailed behind her with the dog. Blanche and Sophronia ran up to her as she neared, both talking at once, repeating the story of the imprisoned kittens. Alafair could see the small calico barn cat pacing up and down in front of the store room door, mewing loudly. She suddenly felt a pang of worry that she was going to open that door and find a litter of dead kittens. After the recent stress of their uncle's death and his murderer uncaught, and the long day of waiting for their sister to give birth, losing the kittens might be just the catalyst to send her younger ones into fits of hysteria all at once. She hesitated, key poised over the lock, considering whether she had the energy to deal with this right now.

Well, whether she did or not, it was going to have to be done. She slid the key into the lock. As soon as the door was open an inch, the cat oozed into the store room, and the kids and Charlie-dog nearly knocked Alafair over trying to all get inside at the same time.

"Here they are! Here they are!" Blanche called.

"Don't touch them!" Alafair cautioned, even before she got inside to see the knot of children leaning over a pile of burlap bags in the corner.

Sophronia flitted over to her and grabbed her skirt. "But, Mama, they're barely moving. We got to feed them."

"Are they alive, Charlie?"

"Looks like they are, Ma, but just barely." He was squatting down near the floor, still holding on to Grace, who was practically doubled in two over his arm in her desperation to see what was going on.

"Can't we do something for them, Ma?" Blanche asked, close to tears.

"No, come on, kids, leave them to their mother. She knows way better than us what to do for them. If we get to messing with them, it'll just make things worse. We did the best thing we could do by getting them back to their mama."

After some protest, the children finally acquiesced to their mother's greater wisdom in these matters, and followed Alafair back to the house, all in a row like preoccupied ducklings, considering the fate of the hapless kittens.

Life for a young creature on the farm was precarious at best, especially for barn cats, who were just the right size to make a tasty snack for coyotes or a passing stray dog. But it did seem to Alafair that they had been having a particular run of bad luck over the past few months. Thinking of coyotes brought to mind the previous February when one of the new foals had managed to get out of the pasture and away from her mother and the coyotes or a bobcat got her. She had gotten away somehow, but her muzzle was so chewed up that she couldn't eat and Shaw had had to put her down.

The Eichelburgers on the next farm got worried about their calves and put out poisoned horse meat for the predators, then, way out in the back forty. But blamed if one of them didn't haul a big chunk of it from the neighbor's place right up to the house one night and leave it almost in the yard. If Gee Dub hadn't found it right off when he went to milk that morning, they'd have lost one of the dogs for sure. Alafair shook her head. A coyote was smart, and sometimes just as spiteful as a man.

Charlie moved up to walk beside Alafair. "Do you suppose they'll die, Ma?" He spoke quietly, so as not to alarm his sisters.

It took Alafair a fraction of a second to come back into the present. "I don't know, son. Some of them might, but I expect we got their mother to them in time. Animals are mighty good survivors."

"Why do you suppose she moved them from the barn in the first place?"

"Something in the barn probably spooked her. Who knows what? The cow lowed out of the wrong side of her mouth or a feed sack fell over. Or maybe she just got a notion that she'd like some new scenery. I'm guessing that she'll move them again, as soon as she's able."

"Back to the barn?"

"Maybe."

"You know, Ma, they was all there but that little gray one I saw the other day, the one that Mary likes. What happened to that one, you suppose?"

"The door probably got shut before the cat got the last kitten moved. The gray one is probably still in the barn somewhere, a lot fatter and happier than her brothers and sisters."

"I never did see her, though."

"Nevertheless…"

They had almost reached the house when Charlie-dog broke out of the pack of kids and trotted purposefully toward the bushes at the corner of the front porch. He disappeared behind the ragged forsythia for an instant, then reappeared and loped back to Charlie.

"What are you up to, boy?"

The dog looked up at him, then headed straight back to the bush and began nosing the ground behind it.

"What's that dog doing?" Charlie wondered, drawing his mother's attention away from the flitting Grace and to the dog for the first time.

Alafair didn't bother to answer. She was tired and supper was waiting. She had no interest in any more animal adventures.

Charlie-dog, however, had different ideas. As soon as the family had cleared the front gate, the dog trotted up to Alafair and circled her feet so closely that she nearly tripped over him. She stopped, exasperated.

"He's found something!" Blanche leaped out of the queue and ran to the forsythia bush, Sophonia and Grace hot on her heels.

Alafair looked down at the dog, feeling resentful, but he calmly moved off to join the children, content that she would follow. He may have been the children's dog, but he was perfectly aware of who was in charge of the family.

Oddly, a verse of her mother's old lullaby jumped into her head.

> I saw a boy trundle away with a bundle
> and carry it down to the brook.
> Could that be my kitty, so cunning and pretty?
> I guess I'll go down there and look...

It suddenly occurred to her what Charlie-dog had found. "You kids hold up," she called, and they stopped instantly, frozen in position, a tableau of running little girls.

Alafair strode past them and hunkered down, pushing forsythia branches aside to get a clear look at whatever the dog wanted her to see. She straightened and backed out of the foliage right into the four kids, who had crowded in behind her.

"What is it, Ma?"

"I'm afraid it's the little gray kitten, Charlie. Looks like she's been dead for a day or two. I guess Charlie-dog heard us talking about her and reckoned on letting us know where she'd got to." The fact that the dog had apparently understood what they were talking about didn't strike her as unusual. She had known dogs all her life. Some were more human than others, and Charlie-dog was more human than most.

Charlie shook his head, and Blanche and Sophronia snuffled. Alafair looked down at Grace. She expected she was going to have to explain the word "dead" to the two-year-old, but Grace surprised her by opening her mouth and wailing like her heart would break.

"Poor kitty!" she sobbed. "Poor dead kitty!"

Taken aback by the baby's grief, Alafair nearly burst into tears herself. She scooped Grace up and pressed her to her heart. "It's all right, honey," she crooned. "It's all right."

Now Sophronia started to cry. Alafair gestured to Charlie to take the girls inside.

He nodded, but he wasn't letting her off that easily. "What do you suppose happened, Ma?"

"I don't know, darlin'. It's hard to tell after all this time. But her little side is stove in, like she was kicked. She probably got stepped on by one of the horses, or some such."

"Oh, Mama!" Sophronia blubbered. "Can we have a funeral for her, like Uncle Bill?"

"Of course you can, shug. Y'all can have you a little funeral while supper is finishing up. Charlie, you go get a spade. You can bury her back there in the woods where we put old Timmy and that rabbit…"

"Cotton," Sophronia interjected helpfully.

"Cotton. Girls, go get a box from the tool shed. Here, take Grace with you."

As the children sped off, Alafair thoughtfully eyed the dog sitting at her feet. "Well, you found her for us. Why don't you just go on ahead and tell me what happened to her, and when?"

The dog gazed at her, his brown eyes willing, but kept his peace.

It was sad that the kitten had met with an accident, Alafair thought, but perhaps the timing of her demise wasn't all for the bad, after all. The young girls had not gone to Uncle Bill's funeral. Having the kitten to bury and mourn might be a good outlet for their unexpressed grief.

She heaved a great sigh. She was always looking for reasons why things happened, and maybe there weren't any. Maybe everything that happened was just an accident. As the thought arose, Alafair shook herself. No use to think like that. She went into the house to retrieve an old towel to use as a kitten shroud.

After the kitten funeral and a long supper in which Sophronia and Blanche relived the ceremony in excruciating detail for their father, Alafair left the family to their popcorn and stories in the parlor and took Grace outside. Her original intention was to make up the beds on the front porch, but when she went out the front door and passed the porch swing, her body simply sat down of its own will, and she let it. When she put Grace down, the girl became engrossed in her rag doll and her wooden animals, and just as dusk was gathering, Alafair found herself as alone as she could be given the size of her family. She watched the baby play and let her mind wander. Why did that cat move the kittens out of the barn, anyway? Did the death of the gray kitten have something to do with her decision to relocate? Alafair must have become mesmerized watching Grace and her dolls, because when someone called her name, she started, and looked up to see a tall figure standing at the gate.

"Good evening, Miz Tucker," the figure repeated.

"Kurt," she acknowledged. She eyed him, unsure how she felt about his appearing at her front gate. She decided to withhold judgment, for the moment. "What brings you about? Why aren't you with Micah, having some supper?"

"I was," Kurt told her. "We just finished up, and I was on my way back to the barn to see everything is locked up when I saw you out here, ma'am. I want to ask after Miz Day and the baby."

"They are fine," Alafair said.

"Is a name decided?"

"Not that I've heard."

"And how is Miz Mary feeling?"

Why do you want to know, Alafair thought? Are you just a nice fellow, or are you concerned that she might have remembered something you'd rather she didn't? Her inclination was to give a short answer, end this conversation as quickly as possible, and get him away from the house. But after a moment's reflection, she reconsidered. She got up and walked out into the yard, stopping just short of the gate, keeping the fence between them. Grace calmly tucked her doll under her arm and followed her mother down the steps.

"Mary is tired, and her head aches most of the time, but I'm pretty confident she'll mend," Alafair told him. She studied his face carefully as she spoke, looking for either guilt or innocence in his expression, and finding only attention to her words. He was a good-looking man, tall and thin, with sharp planes to his face, clear blue eyes and a steady gaze. The pale scar served to keep his regular features from being too perfect. He didn't seem like the cold-blooded murderer type; but then again, who did?

"Tell me about yourself, Kurt," Alafair asked him, on impulse.

His eyes widened at the question, but if he was taken aback, he didn't otherwise show it. "Not so much I can tell, Miz Tucker. Micah said about all there is the other night."

"Why did you leave Germany? Why did you leave your family to come to a faraway country where you didn't know a soul?"

"I have no family," he answered her simply.

"No one at all? No mother or father?"

"No, ma'am. Once I had a mother, but she died when I was thirteen."

"Who took care of you?"

He blinked at her. "Nobody. I was thirteen."

Alafair looked down at Grace, who was sitting in the dirt at her feet, and pondered Kurt's reply. She looked back up at him. "Where did you live, then? How did you live, just being thirteen?"

Kurt shrugged. He crossed his arms over his chest and leaned one hip against the fence, settling in to tell her whatever she wanted to know. "I was born on a big…what do you say? Like a ranch, a farm, a big piece of land. We call it *ein Rittergut*. *Mutti*, my mother, she was a house maid in the big house. Very big house it was, like a castle. When I was big enough, I went to work in the stable, mucking out the stalls. When *Mutti* died, I stayed on, worked under *der Stabilmeister*. He was called Wilhelm Jaeger, a good man. He taught me about horse, about metalwork, even paid me a little wage. I am a good saver. When I was eighteen he died, Herr Jaeger, but I had saved enough money from the stables and some extra work at the forge that I could travel here. There was nothing for me in Bavaria, Miz Tucker. No future. Here a man can make something of himself."

"What about your father?"

"I didn't know my father," Kurt said, matter-of-fact. He hesitated and thought about this for a moment before deciding to elaborate. "I saw him, sometimes. He was the second son of the *Graf*—the lord, the nobleman, I think is the word. At least this is what my mother told me. I had no reason not to believe her."

Alafair was mildly shocked, but tried not to show it. "And he wasn't inclined to provide something for you?"

For the first time that Alafair could remember, Kurt smiled. "He wasn't inclined to care if I live or die, ma'am. I was not his only little..." He hesitated, his English failing him. He unconsciously touched the scar on his cheek.

"Did he give you that scar, son?"

Kurt quickly dropped his hand and gave her a shallow smile and a shrug. "The *Graf* was a cruel man."

"Your own grandfather did that to you?"

"Things are different where I am from, Miz Tucker. For many years, much of my life, I think, I hate him and all like him, who own much land and the people who lived on it also. My little mother was gentle and helpless, but those rich people, to them she was another piece of property, like their horse or their dog. I didn't like to be a rich man's horse, so I came here."

No one spoke for a long moment. Kurt seemed content to let Alafair digest his tale, and Alafair was in no hurry to comment. Grace stood up from the dirt and skipped to the fence, where she handed Kurt one of her little carved horses over the pickets. He accepted it gravely.

"That's horse," Grace informed him. Unable to pronounce the "th" sound, she had actually said "dat's horse," and Alafair noted with some amusement that Kurt and the baby suffered from the same speech impediment.

"Thank you, Miss," Kurt said. He began to gallop the horse across the top of the fence for the child's amusement, but he looked at Alafair. "So do you think less of me, now, ma'am?" he wondered mildly.

"Why?"

"For how I was born low."

"That's hardly your fault. I approve of your desire to better yourself."

"I'm glad. I thought you should know."

She had in fact wondered why he would tell her something so personal, since she didn't consider his circumstances any of her business. She dismissed his comment as a cultural difference.

"It's a hard feeling I have, maybe, but this war that is happening in Europe…I hope Germany loses," Kurt was saying to her. "I know I am born German, but I want to be American, now, and forget all about Germany. Micah has helped me a lot. He has been a good friend. He taught me about America, taught me English. Rough English," he amended. "Miss Mary has helped me to speak much better, more proper. I am grateful to her."

When he mentioned Mary, Alafair tensed. "You like Mary, do you?"

Kurt's face changed instantly from open to guarded. He handed Grace's horsey back to her and backed off a step. "Miss Mary is good person, good to me. But of course, I know my place."

"Your place?" Alafair repeated, taken aback.

"I am the hired man."

Alafair's first instinct was to reassure him, but in light of her concern for Mary, and Kurt's sudden odd behavior, she said nothing.

Kurt took her silence for dismissal. He bid her good night and beat a retreat toward his little room across the barnyard. Alafair watched him go, torn. She had never paid much attention to Kurt. He had always been Micah's tongue-tied shadow. She had asked him for his tale, after all, and at another time, she would have been touched by his openness and his willingness to trust her. But under the circumstances, she simply wished he would go away.

She picked up Grace and turned to go into the house, when the wind suddenly picked up, stirring the leaves in the elms. Grace dropped her wooden horse, and Alafair was bending to retrieve it when she heard the moaning on the wind. She froze where she was, squatting on the path with Grace on one arm and the other reaching for the toy, listening.

"That lady cry?" Grace wondered, concerned.

"Do you hear it, too, punkin'?"

"Who that, Mama?" Grace asked her.

"It's somebody who is lost, honey, and can't find her way home."

Chapter Eleven

At first Grandpapa used to take Daddy and his brothers with him on those horse-buying trips, then Uncle Howard came along, and finally Uncle Bill. Eventually all the boys grew up and left home, all but Uncle Bill, and for the last few years, Grandpapa hasn't even made the trip. He's just left it to Bill. Well, Bill told us that the very first time he went down to Waco without Grandpapa, he arranged to go with some of his friends: Nix Webb, the Turner boys, and Farrell Dean Hammond. Nix Webb's father has worked for Grandpapa for twenty years, and Nix and Bill knew each other all their lives. The Turner boys are both interested in horse breeding. I guess it's in their blood, since they grew up around old man Turner's livery business. And as for Farrell Dean, well, I expect he didn't know one end of a horse from another. He was just always up for an adventure.

Mary had slept most of the day on Sunday but rose early Monday morning, and, skipping her breakfast duties, slipped out of the house into the murky pre-dawn. The early morning air and misty light felt good to her after the long, anxious hours at Phoebe's. For a long time, she simply stood next to the back door, close to the house, and enjoyed the relative cool. She greeted her brothers when they left the house, heading for the barn to do the milking, but didn't move from her spot. She was aware of her mother checking on her from the kitchen window every fifteen seconds, but thankfully Alafair didn't try to make her come inside, so she tried to ignore the distraction.

When the sun finally arose enough to allow Mary to see what she was doing, she walked out to the vegetable garden to water and perhaps pull up a stray weed. The early morning in mid-August was the only tolerable time of day to move around, and it felt good to Mary to stretch her muscles, keep busy, and avoid thinking as long as possible.

She hadn't been in the garden but a few minutes when she caught sight of Micah watching her from the yard at the corner of the house. He smiled at her and straightened when he caught her looking at him, and casually placed one hand in his pocket. The move drew Mary's attention to the gun belt slung low around his hips. He tipped his hat.

"You must be on guard duty this morning," she said. Taking her comment as an invitation to talk, he walked over to the low chicken wire fence that ringed the garden.

"Mr. Tucker asked us to watch the house while y'all were over at your sister's, but I reckon I'm just on my way to work right now. I seen you over here and expected I'd better come over and see if everything is all right."

"Everything is fine, thank you very much." Her tone was more acerbic than she had intended, and Micah looked slightly taken aback. Mary felt a brief sting of regret that she had snapped at her would-be protector, and determined to moderate her exasperation. She gave Micah a conciliatory smile, and his stance relaxed.

"Are you planning on shooting something?" She nodded at his gun belt.

"I hope not, ma'am. Just seems like a good idea to go armed while there's still a killer on the loose."

Mary nodded and bent back to her task, but Micah didn't seem to be in any hurry to move. "I was right pleased to hear about your new niece."

Mary flicked him a glance. "Thank you."

"I expect you must be tired out."

"I have been, but it's not so bad this morning. It'll probably catch up with me later. Right now the excitement's got me all stirred up, I guess."

"You're looking better," Micah observed.

She stood up. "Than what?" she asked, and laughed, a not-very-happy laugh.

But it seemed to be good enough for Micah. The gray eyes crinkled. "It's nice to hear you laugh again, Miss Mary. I always admired your laugh. It bubbles like water over stones in a Colorado mountain stream."

Mary placed her hand on her hip and shifted her weight to one leg, not bothering to move closer to the fence for a more intimate conversation. She did appreciate the comment more than she might have expected, though. "You've been to Colorado?"

Micah shifted his weight as well, mirroring her stance. "I've been all around."

"I've never been any further east than Arkansas nor west of Enid. Must be interesting to travel."

He shrugged. "It gets tiring. I envy anybody who has his own place in the world—a family that loves him."

"There's no reason you can't have that. Didn't you say your father has a cattle business in Abilene he wants you to go into?"

"Oh, yeah, I guess he does, but I've been having second thoughts about that. I've been footloose too long, I reckon. I wouldn't know how to set down roots." He looked down at the ground, then back up at Mary. "I'd like to. Just don't expect it'll come to pass."

"Seems to me that folks can pretty much do anything they set their minds to."

A blush spread across his cheekbones, and he smiled. "Maybe."

The blush caused something to loosen in Mary, and she took a few steps nearer the fence. "How'd you end up traveling with Kurt? Y'all are about as alike as dirt and Sunday."

"I like old Kurt," Micah assured her with a laugh. "He's a good hearted *Deutch*, even if he is as thick as a plank."

"I don't think he's thick. Just shy."

"He ain't so shy with livestock. No mule can out-stubborn him. Why, I've seen him rassle a iron-headed mule right to the ground."

"That's quite a prodigious feat."

"Why, you needn't sound so skeptical, ma'am, though perhaps I did overstate the case a mite."

Mary rewarded his comment with a snatch of the bubbling laugh he had described, and shook her head. "I thought you were on your way to work."

She was dismissing him, but he didn't seem to take the hint. "Excuse me, Miss Mary, but can you handle a gun?"

This unlikely question gave her pause, and she hesitated before she answered. "I've done some shooting in my time. Why do you ask?"

His face reddened yet again, and his hand automatically moved up to remove his hat. "Well, I been thinking that it couldn't hurt if maybe you had a little target practice. I mean, wouldn't it be good if you was prepared to defend yourself? I'd be honored to go with you out to the back section out there where your dad and brothers shoot cans off the fence, if you'd like."

"Oh, mercy, Micah. I don't care to become a gunslinger over this."

He bit his bottom lip and turned another couple of shades of red. "Well, ma'am, I know that a well-brought up lady like yourself shouldn't have to learn to handle firearms. Any fellow would be proud to be your protector. But you can't have some-body around close to look out for you for the rest of your life. Whoever killed your uncle is skulking around here somewhere, sure as daybreak, and it sure would comfort me if I knew you could blow the snake's head off if it came to it."

"I can handle a rifle. Daddy makes sure every one of us knows enough not to shoot ourselves at least."

"What about a pistol? I was thinking I'd ask your father if I could give you a small sidearm that I don't carry any more. It's got a good safety and it'd fit just about right into the pocket of your skirt, or an apron maybe." He looked down at the ground.

"I sure would hate it if…I mean to say, I'd be distressed if I didn't do everything I can to make sure you're safe."

Mary was amused and touched at his fumbling. "You're sweet."

He looked up. "Then you will?"

While Mary was still considering her reply, Gee Dub walked up with Charlie at his heels. Micah started and looked back over his shoulder at the boys, who were returning to the house after milking with full pails in their hands. The flush on his face spread down his neck.

Gee Dub put his pails of warm, foamy milk down on the ground by the fence. His dark eyes appraised Micah's face, then Mary's, as he flexed the cramp out of his hands. "I see that Ma let you out of the house."

"Well, she's got a weather eye on me."

"She probably sees that Micah is bodyguarding you," Charlie interjected.

"Micah was just suggesting that I do some target practice. I expect he thinks I should hone my shooting skills and go about armed to the teeth so that I can drop an assailant at fifty feet."

Charlie liked the idea. "How about this afternoon?"

"Oh, Charlie, I was just joshing around. I could be the best shot in the county, but it isn't that easy to shoot a…"

"Mary!" Alafair called from the back door, interrupting the conversation. The four young people looked toward her as one. "You'd better come inside now, sweetheart. It's light enough now that you shouldn't be outside in plain sight."

Mary's gaze shifted from her mother to Micah and then to her brothers. "This afternoon sounds fine."

After overcoming Alafair's strenuous objections, Mary, her brothers, and her sister Ruth trooped out to the field in the early afternoon, hauling a sack of empty tin cans, an old-fashioned .44 revolver, and a box of bullets. The heat was oppressive and the myriad tiny buzzing insects were maddening, but at least Mary could be outside and distracted for a little while, even if she had to surround herself with mobs of people before her mother would reluctantly stop badgering her to stay within doors.

The spot they chose was their usual target-shooting venue. A gate in the barbed wire fence that surrounded the horse pasture provided a surface on which to place a row of cans, and the grassy field afforded a long, clear view so no unintended living targets could sneak up on them. One solitary tree, a tall, stringy persimmon, grew a few dozen yards from the gate. It was the perfect place for the siblings to spread an old quilt, sit in the shade, and pick cockleburs off their stockings or trouser legs while waiting their turns to shoot.

Micah had not wanted to intrude on the expedition once Mary's siblings decided to go, but she cajoled him, and he walked up from the stable to join them just as Gee Dub was arranging cans along the top rail of the gate.

"Micah," Charlie greeted him. "Just in time! You can take the first turn if you've a mind."

Micah grinned an ingratiating grin and shook his head. "Not me," he demurred. "I'm afraid y'all will see what a bad shot I am and think less of me."

Mary looked up from loading bullets into the six-shooter. "Well, then, you could use the practice." She handed him the gun, and he shrugged.

"All right, but I wasn't fooling, now." He took aim, slow and precise, and hit five of the ten cans perched on the gate.

"Well, that's not bad, Micah," Charlie said over his shoulder, as he raced to the fence to retrieve and replace the cans.

"Now you, Miss." Micah handed the gun to Mary. "After all, the point of this here exercise is to improve your skills."

Mary reloaded, aimed carefully, and shot five times before she nicked one can. She lowered the revolver and rubbed her forehead. The noise and kick of the gun hurt her aching head worse than she had anticipated. Out of the corner of her eye, she saw Micah step toward her. But it was Gee Dub who placed his hand on her shoulder.

"You want to stop?"

She shook her head. "Just a little more. I don't want y'all to think I can't do any better than that."

Gee Dub nodded, then stepped behind her to help her sight. "Lift the barrel a bit," he said into her ear, "and sight along that notch."

"I remember," she murmured, and he stepped back. She tried again, and hit three of the five remaining cans. She stepped back, surprised but happy, and accepted her siblings' accolades.

"Me next!" Charlie called, as he replaced cans, but Ruth stepped up and relieved Mary of the pistol.

"Out of the way, Charlie. You boys get to shoot all the time." She threw a challenging glance at Gee Dub, but he spread his hands in surrender. Mary backed off, and felt rather than saw Micah move up beside her as Ruth took aim.

Six quick shots, reload, then four more, and three cans remained standing. Ruth gave a triumphant whoop as everyone cheered.

Micah grabbed his hat brim with both hands and pulled his hat down over his ears in an exaggerated expression of humiliation. "Lord have mercy, Miss Ruth! I reckon I'll have to ask you to give me some lessons!"

Ruth handed the gun to Gee Dub before she pranced back into the shade to throw her arms around Mary.

"Your turn, Gee Dub," Mary urged.

Gee Dub looked up from reloading. "It's Charlie's turn."

"I'll bet you can't beat me," Ruth challenged.

There was an instant of silence before Charlie said, "Go on, Gee."

Gee Dub shook his head. He knew very well that his brother and sisters wanted him to show off for the hired man. He was a very good shot, and they all knew it. "Naw. I practice all the time. It's y'all girls who need to be learning."

"Come on, Gee Dub," Mary said. "I'll make you your very own apple pie if you can knock off all ten of those cans in ten shots."

Gee Dub hesitated, clearly torn between his disdain for brag-gadocio and his desire for a pie he wouldn't have to share. "What do you get if I can't do it?" he asked, suspicious.

"I'd say you have to make me a pie, but I expect that wouldn't be much of a prize for me. So I'll just settle for getting to tell everyone you couldn't do it." She looked sidelong at Micah and gave him a sly wink, and was gratified to see his eyes widen and a dark flush stain his sun-browned cheeks.

He turned to Gee Dub. "Come on, Gee Dub. Somebody's got to stand up for us men, here."

Gee Dub reloaded the cylinder, raised the gun, and shot the first can off the fence.

Charlie clapped and cheered, "Hooray!"

Gee Dub cocked the hammer and aimed.

"Watch out!" Ruth yelled as he pulled the trigger. The second can fell.

Gee Dub eyed the red-cheeked fifteen-year-old in mock outrage. "So it's going to be like that, is it?"

"Hey, bragging rights at stake here."

Gee Dub turned back around decisively and took aim.

"Look, it's a giraffe!" Ruth exclaimed, but cans three, four, and five went flying.

Gee Dub reloaded, trying desperately to keep a straight face as Ruth stood there with an innocent expression and waited. He shot once, twice, and then shot again as Ruth waved her arms about and clucked like a chicken.

By this time, Micah, Charlie, and Ruth were collapsed with laughter, and even Mary was chuckling. Gee Dub allowed him-self a bare smile as he plugged another can, then ostentatiously covered his eyes with his left hand and shot off the tenth one.

"I declare!" Micah gasped. "That's some shooting!"

Gee Dub shrugged. "Just cans. They don't generally try to run while you're shooting at them."

In the general fun, no one noticed that Mary had stepped back into the shade and sat down heavily on the quilt. I laughed, she was thinking to herself, horrified. *Bill was just put in the ground and I forgot and laughed.*

Alafair was quite familiar with the place the kids went for target practice. There was no place around that field for a mile for a bushwhacker to hide and practice his nefarious occupation. She had tried to talk Mary out of going, of course, but it hadn't taken her long to see that even the best-natured of her children had just about had enough of her constant concern. And, truth be told, Alafair thought it was a good idea for Mary to hone her gun-handling skills, under the circumstances. She had already considered giving Mary the little two-shot derringer her father had given her when she was sixteen. But that little gun had already been the cause of enough trouble. She'd talk to Shaw about buying a different lady's gun for Mary.

The instant the kids were out of sight, Alafair went into the bedroom and took Mary's journal from its hiding place. If Mary insisted on having an outing over her mother's objections, then Alafair was going to put her absence to good use by checking to see if Mary had remembered anything new since last she looked. She had no intention of telling Mary what she was doing, but neither did she feel an instant's guilt about snooping. One did what one had to do to help her children.

"What you doing, Mama?"

Alafair started. She had been so engrossed in her reading that she hadn't heard Grace come into the bedroom. "Gracious, shug! You gave me a fright." She casually laid the book on the bed beside her.

Grace grinned at the thought of scaring her mother and took a flying leap into Alafair's lap.

"I thought you were playing outside with the girls," Alafair said. "Go into the kitchen and I'll get y'all some cookies."

Grace jumped off Alafair's lap and was out the door without another word, the latest victim of her mother's practiced child-distracting skills.

Alafair shook her head. She should have known better than to try and do something stealthy while any of the children were within a mile of the house. She regretted having to return the journal to its box before she had finished, but at least she had a better idea of what Mary was thinking, and something new to ponder.

Should she tell Scott?

No, not yet. At the moment, Mary was just thinking random thoughts. There was no connection she could see between last Fourth of July, the boys' trip to Waco, and the murder of Bill McBride. If something was working its way toward the light of day from deep in Mary's head, it wouldn't help a thing to try and force it.

Chapter Twelve

I reckon we all remember that trip to Waco Bill and the boys made. They had finished their business and were ready to come home after a week, but they got delayed and ended up having to stay on an extra two weeks. Remember how Grandpapa fretted over that? The trip started out the same as usual, Bill told us. Him and his friends took the train to Dallas, then to Waco, where Mr. Jackson sent somebody to pick them up and carry them on out to the ranch. They spent three days out there, looking over stock—having a good time, too, to hear Bill tell it—trying to teach Farrell Dean the difference between a stallion and a mare, or keep Art Turner from playing his tricks on Miz Jackson's pretty maid.

Bill bought three thoroughbred fillies, and Nix bought a quarter horse foal, since he had plans to start a racing stable. I don't remember if the Turners bought any stock or not, but I expect they did. Johnny especially has a good eye for horses. As for Farrell Dean, maybe he learned the difference between a fetlock and a forelock. I hope so, considering what happened to him.

With only one minor swerve to avoid a flapping charge from the rooster, Martha bicycled past the house straight to the barn when she got home from work that afternoon. She kept her precious bicycle in its own little stall in the barn, next to the milk cow, and she always put the bike away immediately. She would never think of leaving it in the front yard, even for a little while, where it might be exposed to the elements, or where curious dogs might sniff it or pee on it, or horror of horrors, some sibling might play with it.

Martha dismounted at a roll as she neared the barn, and walked the bicycle up the path to the wide open door. She could see both her brothers in the small corral off to the side. Charlie was circling a pinto yearling around and around on a rope in the dusty yard. His left hand guided the pinto and his right twirled the end of the rope over and over, occasionally slapping the ground to encourage the horse to keep moving. The brim of his well-worn tan cowboy hat was turned down in the front, the better to shade his eyes from the harsh summer sun, and he had it pulled down so low on his forehead that he was forced to tilt his head back a little to watch his pony's progress.

Gee Dub slouched languidly on the fence, his own hat pushed casually to the back of his head, watching the proceedings with one booted foot on the bottom rail and both elbows on the top.

"Howdy, boys," Martha called.

Gee Dub smiled at her, but it was Charlie who replied, "Hey, Martha." His body turned away from her as the horse circled, but he kept his sister in sight by looking at her over his shoulder.

"That's Paintbrush, isn't it? Is he already old enough to train?"

"I had my eye on him since he was foaled," Charlie hollered at her as he circled. "Daddy said if I can gentle him, I can have him."

"Well, good luck." Martha turned to enter the barn, but hesitated when Gee Dub unfolded himself from the fence and ambled toward her.

"His own horse," Martha observed, inviting Gee Dub's opinion of Charlie's readiness to care for his own animal.

"He's getting a mite impatient riding old fat Pork Chop," he offered. But that was not what he had come to discuss, and Gee Dub was not one to go the long way around when it came to conversation. He nodded toward the barn. "Mary's in there."

Martha's eyebrows inched up. "I'm surprised she's been allowed to run around unsupervised."

"Her and Ma have butted heads over that one all day. Mary and a bunch of us went out to the horse pasture for target practice this afternoon. Ma about had a conniption, but Mary wasn't having none of it. She's bounden not to be made a prisoner, she says. I don't think she enjoyed herself very much, though."

Martha pursed her lips thoughtfully. "I think she'd just as soon stay at home, but can't abide Mama's fussing. Mary wants to be let alone, and Ma can't help herself."

Gee Dub nodded toward the barn. "This is the deal they came up with, I think."

"And y'all are the guard unit?" She nodded toward Charlie. "I reckon."

"What are you supposed to do if the murderer shows up and starts taking pot shots?"

"My plan is to leap into the air and catch the bullet in my teeth."

Martha snorted a laugh, but she said, "It's not something to joke about."

"I know. Well, I expect we should be glad Ma and Daddy haven't packed us all off to Grandma and Grandpa's in Arkansas."

"Don't give them any ideas. Besides, they'll finally come around to that if the killer isn't caught soon. I'd bet money on it."

"I won't take that bet."

"So what's Mary up to in there?"

Gee Dub shrugged. "Writing in her journal, last I looked."

Martha nodded, and so did Gee Dub. He had apprised her of the situation, and, purpose achieved, he turned without another word to return to Charlie and his pinto.

The first thing Martha always did when she entered the barn was take a deep breath. The sweet and cozy smell of leather, corn, sorghum, dust, and animals was irresistible.

Charlie-dog skidded out of a shadowy corner and trotted up to greet her, his entire hindquarters wagging a hearty greeting.

Martha murmured to him and let him push his wet nose into her hand as she surveyed the cavernous space, looking for Mary.

"Mary," she called, and heard a scuffling and the clomp of feet above her head. Mary's face appeared at the head of the ladder to the loft.

"Well, hey," Mary said. "You're home kind of late. What have you been up to this afternoon?"

"I had some things I had to do in town."

"You have another suffrage meeting?"

"Yes, Alice had it at her house this time. You should come to one."

"I'm sure Mama and Daddy would be delighted."

"Mama and Daddy wouldn't care a bit."

Mary's voice thickened with irony. "Why haven't you told them about it, then? Mama might even want to come."

Martha felt her cheeks grow warm. Why hadn't she told her parents? They probably would be supportive. Probably. She changed the subject.

"What are you doing up there? You have alfalfa all over you."

Mary absently brushed the tail of the flowered bib apron she wore over her faded navy blue dress, but didn't really seem to mind. "I brought one of those kittens up here with me. Looks like the mother cat did move them back into the barn here, but she won't let the litter come out when Charlie-dog's about. He might love them to death."

"Are you being shunned?" Martha asked the dog. He looked up at her, forlorn, and she patted his head.

"Come on up here when you get that bicycle put away." Mary's hand appeared and she beckoned an invitation. "I brought a jar of tea. We'll finish it off and you can help me haul down the jug and the cat when we go back up to the house directly."

Martha slid the bike into its stall, hung her wide-brimmed hat on a handlebar, and mounted the ladder to the hay loft, leaving Charlie-dog to whine once in a vain attempt to rouse pity before he padded back to his corner, resigned to abandonment.

Mary had already resumed her seat in the loose hay, next to a wooden crate she had upended for use as a tea table. The black and white kitten was romping around the loft for no reason other than to burn off some of its baby energy.

"That cat is full of beans," Martha observed.

"Yes, he's a real exuberant one. It's hard to dwell on your troubles while you're watching a romping kitten."

Martha inspected Mary's little hideaway and then cast a critical eye over her sister. Mary looked pale. The blue circles under her eyes bespoke someone who was not sleeping well. She had smiled at the romping kitten, though, and that was nice to see. The smile made her look more like herself, and less like the stricken young woman who had emerged from the field where Bill died the week before. Martha hesitated a moment before sitting down in the hay, thinking of her crisp black serge skirt. But she was already hot and gritty from the bicycle ride home, so she gracefully accepted the inevitable and lowered herself onto the floor next to Mary. The kitten instantly pounced on her, and she laughed. Cat hair on her clothes, to go along with the hay.

"You've got yourself a nice little hidey-hole up here," she acknowledged. "Gee Dub thinks you're hiding more from Mama than from the murderer who's lurking about."

"Oh, Mama means well, I know that. I just don't have the patience to humor her right now. Besides, you'd need a change of scenery, too, if you were cooped up in that house all day."

"I heard you and the kids had an outing this afternoon, though. Did some target practice?"

"Oh, yes, but that was…" She paused, not knowing quite how to describe it. "That was a little too much fun. I guess I'm not ready to be that happy, yet." She gave Martha an ironic smile.

Martha was surprised by a sudden prickle of tears as the meaning of Mary's comment dawned on her. She took a breath and sat up straight, determined not to give in to melancholy. "You're looking better."

Mary shrugged. "I'm still kindly in a fog. I try not to dwell on things. No point in that. But I hardly think of anything else. I don't have a job to distract me, like you do."

"I expect."

"I brought my little journal up here with me." She picked up the small cloth-covered book which was lying in the hay beside her. "I write in it every once in a while, when a useful thought comes to me."

"What kind of a thought?"

Mary hesitated before answering. "Anything useful. Don't know how to say it. Know how it is when you just catch sight of something out of the corner of your eye, but when you try to look right at it, there's nothing there? Well, somehow I've got a notion that I know something about who shot Uncle Bill and kidnapped Laura, but it's buried deep and I can't bring it to light."

Martha's brown eyes opened wide. "I declare! Nobody else has the littlest idea!"

"Now, don't get excited, Martha, and for mercy's sake, don't say anything to Mama or Daddy. I don't know any more than anybody else. I just have the awfulest itch of a feeling that there's something buried in my head—a clue—and if I could just be quiet long enough, it might float right up."

Martha was leaning toward her, looking so intrigued that Mary grew alarmed. "Martha, don't go telling Mama," she reiterated. "She'll plague me, and then I'll never think of it."

"No, no!" The kitten had clawed itself halfway up Martha's sleeve, and she absently pulled the little body off herself and handed it to Mary. "I won't say anything. But I confess I'm excited that there could be an answer somewhere. I won't tell Mama, I promise, but, you know, you might ought to talk to her about it. I don't mean you should tell her you might have an idea. You can wipe that look off your face. I mean Mama's got a way about figuring things out."

"Yes, she gets in there and never lets go."

"Don't I know it. But if you give her something else to occupy her mind, she might not spend all her time trying to cosset you."

Mary laughed. "There's a happy thought. Which, speaking of Phoebe, thank goodness for that new baby. Mama and Grace were over there for hours this afternoon."

"Have you been back to see her?"

"No, not yet. I expect it'll be a few days before I can, too. Mama is determined that I go with them over to Uncle James' for the cotton harvest tomorrow."

"Well, you're just going to have to put up with the fact that everybody is concerned about you right now, and wants to keep an eye on you."

"Oh, I know I shouldn't be so contrary. I caught Micah watching over me when I was in the garden early this morning, and we had a nice talk. He came with us when we went target shooting, too."

"Micah's sweet on you. I've seen the way he turns all red when you're around."

Mary reddened a little bit, herself.

Martha went on. "I think both those hired boys are taken with you, especially now that Daddy's put it into their heads that you need protecting right now."

"Pshaw."

Martha grinned, amused at Mary's discomfort. "I hope they don't end up getting into a big dustup over your favors."

"Now you're just teasing me," Mary accused.

"Well, maybe. But there's truth behind what I say, and you know it. What do you think? Do you favor one of them over the other?"

"I think I don't want to think about that right now." Mary sounded adamant, but then she turned right around and contradicted herself by answering, "Actually, I kind of go back and forth. They're both fine-looking. I think I favored Kurt, when they first came to work here, but he's so shy, he just digs his toe in the dirt and won't look at me, and it's hard to build a friendship on that, don't you know. Micah's a lot of fun, and he really seems to be concerned about me."

"Do I hear my name taken in vain?"

The girls started as a head popped up through the trap. A mischievous black-fringed gray eye winked at them.

"Micah!" Mary's cheeks grew hot as she realized what he might have heard. "What are you doing sneaking around eavesdropping on us?"

One hand appeared and tipped the Stetson on Micah's disembodied head, and he grinned. "Well, ladies, I heard y'all's voices, and reckoned I'd pay my respects." He eyed Mary's cozy setup, and nodded his approval. "This looks like a good safe place for you to be biding your time." He flicked a look at Martha, who was leaning back on her elbows and appraising him coolly. He returned his attention to Mary. "Good to stay out of sight until whoever shot your uncle is brought to justice, that is. Won't be so long, surely."

"Come on up," Martha said, "and don't just hang there between up and down."

"Sorry, Miss Martha, but Mr. Tucker just sent me to fetch a bag of feed for the foals, so I expect I'd better be about it."

"All right, then. We need to get back to the house, anyway."

Micah touched his hat brim again and disappeared down the ladder. The minute he was gone, Mary and Martha tried in vain to suppress an explosion of laughter. The effort caused a searing pain to shoot along the side of Mary's head, and she bit back a moan and pressed her hands to her temples.

Martha put her hand on her sister's arm. "Are you all right, Mary?"

Mary shook her head. "I'll swear, every time I feel better for a minute, God reminds me that evil has been done."

"That doesn't sound like God's doing to me," Martha said grimly.

Chapter Thirteen

I know you remember, Mama, how that trip to Waco ended, because there wasn't one of us sitting by the gazebo on the Fourth of July who hadn't heard the tale of how Farrell Dean Hammond slipped under the train as it was coming into the station and was killed on the spot. Everybody in town was horrified about it. None of the boys could figure out how it happened, either. Bill said the platform was pretty crowded that day, and they were all five standing in a bunch by the tracks, waiting for the train to pull on in, and the next thing anybody knew, Farrell Dean was gone. Bill said he never made a sound.

We all remembered when Farrell Dean died. Bill was pretty shook about that for months. But that awful event had sort of knocked out of everybody's head the reason that the boys were still down there and not at home like they should have been two weeks earlier. Three of them had had to testify at a murder trial.

A pale smear of light streaked the horizon, but the sun had not risen when Shaw and Alafair and their family arrived at James Tucker's cotton farm the next morning. Shaw had driven them in the big buckboard. Ruth sat on the seat between her parents, holding a basket of eggs, while Mary was in the back trying to restrain a wiggly Grace. Blanche rode with her arms around boxes and baskets of food and containers of cream and butter. Sophronia and Charlie and his dog bounced around the wagon, full of energy, generally irritating everyone else. Gee Dub rode behind on his horse, leading a string of three mules.

Mary had not wanted to come. She pleaded fatigue and volunteered to go back to Phoebe's to help with the new baby, but Alafair had told her that since Martha had to work and Alice was with Phoebe, Mary was needed on this expedition. Actually, Alafair expected that Mary would probably get more rest and be as safe at Phoebe's, with Alice and John Lee there as well. The truth was that she didn't want to have Mary out of her sight again.

They were met in front of James' long, low frame house by his two teenage sons, Jimmy and Jerry, who took the buckboard and the stock to the barn. Alafair restrained Charlie from following his cousins for the moment and loaded him and the other children down with food to carry into the kitchen, where James' wife, Irene, was directing the preparation and distribution of breakfast for the pickers.

It was a task not for the fainthearted, and already well underway when Shaw and Alafair arrived. Long sawhorse and board tables had been set up before the row of tents by the edge of the field where the thirty or so black workers, men, women, and children, along with a few infants and toddlers who were too young to work, were eating breakfast by the light of kerosene lanterns. A smaller table had been set up at the side of the house for James' family members and his few white hands who would also be picking, weighing, loading, and driving.

Shaw spotted his brothers James and Howard, and his brother-in-law W.J. Lancaster. He and Gee Dub skewed off to join them, while Alafair and the other children carried the food into the house. Alafair found Shaw's sister Sarah Lancaster alone in the kitchen, at the stove, frying dozens of eggs by the yellow light of kerosene lamps. An enormous platter at her elbow was already piled high with eggs so expertly fried and stacked that while none were cooked hard, not one egg on the platter had a broken yolk.

Sarah glanced back at them over her shoulder when they came in. "Morning, Alafair, kids," she greeted cheerfully. She pushed a stray tendril of black hair behind her ear with her free hand. "Glad y'all are here. Irene and Vera and Josie are hauling out bacon and biscuits and coffee. I need one of you girls to take this plate of eggs on out to your uncles and the boys."

Blanche imperceptibly fell back behind her mother, but Sophronia leaped forward. "I'll do it."

Sarah handed her the platter. "That's my girl. Just put it on the table and scoot on back here. I've got more tasks for you."

Sophronia disappeared out the back door and Ruth handed her aunt the basket of eggs. Sarah began to crack them into the skillet and threw the shells into a bucket beside the stove without missing a beat.

Charlie dumped his burdens on the cabinet and began winding one of Blanche's dark braids around her head to have something to do while he complained to Alafair. "Can't I go with Daddy, now? I brought in all them things you told me to."

"Mama!" Blanche protested, swatting Charlie's hand and trying to lift a ham out of a basket at the same time.

"Go on, get out," Alafair told him, annoyed. "And take the dog with you. Not you, Blanche. Ruthie, why don't you take over frying up the eggs for your Aunt Sarah? Mary, you set up a blanket under a tree outside. You can baby-sit Grace today and keep an eye on your cousin." She was referring to Sarah's four-year-old daughter Katie, whom she had seen crawling around under her father's feet at the breakfast table. "Where's your other kids, Sarah?"

"They're at their Grandma Lancaster's, all but Katie. I didn't feel like riding herd on the bunch of them today."

"I saw a couple of little babies with the pickers," Mary noted. "You suppose they'd let me sit the bunch?"

"Their mamas may have their own arrangement, but you can ask them, if Aunt Irene don't care," Alafair told her.

"You going to let her babysit Grace and Katie and a bunch of little colored babies after what she's been through?" Sarah asked Alafair, after Mary had left with Grace in tow.

Alafair was unconcerned. "It'll occupy her mind. Did I hear you say that Josie is here?"

"Yes, and I was surprised, too. Irene told me that she showed up this morning not long after cock crow. She's been staying at the big house with Mama and Papa for the past few days. Mama told her she's getting underfoot, trying to do for them all the time, so she decided she'd give Mama and Papa a break from herself and do something useful over here for a spell."

"Sounds like your ma is feeling better."

Sophronia reappeared, skipping through the door with her shoes and stockings in her hands. "It's getting hot already," she protested, when she saw the look on her mother's face.

Alafair let it go. Anyone who wasn't tramping around in the field would be barefoot before the day was out, anyway. "All right, Fronie, Ruth has another plate of eggs ready to go. Blanche, pile up a big platter with this ham and take it out to the pickers, and when you get back we'll have a small platter ready for you to take out to the family. I'll make more coffee. Ruth, it looked to me like everybody's just about finishing up. Sun'll be up directly and it'll be time to go to work. Dishes need to be gathered up."

"Mama, I'm hungry," Blanche pointed out. "When do we get to eat?"

"We can eat after everybody's done, sugar," Aunt Sarah told her, "before the washing up. Won't be long."

Alafair snatched a hot biscuit from the pan sitting on top of the stove, slathered it with butter, and shoved it at the girl. "Have a bite of this to tide you over."

She took one of the enormous tin coffee pots outside to fill at the pump beside the back door. The sky was light, now, and the disc of the sun just coming up over the eastern horizon. Alafair could see the itinerant workers standing up from the table in ones and twos and gathering in a group under the elms, putting on hats, adjusting fingerless gloves and toeless old socks over their hands, and draping the long, trailing bags over their shoulders, which they would drag behind them down the rows and fill with cotton. The hand covers wouldn't help much. The only help for what cotton bolls did to fingers was to develop callouses like an elephant's hide.

It made Alafair tired just to look at them. She had picked plenty of cotton in her time, both when she was a girl and when she and Shaw were young and unable to afford to pay pickers. It broke your back. It ripped the skin right off your hands and dyed your fingers black and tore your clothes. It sucked every drop of water out of your body. It blinded you with sun and choked you with dust and grit. And it had to get done in a day, or two, and then it had to be done all over again in another week, or two, sometimes off and on all the way to November. And these people traveled from field to field for months and killed themselves to get other people's cotton in, starting in Texas and following the cotton up to Kansas. Just as the wheat harvesters did in the spring.

The itinerants wouldn't be picking Shaw's crop this year. Shaw had feared this spreading boll weevil plague, and had not put in but a few acres, even though the price of cotton had been excellent the year before. It was just as well he hadn't planted more, since cotton prices were dropping like a stone since this new war had instantly killed the European market. Shaw had already made arrangements for local help when his crop was ready; in only a few days, Alafair suspected. She could see Shaw and James and Sarah's husband W.J. come around the house and walk up the hill toward the workers. Two slender young women at the long breakfast table had begun gathering dishes into piles. A tall, middle-aged black man in overalls broke away from the knot of pickers and went to meet the white men. The foreman of his group, Alafair thought.

Alafair's dreamy reverie and water pumping were interrupted by someone saying her name, and she started and skewed her gaze back over her shoulder.

"I said 'morning, Alafair,'" her eldest sister-in-law Josie repeated, amused. She was carrying an armload of plates from the family's breakfast.

Alafair straightened up and replaced the lid on the coffee pot, eyeing Josie critically for a moment. She seemed her usual self: tall, plump, and lively. Her black hair, barely touched with gray, was usually fluffed and poofed, but today was wrapped in a scarf for work. Her hazel eyes were lively enough, but her face looked drawn and tired, the skin around her eyes pinched.

"Morning, Josie," Alafair said at last. "I was in the clouds, I expect. Sarah told me you were here. How's your folks holding up? How are you?"

Josie's gaze slid away from Alafair's face, and she shrugged. "Glad to be doing something useful." She looked back at Alafair. "I've been over to Mama's most all the time since Bill died, trying to do for them, visiting with the callers when Mama and Papa couldn't face it any more. Keeping the house clean, dishes washed up and all. They've been pretty grieved. I reckon you know how it is."

Alafair did know. Her mother-in-law Sally McBride was no stranger to grief, having lost her first husband and an infant daughter when she was young, and now a grown son. For years, Sally and Alafair had had an extra bond, both having lost children unexpectedly. Alafair smiled, but said nothing. There was nothing that could be said.

"Mama and Papa both seem to have perked up some in the last day or so, though," Josie continued. "They want to be doing things, keeping busy again. Ma said she appreciated me wanting to be of help, but I ought to get back to my own life. I was getting underfoot, now." She gave an ironic smile. There was no explaining Sally McBride, so Josie changed the subject.

"How's my new grandniece? Does she resemble her mama?"

Alafair couldn't keep from grinning. "She's a beauty, even if I do say so. She looks more like John Lee to me, with big old eyes and a mess of black hair."

"What are they calling her?"

"They haven't come up with anything yet, at least not that I've heard."

Josie sighed. "It's funny, ain't it? One goes out, and one comes in." She moved up next to Alafair as though she wanted to tell a secret. Alafair leaned in toward her, curious. "You know, Mama told me she hears him sometimes, Bill. At night, mostly, she hears him, just next to her. Trying to whisper something to her, but she never can quite hear what it is."

Alafair drew back a little and looked Josie in the face. "What does she think he's trying to say?"

"Well, she said she can't quite hear him," Josie reiterated. "But from the way Mama was acting, I just feel that he's trying to tell her something about Laura—that something needs to be done about Laura."

In spite of the already sultry heat of the August morning, Alafair felt a chill around her heart. She gazed at Josie's face, unable for a moment to form a thought. Alafair had no doubt that Sally was sensing something about Bill. The woman had spent most of her life deep in the Ozark hills where the ordinary rules of nature didn't apply. She was half Southern Appalachian white and half Cherokee Indian. Sally knew for a fact that the veils between the world of the living and the world of the dead were mighty thin, and this wasn't the first time that she had admitted to contact with someone on the other side.

Alafair was not quite so sanguine. Not that she didn't have perfect faith in her own senses. She knew what she knew and would have scoffed at anyone who tried to talk her out of it. But she wasn't inclined to share her otherworldly experiences so readily. Still, since Josie had brought it up…

"Have you been to see Laura?" she asked Josie.

"No, I meant to sooner, but I didn't have the heart. I'm afraid it's too late now. I hear that Calvin sent her off to some folks of his after the fire the other night."

"Did he, now? Well, that makes sense. I'm sure he'll bring her home as soon as this murderer is caught."

"I was hoping that she'd come out of the darkness, though, and tell Scott who did it."

"Mary and I went to see her before the funeral," Alafair said. "She's not doing well at all. Not dead, but not quite alive, either. I think she's lost her soul. I think maybe whatever happened to her was so awful that she couldn't deal with it and now her spirit is wandering around lost." She hesitated, but Josie was gazing at her attentively, without skepticism. Alafair took a breath and continued. "I've been hearing her, you see. I can hear her crying in the night."

"Are you sure it's Laura?" Josie asked.

"I recognize her voice."

"And she isn't trying to say anything?"

"No, she's just crying like her heart will break."

Josie thought about this before she replied. "Do you suppose this is what Bill is trying to tell Mama?" She suddenly straightened to her full height, and the dishes in her hands rattled alarmingly. "Maybe he's trying to tell her something that will help Laura find her way home, and until then he won't consent to go to his reward."

They were interrupted by James' wife, Irene, who came around the corner of the house with her own armload of dishes. Josie and Alafair turned to face her, both looking so shaken that Irene stopped in her tracks. "What's wrong?" she demanded.

Josie shook her head tightly. "We're just grieving about Bill." Irene relaxed and nodded.

After the dishes were gathered up, the women ate their own breakfast. Cleanup occupied the next couple of hours, and then it was time to begin preparing a dinner to be taken to the workers in the field. The younger boys, black and white, served as water bearers, spending the long, miserably hot day running between the field and the well, hauling buckets of water to the hands as they picked the cotton. Alafair kept a weather eye on Charlie as he lugged the heavy buckets back and forth on a yoke, each trip under the blazing sun longer than the last as the workers moved further and further into the field. She could tell that he was flagging as the afternoon dragged on, but he persevered. He would earn the two bits he had been promised for his labor.

Gee Dub and his cousins began the day picking cotton beside the laborers, but as the afternoon wore on, the older boys loaded cotton into wagons. As the pickers brought them in, the men weighed the full pokes by hanging them on a spring scale suspended from a sturdy tree branch, then entered the weights into the record book next to the worker's name. Then the bag was dumped into a wagon and the worker returned to the field with his or her empty poke to start all over again.

Late in the morning, the girls and their aunt Josie washed the worker's dishes in a couple of washtubs in the back yard, while the rest of the women did the family's dishes in the kitchen. They hauled a meal of cornbread, chicken, ham sandwiches, and jugs of buttermilk and sweet tea wrapped in wet burlap out to the field on little wagons. Dinner was usually the main meal of the day, but nobody was going to stop for a sit-down meal while there was still daylight. When the shadows grew long in the afternoon, James, Gee Dub and his cousins, and the black foreman drove the first wagon loads of cotton to James' gin, half a mile down the road.

Mary spent the day with her little sister and four-year-old cousin under the shade trees by the side of the house. The workers had declined her offer to watch their children. They had left their babies on a blanket under a few big sycamores closer to the cotton field, tended by a girl who looked to be about twelve. Every few hours throughout the day, one woman came in and lay her bag aside to nurse her infant, then trudged back to work. After nap time, when the children were hot and bored and full of energy, Mary herded her ducklings over to the group under the sycamores. The little children played together for half an hour, then Mary shepherded her charges back to their spot beside the house.

About the time the wagons drove away, the women started supper. It would be an enormous meal for forty very hungry and exhausted people. As the sun was westering, Alafair left the sweltering kitchen for a few minutes to check on Mary and the children.

Mary was sitting in a straight-backed chair, languidly fanning herself with a paper fan adorned with a picture of Jesus delivering the Sermon on the Mount. Grace and four year old Katie were stretched out on their bellies on the quilt, playing some desultory game of pretend with several round rocks. The air hung heavy, smelling of dust and the sweetness of dry grass. The shrill singing of the cicadas was relentless.

"Looks peaceful out here," Alafair observed.

Mary looked up at her, red-cheeked, and smiled. "Nobody's got the energy to be getting in trouble."

Alafair put the back of her hand against Mary's face. "How you feeling, honey?"

"My head's like to split. It's the heat, I reckon."

"Katie, go into the house and ask your Aunt Irene to give you a glass of water for your cousin Mary," Alafair instructed. Both Katie and Grace leaped to their feet.

"Me too, Mama!" Grace exclaimed, and the two girls ran off toward the kitchen.

"They been behaving themselves?" Alafair wasn't really concerned about the little girls. She was just making conversation while she inspected Mary's face for any signs of illness or other trouble.

"They've been very good, considering. They've been wanting to go back down to the field and play with the little colored babies some more."

"Now, sugar, I doubt if their mamas minded y'all going down there once, but they may not want you pestering them. They ain't baby dolls for the girls to play with."

Mary was mildly insulted at the uncalled-for admonition, but before she could comment, the little girls reappeared, both carrying tin cups of water clutched gingerly in two hands. Apparently there had been a disagreement over who was to be the water bearer, which Aunt Irene had solved in the most egalitarian manner possible. Katie arrived with the water she had started out with, but most of the contents of Grace's cup was left in a damp trail from kitchen door to Mary's side. Mary drank down Katie's offering and Grace's too.

"Thank you," Mary told them. "I feel much better now. Y'all girls can take these cups back to Aunt Irene, now."

Delighted with their accomplishment, the children skipped away. As soon as they disappeared around the corner of the house, Mary turned back toward Alafair and took a breath to speak.

Years later, thinking back on it, Mary never did remember how she got on the ground with her mother sprawled on top of her. There was a loud crack, she remembered that plainly enough. Then she found herself lying face down on the ground without ever being aware of leaving her chair. Alafair was lying over her, pushing her into the quilt, holding her down and screaming for Shaw. Out of the one eye that could see over a wrinkle in the blanket and out from under Alafair's arm, Mary could see movement in the distance, in the field, where pickers were straightening up, looking toward them. She saw the blur of someone beginning to run in toward the house; a white man, Uncle Howard, or Daddy, maybe. She had a strange feeling of dislocation, of having skipped a portion of time, of suddenly waking up in a foreign land, or a hundred years in the future.

"Mama, you're smothering me," she said calmly.

"Sarah, get back in the house with them girls," Alafair was yelling. She seemed not to have taken notice of Mary's statement, but she shifted, and Mary's lungs expanded.

"What's happening?" Mary asked, still in a state of unreality.

Alafair lowered her face down next to Mary's, practically cheek to cheek on the ground. "You just stay still," she whispered. "Somebody's shooting at us."

"Shooting," Mary repeated. She remembered the cracking noise and, suddenly enlightened, exclaimed, "Oh!"

Shaw was on them by now, closely followed by his brother Howard. He fell to his knees beside them and put his hands on the women's heads, feeling for wounds.

"We're all right," Alafair informed him impatiently. "Did you see him?"

"No." Shaw was breathless from the run. "Just heard a shot. How many shots? Could you tell where they came from?"

"Only one shot." Alafair raised herself up on one elbow and pointed to the west. "That way."

That way was the barn, three grain silos, and several outbuildings a few hundred yards away.

"I'll get the guns," Howard said.

"Get some of them men in the field to help us find this…" Shaw hesitated and looked down at his wife and daughter. "… shooter. I'll pay a dollar to anybody who'll help us, and twenty dollars to whoever finds him. Send somebody into town to find the sheriff. Go on, Howard, I'll get the guns." Shaw hunkered down over Alafair and Mary. "Come on, now. Get up and let's get to the house." The three of them stood and scuttled toward the house in a tight huddle, with Shaw on the outside acting as a human shield. They hurried around the corner and up the back steps into the kitchen, where they found the other women and girls standing far away from the windows next to the stove at the back wall, in a wide-eyed bunch with their arms around one another.

"What in the name of gingerbread is going on?" Josie managed. "Who's shooting? Is everybody all right?"

"As near as I can tell everybody's fine," Shaw assured them. "Somebody took a shot at the house." He looked at Alafair when he said this. Neither had said so, but their common opinion was that somebody had taken a shot at Mary. "It was just the one shot," he continued, "so I expect it was a stray. Me and Howard are taking some men to hunt for the chucklehead that done it. He's long gone by now, probably, but it's best that y'all stay in the house for a spell 'til we get this straightened out."

"What about the boys?" Sarah wondered, distressed. "What about the pickers?"

"I don't think anybody is out to get the boys or the hands," Shaw soothed. "Just don't go outside until we get it taken care of. Irene, where does James keep the key to his gun cabinet?"

Chapter Fourteen

Bill told us that just before they were scheduled to start for home, him, Nix, and Farrell Dean had decided to go to the blacksmith's in Waco to look into getting Nix's foal re-shod before they left. The smith was situated at the edge of town, a bit away from other buildings because of a pretty good-sized corral he had next to his stable. It was late in the day, about dusk, and Bill said that as they walked up, they could hear a ruckus coming from inside the blacksmith's workshop. Men hollering, a bunch of whomps, then a yelp like somebody kicked a dog, is how Bill described it. The fellows ran inside to see what was going on and to see if anybody needed help. Didn't even think twice about the danger, I expect. That's how young men are, to my observation.

It was a long evening for the women and girls, stuck in the sweltering house, not knowing what was going on outside, unable to even go to the windows in hope of a breeze. The women cooked. No matter what happened, when it became so dark that the workers in the field could no longer see to pick cotton, they were going to have to be fed. The women simply proceeded in faith that one of their men would give them the all-clear eventually, and they could fulfill their obligations. Grace became so hot and bored and impossible to live with, and Alafair so annoyed, that she considered giving the child a teaspoon of Mother's Helper. Finally, she and Sarah put the tin bathtub in the middle of the kitchen and filled it with a few inches of cool water and let the two little girls splash around in it. They were messy and noisy, but at least they were out from underfoot.

Alafair volunteered to venture out the back door and pump more water when they ran low. She was priming the handle with water from the little bucket that was kept by the pump for that purpose when she heard voices around the side of the house. Curious, she set her bucket down and moved close enough to the corner to be able to see a huddle of men standing under the elms, close to the spot where Mary's blanket had been. They were bringing each other up to speed on the hunt and planning their next move. Shaw was in the group, along with his relatives, including his cousin Scott, the sheriff. Close to the house where the horses were tied, very near her corner, the deputy Trent Calder stood alone with his thumbs hooked in his belt, watching the older men parlay. He had already offered his opinion, Alafair speculated, and was anxious to carry on.

Alafair liked Trent. He was a tall, serious young man with a dry sense of humor—a redhead, like Bill, but where Bill's hair had been a coppery auburn, Trent was a true strawberry blond, with blue eyes that sized you up one side and down the other. Trent had been a friend of Bill's, Alafair remembered. He was also a friend of Art Turner's, and Scott had sent him down to Tishomingo on the day of Bill's funeral to talk to Art. She had not known until this minute that he had returned.

Alafair sidled up to the corner, careful not to expose herself too much. "*Psst,* Trent," she called. His head turned toward her and he eyed her curiously.

"You'd better step back in, Miz Tucker. Don't know who's watching."

"I could say the same to all of y'all out there," Alafair chided. "Being men don't make you bullet proof."

Trent tried to look stern, but his mouth twitched. "Now, Miz Tucker…"

"Oh, hush up, boy, and come on over here. I want to talk to you."

Trent blinked at her. He glanced back at his boss, Scott, who was still conferring with the others, apparently in no hurry to leave. Trent looked back toward Alafair, his decision made, and came around the corner. He spread his arms and shooed her back from her exposed position as though she were a recalcitrant duck. "Let's move on back, now, ma'am."

"I ain't a fool, Trent," she said, short, but not really offended. "Now stand here with me a minute and tell me what's going on."

Trent shook his head. "Ain't much to tell. We got folks searching the silos and looking for a trail. He's long gone, I expect, but it would be foolish not to be careful. We got a lot more searching to do."

"When did you get back from Tishomingo?"

"This morning."

"What did you find out?"

Trent pondered a moment before he answered her. "I'd rather not say just yet, Miz Tucker. Wouldn't do for anybody to go to forming opinions at this early date."

"Now, if you've found out something, son," Alafair urged, "I want to know. I want to know who's shooting at my girl."

"Miz Tucker," Trent soothed, "Mary is my friend. So was Bill. I want to get the man who killed him as bad as anybody. But I want to be dead sure we got the right man. Please be patient, ma'am."

Silence fell for one uncomfortable minute before Alafair nodded. "I swear, you're the most close-mouthed youngster I ever saw. But I understand, I guess." She found herself admiring the deputy for his fairness and discretion, but at the same time, she was plotting ways to get him to spill some information that she could use.

"Well, answer me this, then. At Bill's funeral the other day, Mary was talking to Johnny Turner and he told her that Art and Bill had words the morning Bill was killed. Johnny didn't want to tell Mary what the fight was about. I was wondering if you had heard anything about that."

Trent's eyes widened. This was not the first time in his life that Alafair had surprised him with how much confidential information she knew. He considered a long time before he answered. "I'll tell you, Miz Tucker, to set your mind at ease, but only if you'll give me your solemn promise not to spread it around. Art don't need to be tried by gossip before he's ever charged with a crime. Do you promise?"

"I promise."

"All right then. But first I'll tell you that it wasn't Art who told me this, it was Bill himself. He come by the office to visit with me the afternoon of the very day he got shot. He told me that he had just had a big dust up with Art right on the sidewalk in front of the drug store. He didn't seem upset about it. In fact, he was laughing about it when he told me the story. Said that him and Art and Johnny had been on their way to get a soda pop when they spotted Shirley Kellerman coming down the street toward them. He told me that he wasn't sure whether Shirley was stubborn as a mule or just not very smart, but it seemed to him that she just refused to get the idea that he was going to wed Laura Ross. He wasn't in the mood to go around with her about it, so he was fixing to duck into the drug store and hide when Art called out to Shirley to come over. Bill was spitting mad that Art would do something like that to him, but he figured that the likelihood of fireworks was just too tempting for Art to resist.

"Well, it fell out just as Bill feared. Shirley lit right into him about breaking her heart, and Bill got all exasperated and told her that he'd never said anything that any sane girl would take to mean love, and that Shirley had broke her own heart. So Shirley went to crying, told Bill that she hoped Laura would leave him at the altar, and ran off. Bill felt mighty bad about this, as you can guess, but Art thought it all great fun and started to laugh. Then Bill really did get mad, and told Art that was a dirty thing to do. But Art said that Shirley was just a silly cow and deserved to be made sport of, and the next thing you know somebody took a swing and Johnny flung himself betwixt them, trying to keep them from pummeling each other right in the middle of Main Street. Art stalked off in a huff, all bent out of joint, but by the time Bill told me about the incident a couple of hours later, he was chuckling about it."

Trent paused when his tale was finished and smiled at Alafair. "Don't sound like a killing kind of fight, does it?"

"Not the way you tell it," Alafair admitted. "What did Johnny Turner think about all this?"

"At the time, he was perturbed that he didn't get his soda pop." The sheriff called his name, and Trent cast a glance over his shoulder. "Got to go now, Miz Tucker. Remember, don't be telling that tale around, now."

"But what about Art?" Alafair asked, as the deputy turned to go. "What did Art say about the fight?"

"Just be patient, Miz Tucker," Trent called back to her before he rounded the corner.

An enormous meal was sitting under covers on the kitchen table and cabinets, ready to be transported, when the last of the light finally faded from the sky, and Shaw, James, and Sheriff Scott Tucker came into the house.

"Whoever it was got plumb away," Scott told his attentive audience. "We dug a 7 by 57 slug out of the side of the house, like the one killed Bill. Looks like it was near to spent by the time it hit the wall, so the shooter fired it from a ways. We're thinking it was from that westernmost silo beside the barn yonder. The dust and chaff had been disturbed under the window in the upper loft. Probably laid his rifle on the sill to steady it. He was on horseback. Must have taken his shot, shinnied down the ladder, jumped on his mount and took off. We tracked him to the road, but he skewed off and went to the creek again. He did the same thing after the fire at the Ross place. We lost the trail. I've got Trent riding up past the gin to see if he can pick it up, and Skimmingmoon and his hounds are following the creek bank."

"So it wasn't a stray shot," Alafair said.

"Afraid not," Scott confirmed. "Seems our murderer is still around."

A cold, shrinking feeling came over Mary's heart. It wasn't over. "What have you found out, Cousin Scott?" she asked, sounding infinitely more sane and reasonable than she felt. "Do you have any idea yet who is doing this, or why?"

"Not yet, darlin'. I have a notion or two, but nothing I'd want to be spreading about just yet."

"Do you think it's safe to be outside?" Howard's wife, Vera, asked anxiously. "Can we go home?"

"I think he's long gone, Vera," Scott reassured. "If you want to be careful, though, hang your wagon light way forward, so nobody can see from a distance who's in the wagon. And now, if you ladies will excuse me, I've got to catch up to Trent." He touched his hat brim with his fingers. "Irene," he said to the mistress of the house, by way of leave-taking. "Josie, Alafair, Sarah, Vera," he acknowledged the matriarchs. "Mary, Ruth," he added, his blue eyes twinkling as he began to enjoy blowing his good-bye all out of proportion. "Blanche, Fronie, Miss Katie." The young girls giggled and blushed at being included. Scott looked down at the two-year-old clutching his pants leg with a honey-sticky hand. "And good evening to you, young lady."

Alafair shook her head, amused. Scott was an excellent lawman, but he could make a joke out of anything and often did. Shaw followed Scott outside, and Alafair slipped out behind him.

"I think he was shooting at Mary," Shaw was saying to Scott as Alafair came up to them.

Scott's gaze switched to Alafair, and Shaw turned his head to look at her. "Don't be delicate on my account," Alafair said. "Do you think we should be keeping her hid for the time being?"

"I don't know what he was shooting at," Scott told them, as he untied his horse from the porch railing. "But it does look suspicious, like maybe he was trying to get rid of a witness. You might want to get her out of town for a spell, like Calvin Ross did with Laura, or at least keep her inside until we catch this man."

Alafair nodded. She had already decided on her own to do just that.

"Speaking of getting out of town, when did Trent get back from Tishomingo?" Shaw wondered.

Scott grabbed up the reins and stepped up into the saddle. "This morning."

"Did he talk to Art Turner?" Alafair asked.

Scott looked down at them from the back of his horse. Alafair could tell from the pale light coming from the kitchen door that the look in his eyes had sharpened. He was pondering whether or not to tell them.

"Did he?" Shaw urged, and Scott acquiesced.

"Art ain't in Tishomingo," Scott said. "Seems the only time anybody in town saw him was for a little while on the day after Bill was shot, and not since. He never made it to his grandma's."

The black dress was back in the clothes press. Sally McBride had dealt with her tragedy the same way she always did. She took action.

What was the point, after all, of giving in to the ennui that had threatened to overwhelm her since Bill had died? Nothing was going to soothe the bloody gash of grief but time. This she had learned from hard experience. She knew she couldn't run away from it, or pretend it wasn't there, either. Therefore, she might as well do something productive.

When Sally had first broached to Peter the idea of taking Laura in, he had resisted. Bill's death had hit him hard. When their little daughter had died at birth thirty years before, that had been bad, but not like this. When you spend a quarter-century of your life loving someone, it's nigh on impossible to let him go.

Sally had persevered, however, and convinced her husband that keeping Laura safe would please Bill. And it did, too, she was sure of it, because Bill himself had whispered the idea in her ear.

Calvin Ross had accepted Sally's offer with alacrity. It was the answer to a prayer, he told her, and Sally believed it. They had concocted a clandestine scheme, moving the girl to the McBrides' before the first hint of dawn, where they had ensconced her in a small but bright and airy attic bedroom.

As for what Laura herself thought about the arrangement, well, that was anybody's guess.

She slept at night, woke in the morning, ate when fed. She used the chamber pot when led to it, but otherwise had to be diapered like a baby. If taken to a chair, she sat. If taken to the bed, she lay. She would stand and stare at the wallpaper for hours. Yet Sally had to keep the bedroom door locked, for if left alone too long, Laura would wander aimlessly, and was as like as not to end up walking clean to Muskogee.

But Sally was more than content to tend the girl who was to have been her daughter-in-law, for Laura's own sake as well as Bill's. Sally loved the once shy and clever girl who had brought such happiness to her murdered boy.

They kept Laura's presence in the attic a close secret, to foil her would-be killer. Sally expected she would eventually have to tell her eldest daughter, Josie, but no one else. Sally and Peter were still receiving daily well-wishers, and with Josie's help, they could take turns entertaining their visitors and caring for Laura.

Early in the afternoon, Sally brought a tray of soup upstairs— the only nourishment she could manage to spoon down Laura's throat—and found Laura sitting on the side of the bed, staring out the window. Peter was in a chair opposite, reading Irish poetry aloud to the girl.

Peter paused and looked up at Sally as she closed the door behind her. "I think the lass is enjoying the Yeats, Sally dear."

Sally's heart lifted at the rare smile on Peter's face. Thank you for giving us the chance to help, she thought. We may save each other.

The merest sigh of a breeze stirred the curtains at the window. Or was it Bill whispering comfort to his mother?

Chapter Fifteen

What those boys saw when they walked into the livery stopped them in their tracks. The blacksmith was on the ground, all beat up to a fare-thee-well, and standing over him was a man with an iron poker from the forge. Bill said the smith was about half dead already, but when they came in, he looked up at them from the dirt with such despair in his eyes that Bill's blood turned to ice. Nix hollered, but that iron poker was already in motion, and those three boys stood there and watched as the smith got his head stove in.

Mary was not happy with her parents' decision to intern her. She and Alafair did not go back to Uncle James' the next day. She was kept inside the house under Alafair's watchful eye. Shaw took Ruth, Charlie, and Kurt with him for the second day of the cotton harvest, and dropped Blanche and Sophronia at Phoebe's with dire admonitions to be of help to Alice and stay inside as much as possible. He instructed Micah to stay out in the back forty with the mules and horses. To Gee Dub he gave the mission of watching the house under cover of doing yard chores.

Because the harvest had thrown her off her schedule, Alafair had paid her occasional helper Georgie Welsh a half dollar to do the family's entire wash on Tuesday. And since Martha had to work, Alafair, Grace, and Mary found themselves alone in a very hot house that Wednesday morning, facing bushels of

ironing. Mary and Grace drew pictures in a foolscap tablet, and
sang together, more or less the same song.

> "For there is no knowing what people are doing
> who carry things off in a sack.
> So swift do they hurry, and never do tarry,
> and always they come empty back…"

Alafair traded a cooling iron for a hot one on the stove, then
attacked the work shirt on the ironing board. "I was just notic-
ing that the block of ice is nearly gone," she said to Mary. "A
hundred pound block don't last a week in this heat. Daddy or
Gee Dub will have to take the wagon into town and buy some
more tomorrow. Reckon we'd better make a stew tonight, use
up all the leftovers in the ice box."

"I'm thinking I may go back to helping Miss Trompler at the
school this fall," Mary said to her mother offhandedly, as she
guided Grace's hand in drawing something resembling a dog.

"I hear there's some talk of adding a class this year." Alafair
flicked water with her fingers from a jar onto the shirt, and picked
up the iron again. "The grammar school's got so big that they
may divide out the third and fourth graders. You should talk to
the principal, see if he'll hire you to teach. You have your high
school diploma, and you have experience. Don't see how they
could expect to get anyone better."

"I know you don't think there could be anyone better,
Mama," Mary acknowledged wryly, "but Mr. Voight may have
other ideas. Still…I'll go see him tomorrow, see if they'll hire
me on. School will be starting pretty soon."

"I don't know about tomorrow."

"Oh, Ma," Mary burst out, irritated. "I can't stay cooped up
in the house forever. I've got to get on with living."

Alafair was taken aback. "I didn't say anything about forever.
Just stay out of sight until this murderer is caught. He obviously
ain't giving up. He's already killed Bill and shot at you and tried
to kill Laura twice. I'm afraid he's trying to get rid of anybody
who might have seen him."

"Why aren't you worried about Ruth, then? She was there, too."

Alafair paled. In her mind, she had exempted Ruth, because Ruth had taken off on horseback after the first shot. "Ruth didn't see anything," Alafair said, voicing her reasoning aloud to see if it held up in the light of day. "I expect the shooter never got a good look at her, either, before she took out of there."

"Maybe he didn't. But we don't know for sure."

Mary was sorry for her comment when she saw the look on her mother's face. She was both gratified and annoyed at once at Alafair's constant hovering. Even if the annoyance had won out briefly, she hadn't really meant to add to her mother's anxiety.

"I'm sure you're right, Ma," she backtracked. "Ruth was gone like a shot. I doubt if the killer even paid any attention to her, or maybe didn't even see her."

But that horse was out of the barn. Alafair studied Mary's face for a long minute while she considered what to do about Ruth, now. Should she send Micah to James' to warn Shaw? She pushed her hair back from her sweaty brow and eyed Mary speculatively. "Ain't you afraid?" Ever since this thing had happened, Mary had seemed singularly unconcerned for her own safety.

The question gave Mary pause. If she really considered it, she had to admit to herself that she wasn't afraid. She wasn't anything. She didn't really care one way or the other if she got shot or if she didn't. It was as if the bullet that had creased her temple had knocked every strong emotion out of her, except for a dull, aching sadness. "I'm too tired to be afraid. I can't think about it. I just want to get on with it, whatever it is."

Throughout this exchange, Grace had been drawing busily from her perch in Mary's lap. She seemed unaware of her elders' conversation, but in the way of small children she was also perfectly attuned to the mood in the room and preternaturally attentive. She looked up from her drawing. "Company," she announced, and scrambled down from Mary's lap to head for the front door.

Alafair put the iron back on the stove and followed Grace. Mary started to rise, but Alafair waved her down, and Mary plopped back into her chair, resigned.

Grace was just pushing the screen open with both hands when Alafair came up behind her and saw Gee Dub walking up the porch steps. He had been cutting the grass in the side yard with a scythe, and was flushed and covered with sweat. He halted on the porch and looked down at his mother through the screen. "Johnny Turner is riding up and down the road in front of the front gate."

"What do you suspect he's doing that for?"

"Don't rightly know. Looks like he's pondering whether or not to come in."

Alafair grabbed Grace's arm and pulled her back. "You stay inside, baby." Grace responded with an irritated yip, but obeyed and contented herself with staring through the screen as her mother descended the steps and walked with Gee Dub down the long front driveway that led to the road into town.

The man on the dumpy buckskin mare caught sight of the two people walking toward him long before they reached the road. He guided his horse toward the gate, and was waiting for them calmly when they reached the end of the drive. He snatched his hat off when Alafair stopped walking. "Hey, Miz Tucker."

Alafair crossed her arms and stood behind the closed barbed wire gate, in the middle of the drive, and eyed Johnny speculatively before she replied. Johnny Turner was mostly Creek Indian, and it showed in his compact figure and broad brown face, which made his gray-green eyes all the more startling. Her incongruous first thought was that he was mounted on the sorriest nag she had seen in a long time, and anyone with as good a reputation for knowing horseflesh as Johnny had ought to be riding something smarter. Alafair glanced over her shoulder at Gee Dub, and he nodded at her and leaned against a fence post with the wickedly sharp cutting tool propped casually over his shoulder. She felt herself relax a bit and dropped her arms to her sides.

"Howdy, Gee Dub," Johnny called. "Been cutting grass? Hot work."

"It is, Johnny," he acknowledged laconically. "I'm thinking of getting a goat. What're you riding, there? Looks like she's just about ready for the glue factory."

"Naw, old Tulip here was a fine horse in her time. I just thought she could use some exercise."

"What brings you around, Johnny? You coming in or staying out?" Alafair asked.

"I come to pay my respects to Mary, but I'm a-figuring she might not want to see me. Might not be welcome, right now."

Alafair straightened, half curious and half alarmed. "Mary ain't feeling so well, Johnny. She's not receiving visitors at the moment. But if you have a message for her, I'd be glad to pass it on."

Johnny pondered for a moment, then nodded. "Well, ma'am, tell her I'm sorry I didn't get to talk to her, but seeing all that's been going on lately, I understand. I just wanted to say, Miz Tucker, I know that the sheriff is starting to have suspicious thoughts about my brother Art concerning Bill's murder, and all the other loathsome things that's happened, too." He paused and licked his lips. "But it ain't true, Miz Tucker. Bill was Art's friend. Art would have never done anything to hurt Bill. Why, he admired Bill greatly, and Laura and Mary, too. I know that if he knew what had happened to Bill, he'd be here right now."

Alafair nodded. "I appreciate what you're saying, Johnny. But you've just put your finger on the problem, son. Where is Art? He ain't where he's supposed to be, I hear. And he sure picked a bad time to be disappearing."

Johnny twisted his hat in his hands. The buckskin plug put her head down and placidly began to graze in the tall dry weeds by the gate. "I don't know what's going on, Miz Tucker! But I know for a fact that Art didn't kill nobody. If he said he was going to Grandma's, then he was. Me and Mama and Daddy and the rest of us are mighty worried about him. Everybody knew me and Bill and Art and Trent Calder was tight. Maybe whoever had it in for Bill has done something to Art, too."

Johnny's distress was so genuine that had Alafair been standing closer, she would have put her hand on his arm to comfort him. It hadn't occurred to her that Art's disappearance might bode ill for Art himself. "I expect that it would be mighty hard for you to think ill of your own brother. And I admit that I never much thought of Art as a danger to anybody before all this happened. Just too apt to fly off the handle for his own good. I know it's hard not to fret, but you can trust Sheriff Tucker to get to the bottom of this, Johnny. He won't let it go until he finds out the truth of the matter. Do you believe me, son?"

Johnny eyed her doubtfully, but he said, "I reckon. I sure will be glad when the sheriff catches the murderer. Everybody is looking suspicious at everybody else. I can't hardly stand it. Why, I stopped over to Mr. Ross' place before I come here, and he wouldn't even let me get off my horse. Run me off with a shotgun."

"Don't be taking it hard, Johnny. He's been going through a mighty rough patch."

"Yes, ma'am, I expect. I wish, though, I could see her. I feel mighty bad about what happened to her. Mighty bad. If I could only tell her, why, she might feel better. I know I would, for sure."

"Why, Johnny, I didn't know you held Laura in such high regard."

"Why, of course I do, Miz Tucker. Who wouldn't? She's such a fine, gentle girl. It just hurts me to hear she's suffering." He blinked rapidly and looked off into the distance for an instant before turning back to Alafair. "But I wanted to tell Mary that I'm sorry about what happened to her, as well, and that it just couldn't have been Art who done it. Will you tell her, Miz Tucker?"

"I will. But before you go, will you tell me what Bill and Art fought about the morning Bill got shot?"

A pained look crossed the young man's face. "I'd rather not, ma'am. There's talk enough as it is."

"You don't have to tell me, Johnny, but have you told the sheriff?"

"I reckon I had to." He eyed Alafair, considering. "Well, if you promise not to spread it about, I'll tell you, but just so you'll know it wasn't much of a fight. They had sharp words about Shirley Kellerman. Art don't like her. She really gets his dander up. He said some disrespectful things about her and Bill took exception. That's all there was to it."

Alafair compared his story to Trent Calder's and thought to herself that there was a lot more to it than that, but to Johnny she said that she appreciated his confidence in her before he plopped his hat back on his head, took his leave, and rode away on his spavined mare. Grace and Mary's song echoed in her mind: *There is no knowing what people are doing...*

Gee Dub was still standing silently beside Alafair with his scythe over his shoulder. She turned around and eyed him. "What do you think about that?"

He shook his head, and his mouth quirked. "Beats all."

"I didn't know Johnny was such a tenderhearted youngster."

He removed his hat and wiped his brow with his forearm while he considered Johnny's behavior. "Or a pretty slick liar," he offered.

"Phoebe's just reeling with happiness, Ma," Alice told Alafair, who flopped herself onto the settee in Alice's parlor and pulled off her hat. She and Grace had stopped by the very pretty white frame house in town on Thursday morning to visit Alice while Shaw and Charlie drove the buckboard on to the ice house to buy another block of ice. Alafair had not been able to pass up the opportunity to come into town and update herself on the latest unofficial news, which some unenlightened persons might have regarded as gossip. In Alafair's experience, though, the underground information network was often much more informative than the official sources. The extremely disgruntled Mary was at home with her guardians Gee Dub, Kurt, and Micah, apprised of the locations of all the family's firearms, and sworn to stay indoors with Ruth, and out of sight.

Alice lived with her husband, Walter Kelley, in a gingerbread-trimmed and leaded glass-enhanced white frame house which sat on the shady corner of Elm and Second Streets. Walter was quite a well-to-do businessman, and Alice had taken full advantage of that fact by completely redecorating his house after their wedding. Not one piece of furniture remained that had belonged to Walter's first wife, the late and sadly unlamented Louise.

Alice had pretty much redecorated herself as well since her marriage, Alafair thought. Her blond hair was winged and swooped stylishly, and her clothes looked like they were custom made just for her, using the latest New York designs. Which they may very well have been, since Alice was a talented seamstress and an avid reader of *The Ladies' Home Journal.* Today, she had a sky blue silk scarf draped fetchingly around her neck and fastened at the shoulder with a pearl pin. Two rotating electric fans in the room created a refreshing breeze, which ruffled her hair and lifted the scarf tantalizingly with each pass. The color of the scarf perfectly matched her eyes. Alafair wondered how Alice could stand anything around her neck in this heat—especially anything as expensive and hard to care for as silk.

Alice seemed as happy as a whole sky full of larks, though Alafair worried that she was putting herself out for her husband to an extreme degree. Well, she expected to be treated like a queen in return, Alafair mused, so maybe that was all right. What's sauce for the goose is sauce for the gander, after all. And even if Alafair hadn't noticed that Walter had mended his flirtatious ways, he did seem besotted with his young wife. She did look beautiful. Alafair smiled, proud of her daughter in spite of herself.

Alice smoothed the waves of blond hair over her ears and sat back comfortably in a wing-backed armchair after serving her mother a glass of cool lemonade. Grace was amusing herself hugely at Alice's feet with her doll, some old crocheted doilies, and a tin pot that Alice had given her. "Both of them are crazy for that baby," Alice continued. "John Lee can't get anything done for wanting to rush back into the house and look at her."

"That's the way it ought to be, especially with the first, when nothing but the promise of a bright future stretches out in front of you, and you don't have enough experience to know how much trouble that innocent little creature is going to cause you."

"Are you making sport of your darlin' children? I always thought we made your life an endless joy," Alice teased. She ignored Alafair's snort of derision. "I wish I didn't have to leave Phoebe just yet, but I'd been away from Walter for two days and a night, now, and I shudder to tell you what condition the house was in, or what Walter had been feeding himself. Besides, Aunt Josie is at Phoebe's now, and she said that Cousin Reginia wants to come out and help Phoebe for a while."

"As soon as Daddy gets the ice and we pick up Martha from work and get home, I'm planning on going over there for a while myself," Alafair said. "How does the baby look today? Have they named her yet?"

"Well, they're about to decide to call her Zeltha, after John Lee's grandma."

"Zeltha!" There was a moment of silence as Alafair decided whether or not she approved.

"Ain't it an interesting name though? She's a real sweet-natured little baby. Doesn't cry much. Just sleeps and looks around a bit. She seems small to me. Grace was a lot bigger, and the other kids, too, if I remember right."

"They were. But neither Phoebe nor John Lee is very big." Alafair smiled. "I expect my darlin' granddaughter Zeltha comes by her size honestly."

"I'm glad you're going over, though. I think Phoebe is having a little trouble nursing, and she's too shy to ask anybody else about it."

"Why, she's got the expert over there right now in Josie," Alafair said, all the while listing in her mind the creams, lotions and herbs she would need to take when she made her visit.

Nettle tea, she thought, to make the milk come, and a good goose grease salve.

Alice shrugged. "You know Phoebe." She stood up and carefully placed one of the old doilies on Grace's head. Grace immediately ran to the mirror on the back of the bedroom door to admire her new chapeau. "By the way, Josie brought some interesting news." Alice looked over at Alafair. "Seems Shirley Kellerman has disappeared." She paused to enjoy the effect this piece of information had on her mother, who sat bolt upright in her seat. "Yes, Miz Kellerman ran over to the sheriff's office this morning all in a panic because she had just heard that Shirley never did make it to her aunt's in Oklahoma City. She got on the train in Okmulgee all right, but she never arrived. Scott's been telephoning every train station between here and the City to see if anybody can remember seeing her get off."

With Grace in her arms, Alafair walked the two blocks from Alice's house to the First National Bank of Boynton in silence, ruminating on the new information that Alice had given them. Mr. Bushyhead, the bank manager, was just locking up when they arrived, and Martha stepped out the front door onto the boardwalk to meet them. She looked very neat and businesslike, tall and trim in her navy blue drop waist dress with the white knife-pleat placket inset into the bodice. Her cheeks were rosy with the heat, and as they walked up, she smiled at them as she smoothed up off of her neck the tendrils that had fallen from the twist of dark brown hair at the back of her head.

"Did you hear about Shirley Kellerman?" Alafair said to her, in lieu of a greeting.

"Marfa, Marfa!" Grace was squealing joyfully, as though she had feared she might never see her sister again. Martha relieved Alafair of the squirming toddler and they began walking down the street in the general direction of the ice house.

"I did hear," Martha assured her. "Alice dropped by the bank to tell me when she got back into town this afternoon. I've seen

Miz Kellerman through the bank window two or three times already today, marching from hither to yon up and down the street. I reckon she's torturing whoever's on duty at the sheriff's office, begging for news."

"So has Scott come up with anything?"

"Not that I've heard," Martha said, "but speak of the devil and up she pops!" She nodded toward the sheriff's office just as the door opened and Mrs. Kellerman herself stepped out onto the boardwalk ten feet in front of them.

Martha may have been taken aback by the coincidence, but Alafair, who rather expected that the universe was organized for her convenience, was unsurprised. "Miz Kellerman," she called. "We just heard about Shirley. Is there any news?"

Mrs. Kellerman looked over at them when her name was called. Her expression was distracted and distressed. She blinked at Alafair without recognition for an instant, trying to force her mind back into the everyday world. "Oh, Miz Tucker," she said, as her thought processes re-engaged. "Oh, my goodness. Oh, gracious me. I'm just about beside myself, Miz Tucker. Howdy, there, girls."

Alafair reached out and touched Mrs. Kellerman's arm. The poor woman seemed beside herself, indeed.

"Yes, Miz Tucker," Mrs. Kellerman was saying, "Deputy Calder has just told me that the station master at Shawnee spotted somebody who looked like Shirley get off the Oklahoma City-bound train last Saturday. Said he noticed her because a young fellow come up to her on the platform and they got into a fracas. He tried to latch on to her, but she jerked away and strode off into the crowd, him right on her tail, the station master said, and he didn't see them no more. Oh, Miz Tucker, what am I going to do? Sheriff Tucker says that the sheriff over to Shawnee will find her right quick, now that he knows to look, but it's been days since she was seen! What am I going to do?"

Alafair was patting the woman's arm smartly, partly to comfort her and partly to get her attention. "Now, Miz Kellerman, Scott usually knows what he's talking about, believe me. Did the station master describe what the man who talked to Shirley looked like?"

"Said he looked like a Injun," Mrs. Kellerman said venomously. "I hate 'em! I hate them Injuns! I told her to keep away from them kind. She'd have never spoke to no Injun of her own accord."

The Tucker women, enrolled members of the Cherokee Nation, drew up and moved back a step, but made no comment. After a moment of uncomfortable silence that the muttering Mrs. Kellerman appeared not to notice, Alafair said, "Well, we've got to be moving on. I'm sure Shirley will turn up just fine. We'll be praying for her."

Mrs. Kellerman gave them an offhanded thanks and scuttled off down the sidewalk.

Martha huffed a dry laugh. "Ever since the Indian Territory joined up with Oklahoma and became a state, they're just letting any idiot in."

But Alafair had other things on her mind. "Honey, let's stop in at the jail for a minute before we have to meet Daddy. There's a thing or two I ought to tell Scott that he might want to look into."

Alafair and her daughters met Shaw and Gee Dub just as they were pulling the wagon out of the ice house. A hundred-pound block of ice lay in the wagon bed, wrapped in gunny sacks, layered with sawdust, and laid all about with straw bales. The women hoisted themselves into the back and arranged themselves across the ice, providing further insulation and cooling their posteriors in the bargain. Grace started out riding up front on her brother's lap, but ended up in the back with her mother and sister, burrowed down between the hay bales with her back right up against the cool burlap.

Alafair and Martha sat and looked at one another speculatively for some moments after Shaw pulled the wagon back onto the road.

"Why do you think Scott ought to look into those trips Bill made down to Texas? He did that for years."

"I was just thinking that there was some trouble a few years ago on one of those trips, and Art was there."

"So it's Art," Martha ventured at length. "Do you think?"

Alafair shook her head. "Maybe Art has been murdered his own self."

"Now Shirley has disappeared after being accosted by 'some Indian.' And according to his own brother, Art didn't cotton to Shirley."

"Could be that somebody don't cotton to Art or Shirley either one."

"Do you expect that Shirley will show up lying in the road directly, with a bag over her head?"

Alafair made a horrified face. "Honey, I don't know what's happening." She was making a heroic effort to keep her voice calm and reasonable. "I'm afraid, though, that some crazy man may be running around murdering and terrorizing young people. Maybe all you kids should make a visit to Grandma and Grandpa Gunn in Arkansas for a few weeks."

"This is a bad time of year for all of us to go gallivanting off to Arkansas. I'm not going to up and quit my job, either."

"You can stay with Alice or Aunt Josie in town," Alafair decided. "As for the rest of you, I'd rather be short handed at harvest and the kids start school a few weeks late this year than have y'all in danger." She nodded to herself, satisfied with her plan. "I'll talk to Daddy about it tonight."

Martha didn't argue with her, though in her own mind this was far from settled.

"Maybe I can talk John Lee and Phoebe and the baby into coming to stay with us in the house," Alafair was saying. "That way I could help her with the baby and she wouldn't be all alone out there in that little house while John Lee is off working. Grace will have to stay here with me, of course."

When she heard her name mentioned, Grace got up off the wagon bed and draped herself across Alafair's knees. Alafair lifted her up into her lap. "Who's that crazy man, Mama?" Grace asked her, clearly worried.

Alafair felt a pang of remorse that their unguarded conversation had frightened the child, and she patted her dark hair to comfort her. "Don't you worry about that, butternut. There ain't nobody crazy around here. Mama wouldn't ever let anything bad happen to you."

From Alafair's lap, Grace gave Martha a skeptical glance so adult that Martha laughed in wonder. But Grace wanted to be persuaded, and laid her head on her mother's breast, ear to heart, stuck her thumb in her mouth, and closed her eyes.

Chapter Sixteen

After the boys stood there and watched the blacksmith get his skull smashed, Bill said they jumped the killer, but it was too late to help the smith. Him and Nix held the rascal down while Farrell Dean ran for the marshal and the doctor. Turned out that the murderer was the smith's own son, name of Arvid Weiss. Seems old Weiss, the father, was a hard man on his children, and had finally driven his boy to bash in his skull.

Well, no matter why he did it, he did it, plain as day, before three witnesses. The marshal had the boys stay in town and testify at Arvid's trial. Art and Johnny Turner hadn't seen the murder, and didn't have to stay, but they did, out of friendship, I guess. All five of those boys were such good friends that nobody hardly ever saw one without the others, even if they all were vying for Miss Laura Ross' attention back then, same as every other boy in town.

Arvid Weiss was found guilty and was hanged on the day after the boys finally made it home with Farrell Dean's body.

August was ending, and Alafair could finally tell that the days were getting shorter. Still, it didn't become totally dark until close to eight o'clock, and it was difficult to get all the children corralled and interested in bed while the daylight lingered.

After supper, the family repaired to the parlor to read aloud to each other, play the piano or a guitar, perhaps sing or play a game or two before bed. But Grace usually began to fade shortly after she had eaten, so while the rest of the family entertained themselves, Alafair filled a large washtub full of cool water from the pump by the back door. She stripped the baby's clothes off, stood her in the tub, and sluiced her down, all the while discussing Grace's day and singing nursery songs to each other. Grace was seriously drooping as Alafair toweled her off, and by the time she was dressed for bed in an ex-flour-sack nightie, temporarily clean and cool, she was beginning to doze on her mother's shoulder. Alafair put her in her cot, then stood for a moment and admired her sleeping angel before going back to the parlor to gather the next batch of youngsters for bedtime ablutions.

Blanche and Sophronia didn't go gracefully, but they knew better than to argue with their mother. It was miserable enough to wash sheets in this weather; Alafair wasn't having any children complicate the matter by going to bed dirty.

After Alafair managed to get them cleaned up to her satisfaction, the young girls were allowed to sit in the parlor in their nightgowns while she brushed their hair, and the older girls took their turn in the kitchen. Since Phoebe and Alice were no longer at home, this was not as crowded a proposition as it used to be. It was amazing to Alafair what a big hole the twins had left in the family when they married. How had two girls taken up so much space in such a crowd of children? However, their departure had allowed room for Ruth to move up in the hierarchy, and she was now accompanying Martha and Mary every evening as they pulled up kitchen chairs around the used bath water and soaped, washed, and toweled their feet and legs. Then one of the girls would draw some warm water into a big pitcher from the reservoir in the stove, and the three of them went to their bedroom to wash faces and more private parts before changing into night clothes.

The ritual was so well established that the moment the girls disappeared into their room, the boys stood and slipped away into the kitchen, accompanied by Charlie-dog. Since they didn't have the luxury of a bedroom, though, Gee Dub and Charlie had established a practice of tossing out the grimy water, filling a bucket or two at the pump, and cleaning up on the back porch.

By the time the boys came back in their night shirts, the girls reappeared to make the goodnight rounds in the parlor, kissing their parents and each sibling, even Charlie, in spite of his many protestations of disgust. It was the same every night. No matter how he objected, Alafair suspected that he enjoyed both the game and the affection. The girls withdrew to their room, the boys to their corner of the parlor, and Alafair and Shaw put out all the lamps but the one they carried as they drew a pitcher full of water of their own and retired to their bedroom.

It felt good to lave her body in the cool water and slip into a light gown. It was too hot to sleep with her hair down, so while Shaw lathered his arms over the wash bowl, Alafair stood by the window, gazing into the yard and twisting her hair up off her neck. She was just sticking in the last hair pin when she saw a movement close to the garden fence.

She froze, her hands at the back of her head, and blinked. Surely not. You've been seeing things for days, she scolded herself.

It's the wind stirring the branches.

But there was no wind. Just hot, heavy, sultry stillness.

It's the shadow of a cloud passing over the moon.

But the moon was dark.

If someone was walking about outside, she couldn't hear it over the shirr of the cicadas. She held her breath and peered into the gloom.

There it was again. A definite shift in the darkness, a movement.

"Shaw!"

She had whispered, but somehow she had conveyed her alarm, because he was at her side before his name was quite entirely uttered.

"There's somebody out there," she breathed.

"Where?"

"Over by the fence."

"I don't see anybody."

"No, he's gone, now, off toward the woods."

"A man?"

"I hope not! But I think so, the way he moved."

Shaw didn't try to talk her out of it. Shirtless and barefoot, he pulled his galluses back up onto his shoulders, grabbed the key to the gun cabinet out of a drawer in the chiffarobe, and disappeared.

Alafair stood at the window, holding her breath, for several minutes, watching the night for any sign of something sinister.

After some time, Shaw appeared around the corner, still half-dressed and pistol in hand, searching the yard. He waved at her, then moved out of her line of sight.

Alafair stood there at the window for another fifteen minutes, until she heard the back screen creak, and Shaw came back into the bedroom. She sat down on the edge of the bed, still stiff with tension.

Shaw sat down next to her. "I didn't see anything that shouldn't be there, honey, but I expect you did see something. I went down to the shed to roust out them hired boys, and sure enough, I met both of them out and about. They said they had heard something outside that sounded funny. Micah was standing a watch, anyway. Could be that you saw one of them."

Alafair relaxed a little. "I was wondering why the dogs didn't bark. They wouldn't if it was someone they knew prowling about. Did either of them say if they'd seen anything?"

"They had not. But when I come back in, they were still looking around."

"That's good. But I would feel better if you'd bring in one of the hunting dogs tonight."

Shaw looked over at her, surprised. If she was willing to let one of his hunting dogs spend the night in the house, she was more nervous than he had realized. Neither hound had nearly the house manners of Charlie-dog.

"I don't like you being so scared, honey."

"I don't like it, either, Shaw. I don't want the kids scared, and they look to us for an example of how scared to be. I try my best to be a comfort, but it's getting harder and harder. This afternoon, I was talking to Martha about sending the kids to Arkansas to my folks. Especially Mary, though we may have to hog-tie her to get her to go. Yet, if she stays, I'm like to get so nervous and chary about this murderer on the loose that I'll drive her to distraction. She's as like to poke me as look at me as it is. What do you think, Shaw? They'll go if you say so."

Shaw agreed that it was a wonderful idea to send the children to their grandparents in Arkansas until the murderer was caught. Charlie and Blanche were thrilled. Ruth and Sophronia were sorry that they might miss the beginning of school. Gee Dub, who was to accompany his siblings on the train to see that they arrived safely and then return on his own, kept his feelings to himself.

Mary was exasperated almost beyond endurance. This plan would put an end to any possibility of her teaching this year. She considered refusing outright. She was of age, after all. And yet in the end, she didn't even protest very loudly. She was still emotionally and intellectually impaired, and she knew it, and in spite of everything she trusted her parents' judgment.

But she didn't like it.

On the afternoon before the children were to leave, Phoebe and John Lee moved in with their newborn and Martha moved out to stay with Alice in Boynton. Alafair was running at full throttle, directing the action. There would be plenty of room in the house once the travelers had departed, but for tonight, they were all going to be packed in like sardines. Mary sat in a corner and tried to keep out of the way. She let Alafair pack her little bag for her—her mother wanted to do it, anyway. As the day progressed, the noise and excitement became almost more than Mary could bear.

Grace was beginning to tire and fuss, and Martha picked her up and sat down in the rocker close to Mary. Martha pressed the child's little head to her chest as she began to rock and sing:

"Let me tell you the story of sweet Betsy from Pike
Who crossed the wide prairie with her lover Ike
With a pair of white oxen and a big spotted hog,
A tall Shanghai rooster and a ol' yeller dog..."

Thank God for a cheerful song, at last, Mary thought to herself. She was getting pretty tired of that kitty song that kept playing itself over and over in her head.

She shook her head unconsciously. Two weeks ago, all this happy noise and activity would have been great fun for her.

Alafair was in the girls' bedroom helping Blanche and Ruth fold their dresses properly, and Phoebe was busy with her baby. The boys were out in the stables with their father and John Lee. Sophronia was trying to cram herself onto Martha's lap along with Grace, making all three of them laugh hysterically. Mary stood up, easy as you please, and took herself out of the house. She paused at the front gate and took a free breath before she began walking toward the barn.

S.B. Turner, owner of Turner's Livery and father of Art and Johnny, puffed down the center of Main Street as fast as his short legs would go without breaking into a run. Just down the block, he could see Sheriff Tucker and Trent Calder adjusting their saddles and untying their reins as they prepared to mount and ride off. As soon as he judged himself to be within shouting distance, he called the sheriff's name, and Scott paused, one hand on his saddle horn and his left foot hovering half-way between the ground and his stirrup.

"Hang on, there, Sheriff, hang on! I got some news..." Turner came to a winded halt and placed his hands on his hips, trying to catch his breath.

Scott lowered his foot to the ground and peered aslant at the gasping man. "Where's Johnny, S.B.? We've been looking for Johnny all morning. I want to ask him a few questions about that trip to Waco he made with Bill McBride."

Mr. Turner shook his head, distracted. "I ain't seen him since last night. I never know where he is half the time. But, listen, Sheriff…"

"We have to be on our way, S.B., but I expect you and me need to talk as soon as we get back."

Scott made a move to mount, but Mr. Turner grabbed his stirrup. "No, listen to me, Sheriff. I just heard. I have some news you better hear. About Art."

◇◇◇

Martha, Sophronia, and Grace were alone in the parlor when Sheriff Tucker and Deputy Trent Calder appeared in front of the house on horseback. Martha peered at them curiously through the front window and handed Grace to Sophronia before she went outside.

"Hey, Cousin Scott, Trent," she greeted as she walked down the path toward them. Trent doffed his Stetson and Scott touched his hat brim and grinned at her, but neither man dismounted.

"Hey, Martha, honey," Scott replied. "Where's your daddy?"

"Him and the boys are at the stables. What are y'all about? Have you caught the murderer?"

"Pretty soon, I think," Scott said. "Your ma and the rest of the kids in the house?"

"Yes. Phoebe and John Lee are moving in for a bit. Ma and Daddy are sending Mary and the kids to Arkansas till this blows over."

Scott pulled his horse's head up and the animal danced a bit. "Good idea. You seen Kurt Lukenbach around?"

Martha blinked. "Not all day. What do you want with Kurt?" she asked their backs as they rode off toward the stable.

But Trent called back to her over his shoulder. "Just got some questions for him."

When Martha turned around to go back into the house, Alafair was standing on the porch with Sophronia and Grace. "Did I hear him say he wants to talk to Kurt?"

"So I gather. He asked for Daddy at first. Asked me if we were all in the house."

Alafair immediately counted off the children. Gee Dub, Charlie, and John Lee were with Shaw. Martha, Grace, and Sophronia were standing before her, and she could see Phoebe with baby Zeltha watching through the screen door. She turned and went into the house and checked the kitchen and bedrooms. Blanche and Ruth were still laying dresses out on the bed.

Alafair returned to the parlor and planted herself in the middle of the floor with her hands on her hips. "Where's Mary?" she asked anyone within earshot.

"She was sitting right here on the settee, last I saw," Martha said, "not five minutes ago."

"I seen her, too," Sophronia affirmed.

"I saw her myself," Phoebe interjected.

For a long minute, all the occupants of the parlor gazed thoughtfully at the settee, where Mary plainly was not sitting.

"No one saw her leave?" Alafair asked.

Martha, Phoebe, and Sophronia shook their heads and murmured feebly, bewildered.

Alafair turned quickly on her heel and headed outside. "Ya'll stay inside," she ordered over her shoulder, too loudly, as she banged out the front door. "Martha, make sure everybody stays inside!"

Grace started to cry, frightened by her mother's tone and the sudden atmosphere of dread in the room, and Phoebe's infant emitted an empathetic wail.

Shaw and his son-in-law John Lee Day were standing just outside the big stable doors when Scott and Trent arrived at a gallop and slid out of their saddles.

"We heard y'all coming all the way from the house," Shaw opened, concerned. "What's going on?"

"I hope nobody else has been kilt," John Lee said.

Scott removed his hat and wiped his glistening brow with his forearm. "Not that I know, John Lee, but we have had a break." He turned and addressed Shaw directly. "I went over to Okmulgee this morning and did a little research on the gun markings we found in the dust outside of Calvin Ross' house. I took the drawings to Mr. Vann the gunsmith over there and showed them to him, and we pretty well got a handle on it. Mr. Vann thought he recognized the general shape of the rifle and a thing or two like the rounded pistol grip. Those markings that I thought were two sets of X's Mr. Vann said are probably a 'WM,' and what we've got is a bolt-action Mauser '98 rifle. Takes a five bullet clip, which Hattie tells me no one has bought lately in the caliber we're looking for. But, the caliber of the slugs we have from the murderer's rifle would be right for a Mauser '98."

"A Mauser?" Shaw repeated. "That's a military gun. The same gun the Spanish used in Cuba, ain't it?"

Scott nodded. "They make sporting guns, too, for game hunting. But what's important is…"

"…it's a German gun," Gee Dub finished for him. The men turned and looked at Gee Dub, who had come out of the stable with Charlie and slipped up behind his father unseen.

"A German gun," Scott affirmed.

Shaw blinked. "Scott, there is no reason on this green earth that Kurt Lukenbach would have to go around murdering my brother Bill and committing mayhem on Bill's particular friends."

"Well, because of something Alafair said to me just the other day, I got to looking into the trip that Bill made down to Waco a couple of years ago, along with some of his friends, that time they got delayed because they had to testify at a trial. Strange things have been happening to the boys that went on that trip."

"What does that have to do with Kurt?" Shaw was unable to grasp a connection. His forehead wrinkled as he pondered the problem. "But Alafair and I have noticed of late that the boy has been acting mighty odd."

"Maybe he's just insane," Trent speculated.

"Well, if he is, he's done a good job of keeping it to himself."

"I'm wondering if maybe he's not who he says he is. In any event, I reckon I'd better have a talk with him," Scott said. "Where is he?"

"I haven't seen him since this morning," Shaw told him. "I sent him out to the back pasture with a pickax to bust up some caliche where we're aiming to dig out that new well. Alafair has had her suspicions up about him lately, and I've been setting him tasks away from the house."

Scott nodded. "Show me where he sleeps. We'll have a look for that gun while he's away from the house."

"John Lee, Charlie, go back up to the house and stay with the women," Shaw ordered. "Gee Dub, go with them and bring us back a couple of rifles." He turned back to the sheriff. "Scott, you and Trent come on with me."

Chapter Seventeen

Alice wasn't much impressed with Uncle Bill's story. "But Arvid Weiss was hanged, Uncle Bill. Do you suppose his ghost is revenging himself by going around and pushing his accusers to their deaths?"

"Naw, he's met his maker," Bill told her, "and has other things on his mind now that he's consorting with Old Scratch." But he admitted that he did wonder about it. At the trial, Arvid's lawyer said that he'd practically raised up his brother and sister without any help from his dad after their mother died, and whereas old Weiss never beat on them, he never had a good word for any of them, either. Bill thought the lawyer never did say exactly what the smith did to set Arvid off, but he did try to lead the jury around to thinking that Arvid was protecting his brother and sister from something.

The barn was big and cool and dim after the hot early evening sunlight outdoors. Mary sat down on her favorite feed sack next to the byre and sighed with relief at the quiet. The family's three milk cows had come home a couple of hours ago and had already been milked and fed. They watched Mary with equanimity while they chewed their cud. Specks of dust floated in the shaft of sunlight that cut a swath across the packed earth floor. After a silent minute or two, after they had thoroughly checked her out from their nest behind the hay bale, the kittens came skittering, rolling, and tumbling out to play. Their mother, too dignified to frolic, followed them at her own speed and daintily rubbed against Mary's ankles as her kittens pounced on Mary's feet and clawed their way up her skirt. There had been seven kittens in the litter when they were born. Now there were four. Mary shook her head. It wasn't unusual that so many had met an early end. There were plenty of hazards for barn kittens on a farm. She picked up a black and white kitty and set it in her lap.

A shade moved across the sun trail on the floor, causing her to look up. Since the light behind him threw his face into shadow, it took her an instant to recognize the figure standing at the barn door, looking at her. She smiled. "Micah. What are you doing out here this time of day?"

Micah walked into the barn, scooping his hat off, and came to a halt before her. "Afternoon, Miz Mary. I was looking for Kurt. We were together in the paddock earlier in the day, but now he's got clean away from me. We still got some mares to move before sundown."

"I haven't seen him."

Micah gazed at her, a speculative expression on his face. "What are you doing out here in the barn all alone? Your folks know where you are?"

Mary heard accusation in his voice, whether it was there or not. "Reckon I'm old enough to walk out of the house on my own," she replied, sounding pettish.

Micah made a conciliatory gesture. "I reckon." He put his hat back on. "Them kittens like you."

"You have to just sit and be quiet, and they'll get so curious they can't resist."

"So are you wanting to be alone?"

"I was wanting to be out of that madhouse for a bit. I'm hoping I'll have a few minutes of quiet, at least, before my mother notices I'm gone."

"Mind if I sit with you for a spell?"

She tried to look uninterested, but the quirk of her mouth told him she was not displeased by his offer. "Suit yourself."

◇◇◇

Alafair searched for Mary in ever-widening concentric circles from the house, thinking that in the very few minutes Mary had been missing, she couldn't possibly have gotten very far. Alafair's search pattern took her through the vegetable garden, around the outhouse, by the root cellar and the smoke house and the chicken coop. There was nothing in the tool shed that wasn't supposed to be there, all neatly arranged as Shaw insisted.

She strode briskly to the room at the back, just in case Mary had decided to seek out the comforting presence of one of the hired men. Alafair didn't even knock before she entered. No one was there, either. The room was not as messy as Alafair might have expected, considering that two bachelors lived there. One bed was made and one unmade. A tan cowboy hat adorned the middle of the table between the beds. She recognized the hat as Kurt's, which gave her pause. Night or day, Alafair had never seen Kurt outside without his hat. He had been here recently, but where was he now? She went outside and looked up the rise toward the stable, where she could just see at that distance that Scott and his deputy had arrived and were standing by the door with Shaw and John Lee. She turned and started walking briskly toward the corral and the barn, where she knew Mary loved to go to be alone.

◇◇◇

Micah sat down next to Mary on a feed sack of his own. The mother cat and most of the kittens had disappeared, but the black and white kitty seemed to take into account Mary's good opinion of the hired man, because it immediately began to climb up his pants leg. "I hear y'all are headed to your grandfolks' in the morning."

"Yes," Mary affirmed. It occurred to her to elaborate, but she didn't have the energy to go into it, and said nothing more.

"How long you reckon to be gone?"

She shook her head. "'Til the murderer is caught, is what my mother says."

"It's a shame," Micah opined. "It's an awful thing to say, because I wish your uncle hadn't been murdered, but I'll miss watching over you." He blushed and amended. "All y'all."

Mary smiled, but said nothing.

"Kurt was just asking me this morning how you was doing, if any more of that bad night has come back to you, that might help to identify the scoundrel."

She shook her head again, her attention intently on the kitten attacking Micah's leg. "I try not to think about it."

"I don't blame you," he sympathized. "Kurt asked me, too, if you had seen Miz Laura Ross recently. I heard her dad sent her off somewhere. We wondered if she's doing any better."

"I haven't seen her since the fire, but last I heard, she's about the same." Mary looked up at him. "Kurt does a lot of wondering, doesn't he?"

Shaw and Gee Dub stood at the door and watched as Scott and Trent searched the tool shed apartment. Kurt's hat on the bedside table had caused them some concern, as well.

"What makes you think he'd hide the gun in here?" Shaw asked. "I've never seen him with such a rifle. I'd think that Micah would have noticed it, them living together and all."

While Trent searched the footlockers, Scott paced around the little room carefully, prodding the floorboards occasionally with his toe, looking for loose boards. "Human nature," he replied. "Folks usually want to keep an eye on something important to them, something they want to keep hid. Make sure nobody's found it. He'd sneak the thing around, only take it out when he was sure Micah wouldn't see him." He paused and put his hands on his hips, thinking. "Most criminals ain't geniuses, in my experience. They'll do the most obvious things..."

He leaned over and began poking the mattress on the messy bed. He looked under the bed, sat down on it and bounced, then overturned the mattress to examine the springs. He dropped the disturbed pallet back down on its springs and repeated the process on the neat bed. Trent looked up from his footlocker examination, intrigued.

Scott never reached the point of looking under the bed. After a few random pokes, he upended the mattress and bedclothes onto the floor. Wedged tightly in the springs, close by the wall, was a rifle. Scott picked it up and examined it before he handed it to an ashen Shaw and pointed at the marks on the butt plate—WM. "Mauser," he stated. "Shaw, where is this well you're aiming to dig?"

It took Shaw a couple of tries before he could get any sound to come out of his mouth. "In the pasture south of Cane Creek."

"Let's go find him."

Chapter Eighteen

Bill said that folks around Waco knew that blacksmith's family too well. After he heard the testimony, Bill figured the old man was rough, but the boys were hell-raisers and nothing much to write home about; mean to animals, kids, old folks, anybody weaker than they were. So the lawyer couldn't drum up much sympathy for Arvid.

Now, the sister was there at the trial, but the brother disappeared before the murder, and as far as Bill knew, he hasn't been heard from since. When he found out that Nix died in an accident, just like poor old Farrell Dean, he got to wondering if one thing didn't have to do with the other.

Bill laughed when he was telling us the story, but I didn't think it was all that funny, myself.

While Micah watched, Mary picked up the black and white kitten, a thoughtful expression on her face. "Kurt is asking a lot of questions about whether Laura or I remember anything about Bill's murder? Why do you suppose he's doing that?"

Micah shrugged. "I don't know, but he really is interested. He's always asking me, 'how is Miss Mary, how is Miss Laura,'" Micah said to her, mimicking Kurt's accent. When Mary didn't laugh, he added, "It's starting to make me wonder about the fellow."

Mary shook her head. "I'd just about die of shock if Kurt had anything to do with the murder." She sighed. "I don't know. I just don't know who to point the finger at. What reason could anyone have to do such a thing? I've been thinking and thinking on it, and I'm about to decide it must have something to do with that Fourth of July get-together in town. We were all there—me and my family, Bill and Laura, Art and Johnny and Trent, you and Kurt. Shirley didn't join us, but I saw her over by the bandstand talking to Art after dinner. Maybe Bill said something that didn't sit right with somebody who was there. I can't imagine what, though. Laura and him had just told everybody they were engaged, and we were all so happy. Poor old softhearted Johnny Turner bursting into tears and all. It's been niggling on my brain. I can almost grab hold of it, but it's just out of reach. I know it'll come to me by and by, if I can just…"

She fell silent, and her forehead creased as she thought about it. "Waco," she murmured absently.

"Waco?" Micah echoed. "What about Waco?"

Mary looked over at Micah, surprised. She had almost forgotten that he was there. "Yes. At the Fourth of July shindig. Bill told a story at the Fourth of July shindig about the blacksmith in Waco who got killed."

"I remember that tale. He saw somebody kill the blacksmith with a poker." Micah crossed his legs comfortably and leaned back against the barn wall. "Kurt is a smith, you know. A pretty good one at that."

Mary emitted a snort of disdain. "That has nothing to do with anything. The murderer in Waco couldn't have been Kurt. The murderer was caught and hanged. Bill testified at the trial."

Micah leaned forward. "No, no, I didn't say that the murderer was Kurt."

Suddenly something clicked in Mary's brain, like a piece of rusty machinery finally starting to turn over after long disuse, and Bill's words played in her mind as though he was speaking them in her ear.

At the time, Arvid's lawyer said that he'd practically raised up his brother and sister.

"The killer's brother…" Mary said.

"Maybe."

"How could that be? Kurt's not from Waco, you know that. He's from Germany."

"Well, maybe he lied about where he's from," Micah proposed. "Texas is cram full of German folks who were born there in Texas and can't even speak English."

The machinery in Mary's head rumbled again.

The lawyer never did say exactly what the smith did to set Arvid off, but he did try to lead the jury around to thinking that Arvid was protecting his brother and sister from something…

"No," she said firmly. "Not Kurt. I could believe it of just about anybody but Kurt. But you may be on to something."

Now, the sister was at the trial, but the brother disappeared, and as far as Bill knew, he hasn't been heard from since…

Micah leaned forward. "Could it be that Kurt is wreaking vengeance on them that got his brother hanged?"

When he found out that Nix died in an accident, just like poor old Farrell Dean, he got to wondering if one thing didn't have to do with the other.

◇◇◇

Alafair was moving at a brisk clip toward the barn. The Fourth of July, the Fourth of July. She kept repeating the date in her head. It meant something to Mary, something that might well be the key to this whole mystery.

Bill was telling a story about murder in Waco, and now the witnesses who had condemned the murderer were disappearing, one by one.

That was the connection, surely. The killer had to be someone who was involved in that sorry incident. She had almost reached the corral when she stopped in her tracks, thunderstruck. She had been thinking about it all wrong. This didn't start with the Fourth of July, or with the trip to Waco, or even the murder of the blacksmith. Not with hate. This had to do with an awful, perverted love.

A dusty wind rose suddenly and shook the leaves of the pin oaks at the side of the fence, the sound fading smoothly from a rustle, to a shudder, to a moan. A woman crying.

"Laura!" Alafair said aloud. Her hair was standing on end. "Help me, girl," she called to the wind. "Help me find Mary."

The moan faded, then rose again. A dust devil swirled up to Alafair's right, and began to move in a twisting path toward the barn. Alafair ran after it.

◇◇◇

Mary laughed incredulously. "Why, I think you may be right about somebody wreaking vengeance, Micah. But why does it have to be Kurt? Just because he's been hanging around, watching me? Isn't that what Daddy told y'all to do?"

"Well, your uncle said that his friend died at the oil field up around the Glenn Pool. I got to thinking, Kurt and me worked up there before we came here. Oil field work is mighty dangerous. Roustabouts were dying right and left, and I don't remember that particular accident, but the timing…"

"No, no, I won't believe it. He said he's from Germany, and he has no brother," she reiterated patiently, as if to a slow child.

Micah bit his lip and blushed. The remaining kitten leaped from his pants leg and pounced onto his boot, and he casually kicked it away. The kitten yowped in surprise and skittered off to join his family in hiding.

Mary forgot what she was saying for a second.

The boys were hell-raisers, and nothing much to write home about, mean to animals…

She blinked, and shook her head. "And besides, this tale of yours doesn't even take into account why he would kidnap Laura."

Micah said nothing for a moment, then sighed. "Well, that was just for fun."

Mary's newly activated thinking processes came to a sudden stop. She sat bolt upright. Micah's perverse comment was like a slap in the face. All at once, Micah's blush looked to her less like charming diffidence and more like rage. Suddenly the light of truth nearly blinded her, and she knew everything. "It was you. The blacksmith that got killed is your daddy. You're Arvid Weiss' brother…" She leaped to her feet in alarm. "Why are you telling me this?"

Micah's gray eyes looked up at her from under black lashes, but he said nothing. He didn't have to. There was only one reason he would tip his hand to her. She had betrayed her thought processes to the wrong person.

He reached up and absently adjusted his hat. "You know, I thought I'd killed Laura the first time, but I'll be durn if she didn't crawl out of that hole where I stashed her and into the middle of the road. And then, the Devil take me, her pa found her. I couldn't manage to finish her off the second time, either. Now they've hid her, and I figure she'll come around one of these days. Even if she don't, Gee Dub will remember something he seen at the Rosses', or the sheriff will figure out something from the trail I didn't have time to rub out. Everything went so well 'til now! Dang, I've had bad luck on this last enterprise. I reckon you and me both are going to have to disappear, now."

Stunned, Mary stood rooted to the spot for an instant, before it occurred to her that she should be running for her life. She attempted to sidle by Micah and head for the barn door.

But Micah was intent upon his tale, now, and had no intention of letting her leave. He stood and blocked her path. "It's too bad to have to do this," he admitted. "I always liked you. You see, Arvid killed our pa after the old man said we were all good for nothing and none of us were ever getting another dollar out of him dead or alive. Arvid was the only person on God's big old earth who ever gave a damn about me. Taught me carpentry and smithing, and how to hunt and track like a Comanche. I thought the least I could do for him was take care of those three sons-of-bitches who got him hanged. And it was easy to get rid of the first two. Nobody suspected their deaths were anything but an accident. After I killed them, I hightailed it, but this time, my idea was to sit tight for awhile so nobody would put two and two together.

"I thought the jig was up when Bill told that story to y'all at the Fourth of July parade, but after a day or two I could see that he had no idea I had anything to do with what happened. I knew then that I'd have to get on with the deed. I'll tell you, I was worried that one of you gals saw me in the woods, but it was a mistake to try and get rid of y'all. I liked that pretty Laura, though, and it was just too tempting…But now, it looks like I've left it too long and you've figured it out." Micah glanced at the open doorway and pulled a bandanna out of his hip pocket. "I was glad I didn't kill you the first time, but now, I reckon it would have saved me a lot of trouble."

Mary made a break for the doorway, but he sidestepped and grabbed her around the middle. They went sprawling across the floor.

Mary started to scream, but Micah stuffed the cloth into her mouth and clamped his hand down over it so tightly that she could hardly breathe. She started to choke. Terror seized her. She knew that she had to fight back however she could.

Micah was sitting astride her, his leg pinning one of her arms to her side. But her left arm was free and she raked his cheek with her nails. He yipped when she drew blood and smacked her in the jaw with his fist, stunning her. Then he stood and dragged her to her feet.

He clamped his arms around her tightly while her mind was still fogged by the blow, and dragged her toward an empty stall. The barn was some distance from the house, but not so far away that he could drag a kicking and screaming woman out of it and not be noticed. He knew he had no choice but to kill her then and there, before she left for Arkansas, and figure out some way to remove the body before her folks figured out she was gone.

But as he put his hand on the stall gate, all hell descended on him. It took him a few seconds to figure out what was happening. At first it seemed like an animal had attacked him, a dog maybe. Except for the fact that it had leaped on his back and was going after his head, screaming like a wildcat. It finally dawned on him that the bare brown feet and skirted legs clinched around his middle belonged to Mary's mother.

The intensity of the attack shocked him, and he dropped the disoriented Mary and reached up, trying to grab the hands tearing at him. Mary had already drawn blood, and Alafair was madly raking his face with her nails, and ripping out clumps of his black hair. After several tries, he was able to grasp the scraping, pounding hands, and frantically smashed his attacker between his body and the barn wall.

Alafair emitted a cry of pain but hung on through two or three more blows, until she was dislodged and slid down his back. Finally free of her, Micah leaned over to grab Mary off the floor. He was taken by surprise when Alafair stood up and gave a swift kick to the back of his knee that forced him to grab the side of the stall to keep from falling.

Before he could regain his balance, she tried to jump on his back. He was really alarmed, now. The woman was like a wounded lion, and her shrieks were sure to draw attention. He jerked his elbow back and caught her in the ribs. The blow knocked the wind out of her, but Alafair wrapped her arms around him from the back and squeezed the breath out of him with every ounce of strength she still possessed. Micah emitted a growl and pried her hands from around his chest. Alafair tried to feint as he turned around, but she was cornered by the wall. He punched her in the stomach and she fell to her knees.

He was running out of time. He saw that Mary was coming around, struggling to sit up, trying to spit the bandanna out of her mouth. He turned back toward her in a panic, but was able to take just one step before Alafair grabbed him around the legs and he went down. He maneuvered himself onto his back. Alafair managed to hang on to one leg, even though he kicked her several times in the shoulder with his boot. With every blow she slid further down, her fingers digging into his thigh, his knee, his calf. She was making a horrifying noise now, yowling like an animal.

"Good God, woman!" Micah panted. He kicked her in the face, and she let go, and was still.

Mary raised herself onto on her knees, trying to stand, wailing, "Mama!"

Micah pulled himself up, and gasping for breath, seized a broken hoe handle that was leaning against the wall. He lifted his arm to strike Mary with it, and her scream awakened a final light in Alafair's fading consciousness. With her last spark of energy, she pulled herself across the floor and sank her teeth into Micah's calf from behind.

He shrieked in pain and surprise, and hysterically began to beat at Alafair with the hoe handle. She barely felt the crack across her cheek, then her ear, then all went dark. But she didn't let go.

Mary was on her feet by then, trying to move to her mother's defense. She barely saw the tall figure with the pickax in his hand appear from behind her. She did see Micah's chest explode with red, and the stunned look on his face as he slowly keeled over onto the floor. She believed that she had never seen anything so beautiful as Kurt's blood-speckled face as he leaned over to check on her unconscious mother, whose teeth were still buried in the late Micah Stark's calf.

It took Scott, Trent, and Gee Dub all three to pull Shaw off of Kurt, who was huddling on the floor with his arms wrapped over his head, trying to keep from being killed. Mary had interjected herself into the scrum as well, reaching through the flailing arms and legs to pat her father's back and cry, "No, Daddy, no, Daddy, no, Daddy!" Shaw's hounds were complicating matters by excitedly bounding around underfoot, baying and barking.

The conclusion that Shaw had drawn was understandable. When the men had entered the barn at a run, they were already alarmed by the sounds of mayhem they had heard from the yard. The sight of gore-begrimed Kurt, already the object of their suspicion, leaning over Alafair's prone form and Micah's bloodied corpse, simply added fuel to the fire of Shaw's rage and terror.

Scott and Gee Dub managed to wrestle Shaw away before he did permanent damage to either Kurt or himself. They restrained him with their bodies and soothing words in the corner while Trent Calder pushed Kurt face down in the dirt and handcuffed his hands behind his back. Mary danced around trying to get someone's attention, torn between attending to her mother and trying to keep her savior from being injured. Finally she crouched down to examine Alafair's wounds and at the same time try to explain to Trent, who seemed to be the least excited person in the vicinity, what had happened.

She leaned her face close to Alafair's. "Mama? Mama, wake up," she urged, gingerly feeling the wounds on Alafair's face.

Trent was kneeling with one knee dug into the small of Kurt's back and one hand holding down his head. "How is your mother?"

"Her pulse is strong, and I can't feel any broken bones," Mary said, loud enough for her father and brother to hear. "She was around behind him and he couldn't get a good angle when he went to flailing at her. She's got some pretty good cuts and whomps, though." She looked up at Trent. "Trent, Kurt isn't the bad man, here. It was Micah. Micah killed Bill, he told me so. Nix Webb and Farrell Dean Hammond, too. He hurt Laura and tried to burn her up, and he was going to kill me. Mama saved me, and Kurt saved both of us. Micah would have done us in for sure if Kurt hadn't come in when he did."

Trent looked over at Scott, and so did Mary. "It was Micah?" Scott echoed.

Mary switched her gaze to Shaw, who had gone quiet even though he was still standing in Gee Dub's restraining grip. The whites of his eyes were red. The sight alarmed her. She had never realized until this moment that her father was quite capable of killing. "It was Micah, Daddy," Mary repeated, in the hope that he could hear her. "He said too much, and I figured out that it was him who shot Bill and kidnapped Laura. He planned to kill me while he had the chance and dump me somewhere. I reckon that he was going to try to pin it all on Kurt."

Kurt, face in the dirt, made a little sound of surprise.

"Mama came on him trying to drag me off," Mary continued, stroking her mother's hair, "and jumped him. She gave him what for, I'll tell you, but if Kurt hadn't showed up when he did, it would have gone the worse for both of us. Kurt's a hero, Cousin Scott."

Shaw shook off Gee Dub's hand and knelt down beside Alafair. He couldn't budge her at first. Her jaws were clamped around Micah's calf like a vise. She moaned when he moved her.

"Run for the doctor, Gee Dub." Scott leaned over Kurt. "Boy, do you own a Mauser '98 rifle?"

One wide blue eye looked up at him from under Trent's fingers. "No, sir."

"Did Micah?"

The blue eye blinked. "I don't know of it, no, sir. He owned two or three good guns that he kept wrapped in sleeves most of the time."

"Do you know anybody who does own a Mauser?"

Kurt considered this for a moment. "Since I been here in America, sir," he said at length, "the only Mauser I ever seen belonged to Mr. Schwartzenfeld down in New Braunfels. It got stole before Micah and me left."

"Which of them two bunks in the shed is yours?"

This unlikely question gave Kurt a moment's pause, but he was in no position to ask for an explanation. "Under the window, sir. By north wall."

The messy one. Scott straightened up. "Why did you plant a pickax in Micah's chest?"

"I told you, Scott…" Mary attempted, but Scott held up his hand to silence her, and she bit her lip.

"Were you trying to shut him up, boy? Were y'all in cahoots?"

"*Nein!*" Kurt was so shocked at the allegation that he could only manage a horrified squeak.

"Tell me what happened, then."

Kurt answered the best he could, considering that Trent was crushing his ribs and he had suddenly forgotten most of his

English. "I am coming back to our room after I break the ground in the pasture when I hear the noise in the barn. I ran, then. But when I went inside, I cannot believe what my eyes see. I stand like a tree for a little minute. Then I wake up and see that he is hurting Miss Mary and Miz Tucker, and I have pick in my hand and I know I must stop him how I can."

"That's just what happened, Scott! That's just what happened!"

"All right, Mary, honey. Well, I guess you can let him up, Trent. But I've got plenty more questions before I'm calling this over."

"But why?" Shaw asked. He sounded out of breath, and hoarse. "Why would Micah kill my brother like that?"

"It's a long story, Daddy," Mary told him, "but it seems that a few years ago Micah's brother killed his own father down in Waco. Bill and his friends were there on a horse buying trip and saw the whole thing. They all testified at the trial, and Micah's brother got hanged. Seems Micah was on a mission to avenge his brother."

"But..." Shaw attempted, but Scott cut him off.

"Not now, Shaw," he admonished. "Let's get Alafair taken care of first."

◇◇◇

Alafair was swimming up from the depths. One whole side of her face felt like somebody had taken a sledgehammer to it, and her ribs hurt so bad that she could hardly draw a breath. She could hear Shaw's voice through the ringing in her ears, and she desperately followed it toward consciousness. Something was in her mouth.

"Let go, honey," Shaw's voice was urging gently. "Open your mouth. Let go. It's all over now. Mary's all right. You got him, honey."

She opened her eyes. All she could see was cotton twill material and dirt floor. A man's hand, Shaw's hand, was massaging her jaw, trying to wedge his fingers between her teeth. She relaxed and Micah's calf slid out of her mouth. She could taste blood. The instant she let go, Shaw turned her over and hoisted her into his lap.

"Mary," she croaked.

"Mary's fine, darlin'. I declare, you look the worse for wear." Shaw's eyes flooded with tears of relief, and he started to laugh. "Alafair Gunn, you're going to be the death of me."

Sally had been worried about Laura all day. She had been so restless and upset that Sally feared she might have to tie her to the bed, like Calvin had done. Laura had been doing so much better that this turn for the worse took Sally completely by surprise. She made up a sedative herbal tea and fed it to the girl by the spoonfuls, but by late in the evening, she determined that there was nothing to do but send Peter for Dr. Addison.

Sally was about to turn the doorknob to leave the room when something stayed her hand. A whisper, a sigh, a breeze. And then utter stillness. Sally took a breath and turned around to see that Laura had stopped her flailing and moaning. The girl quietly stood up from the bed and walked over to the window and looked out. Sally stood paralyzed for a moment, watching.

Laura half turned and looked at Sally with an expression in her pale blue eyes that was completely changed from only an instant before.

"It's over now," she said. "My Bill has gone home."

"What about Art Turner and the Kellerman girl?" Shaw asked Scott after Doc Addison had left and Alafair was settled. They were sitting in the kitchen with a couple of glasses of tea while Martha waited on them. "Why did they both disappear? Did Micah do something to them, too? What did they have to do with the situation?"

"Nothing. That was just bad timing. We got word this afternoon that Art did catch up with Shirley in Shawnee. He's one persuasive youngster, because he talked her into marrying him right then and there. They found them a preacher and did the deed and they've been in Oklahoma City ever since."

Shaw guffawed. "Reckon he didn't dislike that gal as much as he let on!"

Both men started when Martha, who was standing behind them at the counter, burst into laughter. "So Miz Kellerman has an 'Injun' son-in-law," she chortled. "The Lord does have his ways!"

Chapter Nineteen

Hexed! Those boys who testified at the murder trial of Arvid Weiss weren't hexed, Mama. It wasn't just that Nix and Farrell Dean and Bill saw the killing, but that they testified against Arvid and got him executed.

Isn't it funny? I opened my eyes in that field and instantly knew that what had just happened was connected to the story Bill told us on the Fourth of July. How could that be? It seems to me that there must be a kind of knowing that has nothing to do with thinking. Maybe that's why the minute I came to and my brain started working again, the answer left me, and I was only just able to grab the tail end of it before it disappeared altogether.

Little bits kept coming back to me over the weeks, whenever I was quiet, or in my dreams. Then, when Micah kicked that kitten, it came to me that it was him who had been tormenting the little animals. No dogs or big critters that might fight back, the coward. Just teasing the rooster to make it spur and picking off the kittens, just for meanness. Who knows what else over the time he's been amongst us? Funny, when he said that, I thought of the last verse of the kitty song:

> *I took my hook, and went to the brook*
> *to see if my kitty was there;*
> *but there I found that she had been drowned,*
> *and so I went home in despair.*

But then when he made that comment about Laura, it shocked me so that I couldn't think, and suddenly I knew as plain as day everything else he had done, as well.

Do you expect that there's a part of a person that's connected right to the truth of things? A part that's halfway between this world and the next—that's standing on the drop edge of yonder?

Mary's story was finished. She sat back in her chair next to her mother's bed and placed her hands in her lap. Alafair turned over onto her side to face her.

Mary had finally told her mother the entire story, from the moment she awoke in the field after Bill's murder to the instant in the barn when everything had come together for her in a flash of insight. Alafair had no intention of telling her that she had already read most of it in Mary's secret journal—enough that she had been graced with her own moment of clarity.

Of course, she had had help from Laura.

A half-smile curved Mary's lips, and her eyebrows arched quizzically.

Alafair smiled back. She could read Mary's expression as plainly as letters on a page. *What does it all mean, Mama?* But Alafair had no answer for her.

Alafair shifted a bit, trying to get comfortable. It had been almost two weeks since Micah Stark's shocking demise, and Alafair was still feeling pretty beaten up. The right side of her face was swollen and covered with yellowing bruises, the eye just a slit. One knee was twice its normal size and her ribs and back were bruised and sore, making her walk crabbed over like an eighty-year-old woman.

She was in high spirits, though. The fact that she couldn't dress herself or brush her hair rather amused her. Normally, anything that interfered with Alafair's perpetual motion would have irritated her no end, but she attributed her good mood to the fact that the lurking, unknown danger to her children was over.

In fact, until half an hour before, Alafair had been in the kitchen. For today, Saturday, September 12, 1914, G.W. Tucker turned eighteen years old, and his mother had insisted on making his favorite dessert herself, in spite of the fact that she was so stiff and sore that she could hardly move.

With so many children in the family, birthdays were generally quiet affairs, marked only by a favorite food and a respite from a chore, but Alafair and Shaw did take special notice whenever one of the heirs turned eighteen. Today, Gee Dub's birthday *soirée* was attended by his parents, his siblings, brothers-in-law, niece, some cousins, and Kurt Lukenbach.

For his special dinner, which this year was cooked by his sisters, Gee Dub had chosen perch that he had caught himself in Cane Creek, rolled in cornmeal and delicately pan fried, roasting ears—corn on the cob roasted in an iron pot over an open fire in a pit behind the house—fried okra, brown beans and fatback, fragrant sliced tomatoes right off the vine, still warm from the sun, fried potatoes with onions, and cornbread. Also on the table were sorghum and sliced raw onion, fresh milk and buttermilk, sweet iced tea, apple cider vinegar and homemade ketchup, piccalilli, homemade pickles, store-bought white bread (since this was a special occasion), and lots of butter for slathering on corn, cornbread, and anything else that struck one's fancy. And on the end of the big table sat a pot of chicken and dumplings, the sad but tasty end of a tough red bird who had competently done his roosterly duty all his life, yet through no fault of his own had ended up a criminal.

In the afternoon, after a nice long layabout to facilitate digestion, and a few games of penny-toss, mumbledypeg, and checkers, Shaw had combined the sweet, custardy base that Alafair had made earlier with a puree of the peaches she had canned in June, and poured them into the ice cream maker. He packed chipped ice and salt into the bucket around the tin container, fitted the revolving paddle into the lid and immersed it into the ice cream mix, and started cranking. Shaw had reason anew to be thankful for such a large family, as one son or daughter or son-in-law or nephew after another took a turn at the crank.

Alafair had finally given in to fatigue and agreed to a brief lie-down while the ice cream made, and Mary had lent her a supporting shoulder when she limped into the bedroom.

But as Mary turned to leave, Alafair had encouraged her to stay and keep her company while she rested. Their talk of ordinary things had turned of its own accord to more serious topics, and for the first time Alafair had learned the complete story of Mary's wander through the darkness of her mind and journey back into the light.

As Mary waited for her mother to comment, Alafair studied her daughter's face. The glaze of grief that had dulled the blue eyes had lifted, and they were clear, peaceful, and alive again. However, the merry sparkle that had always glinted there was still missing, and Alafair feared that it would not return in the same way again. She closed her own eyes and turned over on her back with a sigh.

"I don't know anything, honey," she said. "I'm just like one of Daddy's mules hitched to a plow. I just put my head down and go, come sun or storm. But I do have my opinions, and I think you're right about there being a part of you that's connected square to the truth of things. Thing is, most of us can't get out of our own way enough to see it. It takes something like what happened to you to shock you so bad that you can't think, and then suddenly the answer whacks you over the head like a sledgehammer. That's happened to me, once or twice. You'd think that would be a good thing, to finally understand what 'knowing' really is, and I guess it is. Too bad that sometimes it hurts like sin to learn it."

"How are you feeling, Mama?"

"Pretty stove up," she admitted with a laugh. "But full. What with you girls doing all the cooking and chores I'll be getting fat directly."

"Gee Dub seemed pleased, both with the dinner and with the Winchester Daddy and you gave him." Mary smiled. "That was a mighty fine birthday present, if I do say so."

"Well, Gee Dub's a good boy. It's time he had something nice of his own, and Daddy says that a good firearm will last him a lifetime, if he'll take care of it."

"I can hardly believe he's eighteen now. Has he told you if he has plans for his future? We were talking about it the other day, and if he has something in mind he didn't want to admit to it. Martha mentioned that Uncle Charles is looking for another hand at the sawmill."

Alafair shrugged. "I wouldn't be unhappy if he decided to go to college. It's a new world, sugar, from when Daddy and me was young. Extra schooling would help anybody nowadays; even you girls, if y'all wanted to go. Look what it's done for Martha. She likes working, sure enough, and has her own money. Of course, I notice that she'll be twenty-three years old in a few weeks and seems to have no interest in marrying."

"Well, now, that's her lookout, Ma," Mary chided. "Twenty-three isn't that old."

"No, you're right."

Mary perched herself on the edge of the open window sill. "What about Gee Dub, Ma? I've never heard him talk about going to college. Besides, school has already started."

"Oh, I was just wishing aloud, darlin'. Truth is, I don't really know what Gee Dub wants. He plays it pretty close to the vest."

"He probably doesn't know himself."

Alafair forgot herself long enough to try to stretch, and winced. She turned back over onto her side with a grunt. "I'll ask Daddy to mention it to him. Gee Dub is going with him tomorrow to the big Farmers' Union meeting in Oklahoma City. With Gee Dub, whenever I try to talk to him, I'm the one who does all the talking."

Through the open bedroom window they could hear a clatter and commotion coming from the front of the house. "Sounds like more company has drove up," Alafair noted. Mary stood and walked over to peer out the side window.

"It's Grandma and Grandpapa."

"Oh, good. I was expecting they might show up sooner or later."

Mary straightened and looked back over her shoulder at her mother. "Laura Ross is with them."

"I declare!" Alafair struggled to sit up, and managed to roll herself up onto the edge of the bed before Mary could step over to give her a hand. "I know y'all girls have been over there to see Laura since she come around, but I've been stuck here like an old foundering cow. How does she look?"

"Mostly healed, except for a cast in one eye and a slight drag in her gait. She's looking a lot better, Ma. Better than you, right now. She's mighty pale, though. I'd say she almost glows like an angel."

Alafair expected that was only right, considering that she had spent two weeks between the mortal plane and the heavenly one. She wondered if Laura remembered anything of the other side. She resolved to ask her some day far in the future.

"Orlen Kelso returned the hundred dollars that Bill put down on the property he was fixing to buy," Mary was saying, "and Grandpapa said it should rightly go to Laura."

Alafair reconsidered her plan to stand up and sank back down on the bed. "Well, that's good, then. She'll have a little bit of money to start her a new life. Why don't you go on back outside, sugar? I'll just nap a little while and join y'all directly. Save me some ice cream. By the way, darlin'," she said, halting Mary at the door, "I never did like how that kitty song ended, so me and my mama made up our own ending when I was a girl."

"Leave it to you to make things turn out the way you want, Ma. What happened to the kitty in your song?"

Alafair folded her hands over her stomach and began to sing:

"Your little gray kitty has not been drowned.
I've found her and brought her back home.
But before you take her, a promise please make me,
You won't blame that poor boy no more..."

Mary chuckled. "That doesn't even rhyme, Ma! But I do like a happy ending."

◇◇◇

Mary was glad to get out of the stifling bedroom, and as she walked through the parlor and into the kitchen, it occurred to her that she was actually looking forward to getting back to the party. That ice cream sounded particularly inviting, especially with a piece of pie. It was a relief to have her appetite again.

She opened the ice box and took out the tin pitcher of sweet tea that Ruth had made up that afternoon. She poured herself a tall glass and put in a handful of ice chips as a special indulgence, then leaned back against the cabinet and took a long swallow. She heard the screen door creak open, but didn't see who walked into the kitchen, since her eyes were closed, the better to savor the cool sweetness sliding down her throat.

She choked and sputtered when she opened her eyes to find Kurt Lukenbach standing in front of her.

He snatched his hat off and grinned at her surprise. His teeth were big, white, and even. Mary realized that she couldn't remember ever seeing him grin before. It suited him. She sat the glass down on the cabinet, bemused.

"Howdy, Miz Mary," he said. "Your sister sent me in here to fetch bowls for ice cream. How nice I find you here."

"Kurt, for pity's sake. I've told you a dozen times to call me Mary. I reckon anybody who saves my life is welcome to call me by my first name."

The grin widened, and he glanced away, but he didn't say anything. Mary bit her lip, amused. "How's the eye?"

He looked back at her and fingered the fading shiner. "Much better, thank you. Mr. Tucker has a big punch."

"Daddy packs a wallop. You're lucky he didn't kill you before Scott and the boys got him pulled off."

"He was protecting you, like I tried since your uncle was killed and Miz Laura done so cruelly. It was good. Worth a black eye to me."

Mary's mouth quirked. She set her glass of iced tea on top of the ice box and shook her head. "I never suspected Micah for a minute. I was wondering, Kurt, didn't you ever guess that Micah was up to no good, what with y'all being such good friends?"

"No, I didn't. Never for an eye-blink. I think always that he is my friend. I don't care I killed him, though. I'm happy.

"But since two weeks, I look back on the years I rode with him, and I wonder why I did not know what kind of man was Micah. Twice, he talked me into leaving jobs real fast, in the middle of the night, one time. He would say, 'Kurt, I'm fed up to here with this crew,' and off we go. He was always quick to change like that, so I was not suspicious he did wrong. I hear now that your uncle's friend died while we were at the Glenn Pool. I didn't know. Maybe Micah did something bad in New Braunfels too, steal Mr. Schwartzenfeld's rifle…" He shrugged. "I wonder how I am so blind."

"Good people never expect others to be so bad."

"You think I am a good person?"

"Of course you are."

Kurt reddened, but looked pleased. He started to speak, hesitated, then took a breath and tried again. "I confess, M…Mary, that I did not come into the house for bowls. I seen you through the screen, and I come into the house with no invite, so I can talk to you."

Kurt's statement surprised her, and she felt a thrill of alarm. The events of the past month had made her skittish, she thought. She shook herself. "What's on your mind?"

◇◇◇

Lying on her side, half-asleep, Alafair was roused by the slap of bare infant feet on the bedroom floor. She opened her eyes to find herself nose to nose with her youngest.

"Ma!" Grace's tone was commanding.

Alafair drew her head back on the pillow, far enough to be able to focus her eyes on Grace's face, at least. "What can I do for you, cookie? Why aren't you outside with Daddy? Did you bring me something?"

Grace extended her fist for Alafair's inspection. Since she had been hurt, a concerned and solicitous Grace was continuously bringing treats for her mother's comfort and pleasure. This afternoon's offering appeared to be a slightly squashed piece of white sheet cake. Alafair expected that Sally had brought it, and was currently meting it out with the ice cream on the front porch.

"Birfday," Grace informed her. "Birfday cake. My birfday."

"Not yet, puddin'. Today is Gee Dub's birthday. But your birthday will be coming along right quick."

"Right quick," she repeated, satisfied. "Eat the cake, now, Mama."

Alafair smiled, thinking that Grace spoke very clearly, considering that she was not quite two. She opened her palm and Grace delicately placed the worse-for-wear piece of cake in it. Alafair ate it with a great show of pleasure, not particularly bothered by the griminess of the little fist or the suspicious grittiness of the cake.

The child grinned from ear to ear and crawled up onto the bed, causing Alafair to gasp involuntarily as a small knee grazed her sore ribs.

Alafair gave an exaggerated moan of discomfort. "Oh, Mama's a mess! I reckon I need some good sugar."

Grace's expression changed instantly to one of concern. She grasped Alafair's bruised face between her two sticky hands and covered it with wet kisses.

Kurt shifted from one foot to the other and back. For a long moment, he stared at the hat in his hand as though he didn't quite know what it was. Finally he took a breath and lifted his gaze to look at Mary. "After your uncle was killed, and no one knew where the murderer was, Mr. Tucker set me to guard you."

Mary nodded. "Me and all the family, yes."

"From the first time I watched the house, I realized that if anything should happen to you, my heart would be broke. It made me know how I would feel if…It made me know how I feel about you."

Mary's eyes widened. Was she hearing what she thought she was hearing? "What are you trying to say, Kurt?"

"I got so afraid, Mary. I could not sleep or eat. I hardly could work. I only wanted to watch you, every minute I was free. Hide behind the shadows and watch, to keep you safe." He paled and looked down at his boots. "I know I am not good enough for you."

She reached out abruptly and put her hand on his arm. "Kurt, don't say that. You're a fine man. I like you. I like you a lot. Maybe more than that. There's something about you that makes me feel tender. And it's sure a good thing that you did keep an eye on me, or I'd be dead right now. There are no words to say how grateful I am for what you did. But I'm not looking for a beau right now. I've just started teaching, and I like it. I figure to keep at it for a spell."

"Oh, no, I know that. You should have time, think about how you want your life. We are friends, yes?"

"Yes, good friends."

"Maybe, a long time from now, you will feel more for me, if you know how much I care for you."

Mary was unsure how to respond. She was taken aback by his declaration, but not blind-sided. She was not totally unaware of his regard. However, this entire episode was one more in the parade of surreal events that had twisted and reshaped her life over the last month. She was unable to stop her face from involuntarily forming an incredulous smile.

"I declare…" she murmured. She looked him in the eye. "I have a job of work this year, and I'll be saving my money. I suggest you do the same. If—and I mean 'if,' now,—my feelings for you grow and we ever get around to marrying, I'm not living in that little room behind the tool shed for the rest of my life."

The joy that illuminated his face was blinding. "Now, hang on," Mary cautioned, before he could respond. "I'm not making any promises. If there's one thing I've learned over the last month, it's that you can't predict what will happen in the future."

"No, you must not." His voice was lilting. "You must be sure you are not liking me because of being grateful. You must be sure you will be happy to be with someone so *unwurdig* as me."

"I don't know what that means, but..."

He spoke over her. "And you mustn't worry about money. I have money."

Mary stopped in mid-sentence, taken aback. "What?"

"I have enough money to buy a farm now. In Germany I was a good metal smith, besides working in the stables. And in New Braunfels I bought a fine mare and bred and sold a few foals of my own. I have saved well, but I had thoughts that I should wait a while to buy my own farm. If you should decide, some day, to make me the happiest man, then we can find a place together."

"Why in the frog hops have you been working as a mule wrangler for Daddy for the last two years, if you could have had a place of your own all this time?"

Kurt shrugged. "I like it here. I learn a lot from Mr. Tucker, and here I can save my money for when I decide what I want." He paused and smiled. "I'm a good saver. And as time went by, there was you, and I know now what I want."

◇◇◇

In the midst of being drenched with baby kisses, Alafair caught sight of Sophronia standing in the bedroom doorway. When she saw her mother look at her, Sophronia shrugged apologetically. "Sorry, Ma. I snatched at Grace when she run into the house, but she's got real fast lately. Daddy told us to let you rest. You want me to take her outside?"

"No!" Grace hollered, right into Alafair's ear, which caused her to laugh and grimace at the same time.

"It's all right, Fronie. I'm all rested. Mercy, what happened to you? Your pinafore is a mess, and look at your skinned-up legs! Have you kids been playing rodeo again and letting Charlie rope you? I told him not to be doing that."

Sophronia looked down at herself, apparently just as surprised by her state as Alafair had been. "Aw, Ma, it was fun. Besides, Charlie could never rope me. It was Daddy."

"Oh, Lord have mercy. Come on, help me up. Let's get you washed up and put some marigold salve on them scratches. Then we'll get some ice cream and cake, if there's any left…"

She was interrupted by a peal of laughter, clear and musical as a mountain stream, melodious, exalted, like a thousand larks. Alafair caught her breath.

Sophronia joined in with a chuckle of her own, and a mischievous smile. "Mary's in the kitchen with Kurt."

"What's that, Mama?" Grace asked, as the laughter bubbled and danced through the house.

Alafair grabbed the little girl and squeezed her, her happiness masking the jolt to her bruises and sore bones. "Honey, that's music to my ears."

Alafair's Recipes

OKRA

Is okra an acquired taste? Does one have to be raised eating okra in all its myriad glorious forms in order to be able to appreciate it? Alafair and her entire family loved it however it was cooked, which was a good thing, since okra is a plentiful summer staple for the Southern cook. Once it started to bear, Alafair's family would have had okra in some style at practically every meal. Alafair was perforce creative with her okra recipes, if only to keep her family interested enough to keep eating. Okra would have been used in every soup and stew, boiled with tomatoes, pickled, fried, and served with whatever was going. The uninitiated may be put off by its initial sliminess and prickliness, but if one can endure the preparation and knows the proper way to cook it, it can be quite wonderful. Okra is a good thickener in liquid dishes like soup. As a bonus, it is very soothing to the digestive tract. When picking okra, choose silky, tender pods. Cut off the top and slice into rounds. The pods should be easy to cut. Avoid pods that are dry, tough to cut, stringy, or shriveled.

FRIED OKRA

1 pound tender okra pods   2/3 cup yellow cornmeal
   (4 cups)   1/4 tsp. salt
Lard or drippings for frying

Place the cut up okra in a large mixing bowl. Add cornmeal and salt and mix well, coating each piece of okra. Fresh okra is very…well, slimy. It isn't necessary to boil the okra first or moisten in any way in order for the cornmeal to adhere. Many cookbooks say to boil okra for a few minutes before frying, but if your okra is fresh and tender, this is just a waste of effort and not good for the flavor, either. Fry it raw. It's the Southern way.

Melt the fat in a large skillet over medium heat. When the fat is very hot, add the okra, stir well to coat with grease, and fry until very brown. Stir occasionally, and add more fat if the skillet gets dry, to prevent scorching. The okra will be crispy, crumbly, and tender in the middle, and not gelatinous in the slightest.

FRIED OKRA PIE

Okra "pie" is not pie at all, but a variation of fried okra. The idea is that the entire batch is cooked in such a way that it adheres together in a pie-shaped disk. The finished product can be cut into wedges and eaten by hand, which makes it quite appealing to the younger set.

1 lb. cut up okra	2 eggs, beaten
(about 4 cups)	1/4 tsp. salt, or to taste
3/4 cup yellow cornmeal	Fat for frying.

In a large bowl, mix freshly cut okra with beaten eggs. Add cornmeal and salt and mix well to coat.

Melt fat in skillet. The fat should cover the bottom of the pan to about 1/8 inch deep. When very hot, add the coated okra and spread out so that it covers the bottom of the skillet in a single layer. Do not stir. Let the okra cook until the top looks dry and the edges are beginning to brown, then turn the batch over with a large turner. After years of practice, Alafair could turn the entire thing over in one piece. If the pie breaks into two or three pieces the first hundred or so times you try it, don't worry about it. It's still tasty. Fry the other side until brown, adding more fat if needed. Turn the "pie" out onto a serving plate, cut into wedges, and serve. One's first thought may be that this sounds rather like an okra omelet, but, truly, it is not. It's more like skillet cornbread.

RICE

Rice is one of the most versatile foods in the cook's arsenal, especially if she has an army to feed every day. A pot of rice can be used as a savory side dish instead of potatoes or as the basis for a soup or casserole. It also makes a good dessert. There are endless uses for leftover rice. Alafair's family often ate leftover rice as a warm, filling cereal for a light supper before bed.

The climate in Oklahoma is not generally conducive to rice cultivation, so Alafair would have bought five or ten pound bags of rice grown in the Gulf states. The rice would have been unwashed and un-instant. It was very important that preparation begin with spreading the rice out on the cabinet or table and painstakingly picking out the little rocks and grit, chaff, and insect parts, before rinsing it in clear water.

Cooking times and methods depend on the variety of rice used as well as how the cook wants her rice to turn out. Short-grain brown rice generally takes more water and a longer cooking time than long-grain white. Rice is forgiving, however. As long as it's cooked long enough in enough water and it doesn't burn or boil over, it's hard to spoil. And even then, it can often be salvaged.

The rule of thumb for cooking white rice is to use twice as much cool water as rice, plus about a quarter teaspoon of salt per cup of rice. Use a heavy pot with a tight lid to retain moisture and avoid scorching. Cover and bring to a boil over high heat. Watch the pot during this phase of cooking to avoid boil-over. There's no mess quite like boiled-over rice all over your nice clean stove. When steam begins to escape from under the lid, remove from heat for five minutes or so, then return to very low heat and simmer for about thirty minutes, or until all the water has been absorbed. Don't stir rice during cooking. Remove from heat and let it sit for a couple of minutes, then fluff with a fork before serving. Great with butter or gravy.

If you would like a denser, stickier rice, which is a good way to cook it for cereals and puddings, just add more water and simmer longer until the water is absorbed. Rice will absorb a surprising amount of liquid if you're patient about it. Alafair was known to simmer a cup of rice in six or seven cups of water, or water and milk, for an hour or more in order to make a soft and digestible gruel for a sick child.

RICE CEREAL FOR SUPPER

Reheat 2 cups of leftover rice from dinner by simmering it in a heavy pot with about a cup of water or milk until the extra liquid is absorbed and rice is warm and sticky. Add more liquid during cooking if needed. Makes about 3 cups of warm rice.

Ladle into bowls. Sweeten to taste with white sugar, brown sugar, maple syrup, sorghum, or honey. Plop a good chunk of butter on top to melt. Add warm milk or cream and enjoy.

GREENS AND CORNMEAL DUMPLINGS

Any kind of greens can be used for this delectable dish, but Alafair had a lot of turnip greens in the late summer. Before cooking, wash the greens thoroughly in cool water to remove dirt and sand. Cut off any roots and damaged or yellowing parts. Rip the greens off the stalks by hand and tear into strips. Turnip greens are extraordinarily nutritious, but they have a peppery bite and can be bitter. To mellow them out, blanch them first for ten minutes or so in a couple of cups of water.

1/4 lb. fatback or salt pork
2 lb. turnip greens, torn
1 lb. turnips, peeled and cut into quarters
2 1/2 quarts water
1 tsp. salt

CORNMEAL DUMPLINGS

1 1/2 cups cornmeal	1/2 cup flour
1 tsp. baking powder	1 tsp. sugar
1/2 tsp. salt	3 tbs. melted butter
1 beaten egg	

Bring the water to boil in a large pot. Add fatback or salt pork, greens, turnips, and salt. Reduce heat and simmer, covered, for two hours. Remove meat and discard. Dip out one cup of the broth (pot liquor) to make dumplings.

For the dumplings, thoroughly combine the cornmeal, flour, baking powder, sugar, and salt in a mixing bowl. Stir in the melted butter and one cup of pot liquor. Stir in the beaten egg. Spoon the batter by rounded tablespoonfuls into the simmering greens. Cover and simmer thirty minutes, or until dumplings are cooked through. To serve, ladle soup, greens, turnips, dumplings, and all into bowls and dig in.

ICE CREAM

Hand-cranked, homemade ice cream is not only a rare treat to eat, making it is also great aerobic exercise and a good way to increase upper body strength.

An ice cream freezer from Alafair's era was basically a large lidded tin can that fit down into a wooden bucket. The lid had a hole in the middle, through which was inserted a dasher, which somewhat resembled an oar. The handle of the dasher protruded from the hole and was attached to a hand crank, which had to be turned continuously until the ice cream was frozen.

The recipe for ice cream does not have to be complicated, by any means. An excellent ice cream can be made with a half-pound of sugar beaten into a quart of sweet cream. Add some sweetened fruit puree or just some vanilla extract, freeze, and devour.

For Gee Dub's eighteenth birthday, though, Alafair made a rich peach custard to freeze, which is more work, but the results are worth it.

PEACH ICE CREAM

1/2 cup sugar   3 egg yolks, beaten
1/4 tsp. salt   1 tsp. vanilla
1 cup milk   2 cups heavy cream

Puree four or five peaches, which Alafair would have made by mashing the flesh of the fruit through a sieve with the back of a large wooden spoon. Sweeten the peaches with another 1/2 cup sugar, if desired.

Mix sugar, salt, milk, and egg yolks in a saucepan. Cook over medium heat, *stirring constantly,* just until bubbles begin to appear around the edge of the pan. Cool to room temperature. Stir in the cream, vanilla, and peach puree.

Pour the ice cream mixture into the freezer can. Fill the can only two-thirds full, to allow for expansion as the ice cream freezes. Fit the can into the bucket, insert the dasher and put the lid on the can, then attach the crank.

Fill the freezer tub one-third full of ice, then alternate the rock salt and remaining ice, filling the bucket to the top of the can. Use about four parts ice to one part salt. Turn the dasher slowly until the ice partially melts and makes a brine. Then crank rapidly until it's hard to turn the dasher. How long this will take depends on the weather. If you're lucky, the ice cream will set in ten minutes or so. Or it may take half an hour. Or it may not want to set properly at all. It's all very mysterious.

When it does happen, remove the ice from around the top of the can and remove the dasher. Plug the hole in the lid and replace it on the can. Refill the bucket with ice and salt and leave the ice cream to "ripen" for several hours.

"Ripening" makes a firmer dessert. However, when the day is hot and a bunch of impatient kids are clamoring about, a bowl full of soft, semi-frozen cream that has to be gobbled up before it turns back into liquid is perfectly delicious.

COLD CANNED TOMATOES

When the cook is tired, the night is warm, and it's too late to be messing around in the kitchen, a bowl of home-canned tomatoes right out of the jar is light, refreshing, and delicious.

Sadly, this dish cannot be replicated with an aluminum can of store-bought tomatoes. In order to experience the mild, sweet, flavorful dish that Alafair and Shaw ate one hot night on their front porch, one must begin by growing one's own tomatoes over a long sunny summer on a mound of pure compost. The tomatoes must be picked fully ripe off the vine, and canned in glass jars in one's own kitchen.

Open the jar, pour it straight into a bowl, and eat it. Maybe a little salt, maybe a little sugar, perhaps a sprinkling of chopped onion.

The result of all this care and work tastes like nothing that has been shipped to the local A&P in a refrigerated truck, nor cooked in a big vat in a factory and sealed in a metal can with a dash of citric acid. It will be smooth and mild and sweet and so full of flavor that you'll wonder why you ever thought those things you've been buying at the supermarket were tomatoes.

PICCALILLI

Piccalilli is a kind of relish that can be made with any number of finely chopped vegetables. It's a good way to preserve any garden crop that is bearing to excess, and it's a delicious accompaniment for meat and fish, to boot. Alafair usually made piccalilli out of the green tomatoes she thinned from the vines.

2 quarts chopped green tomatoes
4 finely chopped large onions

1 1/2 quarts vinegar	1/2 lb. sugar
1/2 lb. mustard seed	1 tbs. ground pepper
1 tbs. cinnamon	1 1/2 tsp. ground cloves
1 tbs. ground ginger	1 1/2 tsp. allspice
Dash cayenne pepper	1/2 cup salt

Combine tomatoes, onions, and salt. Let stand in a covered bowl overnight. Drain off liquid, then boil in one quart of water and

2 cups of the vinegar for 20 minutes. Drain through a colander and return to pot. Pour in the rest of the vinegar, the sugar, and the spices. Boil for an additional 15 minutes, until tender, stirring often. Seal in sterilized glass jars.

CHICKEN AND DUMPLINGS

It's a good way to cook a tough old bird. Wash a 4 or 5 lb. stewing chicken and cut it up, removing any excess fat. Put the chicken in a kettle, along with the giblets and neck, a couple of teaspoons of salt, a little pepper, and just enough water to cover. For extra flavor, you may add a sprig of parsley, a bay leaf, some celery leaves, a small sliced onion, and/or a sliced carrot. Bring to a boil, then reduce heat and simmer, covered, for 2 1/2 to 3 1/2 hours, until the chicken is fork-tender and practically falling off the bone.

Remove chicken from the broth and pull the meat off the bones with a fork and cut into pieces. Discard bones, skin, the bay leaf, and any other disgusting pieces of innard that you don't want to eat, then return chicken meat to broth. Bring back to the boil.

DUMPLINGS

1 1/2 cups flour	2 tsp. baking powder
3/4 tsp. salt	3 tbs. butter or shortening
3/4 cup milk	

Mix flour, baking powder, and salt into bowl. Cut in the shortening until the mixture looks like meal. (One may use a fork to do this, or a couple of case knives, or one of those special utensils made for the job. Alafair would have used her fingers.) Stir in the milk.

Drop the batter by the tablespoon-full into the simmering chicken broth and cook uncovered for 10 minutes. Then cover the pot and cook for another 10 minutes, until the dumplings are fluffy and done through.

HOW TO IRON A SHIRT

There is a science to ironing. Each piece of clothing requires its own technique. The well-brought up housekeeper was taught the correct way to iron by her mother, and she in turn did her duty as a parent and taught her daughters. This is how Alafair's mother taught her to iron a shirt. Other women's mothers may have done it slightly differently. There's no use becoming incensed about it.

Cotton shirts should be ironed damp with a hot iron. First, iron the inside of the collar. Then drape the shoulder over the narrow end of the board and iron around the seam from collar to sleeve. When the shoulders are done, iron the inner side of the button plaquets. Drape the left side of the shirt over the wide end of the board and press the front. Rotate the shirt around the back and press (do the yoke first, if there is one), then the right front. Lay a sleeve across the center of the board and iron the inside of the cuff. Iron the front of the sleeve from the shoulder to the cuff, then turn the shirt over and do the back of the sleeve. Press the outside of the cuff over the point of the board. Repeat the process with the other sleeve. Finish with the back of the collar. Button the shirt up before folding or hanging.

Compendium

Bill Tilghman — A famous U.S. Marshal in the Indian and Oklahoma Territories. In the early 1900s Tilghman became a silent movie actor and director. Eventually he formed the Eagle Film Company in Oklahoma City and produced Westerns.

Caliche (ka-LEE-chee) — A concrete-hard layer of soil composed of clay and rock.

Co'Cola — Any American Southerner or Westerner in the earlier part of the twentieth century would be very much surprised to know that this is not the correct pronunciation of Coca-Cola.

Fatback — A chunk of pork fat. May contain a little meat.

Fetlock — A horse's ankle, or the tuft of hair that grows on the back of the ankle.

Forelock — The part of a horse's mane that hangs down between the ears onto the forehead.

The Glenn Pool — In 1905, oil was discovered on the land of Ida Glenn, a member of the Creek Nation. At one time, the Glenn Pool was the richest producing oil field in the world. Site of the present town of Glenpool, located some fifteen miles south of Tulsa.

Mess — A quantity of food that is enough for a meal.

Mother's Helper — A patent medicine that was readily available to mothers of toddlers in the late nineteenth and early twentieth centuries. It was almost pure alcohol. One teaspoon full would put the kid out for hours. It was outlawed in the 'teens.

Pot liquor — The concentrated liquid left after vegetables or meats are stewed or steeped.

Visitation — When someone died, it was customary for everyone who knew the family to call on the bereaved and pay their respects while the body was laid out in the parlor before the funeral. A visitation is akin to a wake.

To receive a free catalog of Poisoned Pen Press titles, please contact us in one of the following ways:

Phone: 1-800-421-3976
Facsimile: 1-480-949-1707
Email: info@poisonedpenpress.com
Website: www.poisonedpenpress.com

Poisoned Pen Press
6962 E. First Ave. Ste. 103
Scottsdale, AZ 85251

FIC
CAS

Casey, Donis.

The drop edge of
yonder.

c.1
$24.95

BAKER & TAYLOR